A CURE FOR KILLERS

A DCI Sidney Walsh novel of suspense
A bomb explodes in a research laboratory in Cambridgeshire, killing a leading scientist. Is this the work of some crazy animal rights activists or the elusive DaSilva, trouble shooter for the international underworld of organised crime? DCI Walsh and his CID team find some Celtic love poems in the dead scientist's desk: had the victim been forced to take his own means of destruction to the laboratory while his lover was held hostage? These questions are soon overshadowed by a concerted wave of terror unleashed on England's ancient seat of learning.

A CURE FOR KILLERS

A CURE FOR KILLERS

by

Richard Hunt

Dales Large Print Books
Long Preston, North Yorkshire,
England.

British Library Cataloguing in Publication Data.

Hunt, Richard
  A cure for killers.

A catalogue record for this book is
available from the British Library

ISBN 1-85389-738-8 pbk

First published in Great Britain by Constable & Company
Ltd., 1995

Copyright © 1995 by Richard Hunt

The right of Richard Hunt to be identified as the author
of this work has been asserted by him in accordance with
the Copyright, Designs and Patents Act, 1988

Published in Large Print 1997 by arrangement with Constable
& Company Limited.

Dales Large Print is an imprint of
Library Magna Books Ltd.
Printed and bound in Great Britain by
T.J. International Ltd., Cornwall, PL28 8RW.

1

The damp foggy mists of winter lay heavy and thick over the bare leafless Berkshire countryside, bringing visibility down to only a few yards. The few hedges, trees and bushes that loomed up out of the blanketing whiteness seemed layered all over with gossamer curtains of spiders' webs, on which tiny dew-drops clung and shimmered in the eerie opaque light.

Yesterday a wan shadow of a sun had feebly tried to dispel the precipitating vapour, but there were no signs of it appearing today—so it was not a morning when wise people set out on long journeys by car, unless compelled to do so by desperate necessity, or from a somewhat less easily definable sense of duty.

One Berkshire country lane seemed to have attracted more than its fair share of such travellers. The first vehicle in the slow-moving line seemed like some ghostly snow plough, as it rolled forward an impenetrable bank of white cloud with the broad beams of its dipped head and fog lamps.

The convoy came to a halt when a pair

of huge closed wrought-iron gates loomed up out of the mist. A signboard announced to those who could see it that this was an entrance to a police training college.

An innocent enough, even a harmlessly useful sort of place, one might suppose, in which case one would have been surprised to observe that the cold-eyed, suspicious guard, who appeared with two young assistants from the gatehouse, was armed.

Their smart uniforms glistened frostily with the clinging fog as they scrutinised the occupants of each car in turn with great care. Seemingly they were not content with a simple verbal acknowledgement of identity, or the display of warrant cards, because they also compared each face with glossy photographs held in an arch-lever file.

Eventually the big gates were pulled open, and the cars allowed to proceed.

Inside the grounds, other shadowy groups of people, some with dogs, could be seen patrolling the high wire security fence.

At the end of a long sweeping drive, those cars joined others parked outside the front of what appeared to be a stately baronial hall. It was certainly a building of classically elegant proportions.

The new visitors were greeted in the

spacious hall with the kind of respectful welcome due to important and influential people, as indeed they were, for among their number was a junior minister from the Home Office and six chief constables.

Clearly the gathering together in one place of many of those people responsible for the maintenance of law and order in south-east England necessitated more than just the ordinary anti-terrorist and anti-espionage precautions, and what safer place should there be, than one guarded by experienced and expert police college tutors, aided by their enthusiastic students?

The last late arrivals for this conference were quickly ushered from the lofty hallway into an even more spacious and elegant room, one decorated in subtle shades of beige and brown, in which waiting groups of people stood conversing near the rows of comfortable Dralon-covered armchairs.

'Right, ladies and gentlemen. Would you please be seated, and welcome to our conference on illicit drugs. Because of the weather we're way behind schedule, and I'd like to get the meeting started,' the tall white-haired chairman explained, easing his gold-linked shirt cuffs fractionally further from the sleeves of his immaculate brown suit. 'Unfortunately Dr Jones, who was to have talked to us about the illegal production of amphetamines, is stuck in the fog on the M1 somewhere, so we will start with a short talk on the latest developments in the treatment of drug addiction. That should take us nicely up to lunch, after which we will examine the main routes by which drugs are moved from producer countries into Europe. Then we'll have another short break before getting down to the nitty-gritty, the main purpose of our meeting—our plans to locate and block the points of entry into this country. So, to our first speaker. Unfortunately Dr Justin Chambers is indisposed, but I welcome instead his colleague, Dr James Wade, from the Cambridge University Medical Research Centre—Dr James Wade.' The chairman waved his hand vaguely in the direction of an individual seated at the far end of the front row.

The man who stood up and peered rather suspiciously at his audience was of average height, in his late thirties, and wore a brown tweedy sports jacket that hung rather baggily from his narrow shoulders. He had a high forehead, a pale face, and gold-rimmed spectacles which perched low down on a long bony nose. He was an intelligent man, obviously, but to those there more used to a military smartness in attire, Dr Wade was undoubtedly sloppily careless about his appearance.

Perhaps that accounted for some of the

mildly hostile looks, or perhaps it was felt that a lecture on such a fringe subject was one that would have to be endured rather than enjoyed, particularly if it alone stood between them and lunch.

Dr Wade clipped a large coloured diagram of a cross-section of the human brain to the nearby display board, coughed to clear his throat a few times, then began to speak.

'My name is Wade, as you've been told, and I work at the Medical Research Centre, in Cambridge,' he announced. His voice was slightly high-pitched, but quite firm enough to carry to his audience.

'Now, addiction is an extended function of this part of the brain—here—near the hypothalamus.' He pointed to the relevant section on his diagram. 'I say an "extended" function,' he went on, 'because under normal conditions this area is concerned with maintaining an adequate intake of those essential chemicals a body requires. It does that by stimulating, when necessary, the reticular formation's gastro-intestinal activity. In simple terms, that causes feelings of hunger and thirst. If the body's diet does not contain all the necessary chemicals for good health, then the hunger or thirst will become a craving for specific foods which contain the missing chemicals, and that will continue until the craving is satisfied. That is perfectly normal. "Addictive compounds", however, are able to penetrate into this area and add themselves to the natural list of essential chemicals.'

Dr Wade paused; most of his listeners were not looking at him, and those that were showed little sign of interest. It was going to be more difficult to talk to these laymen on this subject than he'd realised; clearly such details were way above their heads. He was more used to giving lectures to interested students who were familiar with medical terms. His colleague, Justin Chambers, would have started by cracking jokes and telling amusing anecdotes, but he couldn't do things like that. He looked sadly down at his notes. Was there anything there that might stir up some enthusiasm in this unresponsive crowd of stern faces?

He went on talking for another few minutes, but there was no improvement in the general atmosphere; if anything, it had worsened, so he made the decision to bring his lecture to an early conclusion. It was obviously not a subject to which his audience attached any major importance.

'So, to summarise,' he said firmly, 'current treatment for the rehabilitation of the addict consists, in the main, of the substitution for the addictive drug of one which is less harmful, yet eases the craving. The replacement drug is then gradually reduced in strength until the patient is entirely weaned away from any dependency. That takes a long time and the success rate is poor. Our research project in Cambridge is trying to find methods of treatment that are more effective.'

The audience were now stirring with restless discontent. Wade hurriedly continued.

'In Cambridge we have identified the specific groups of neurones—brain cells, that is—which actually control this whole addiction function,' he blurted out hastily, 'and we've found a blocking agent which successfully suppresses it. I don't know if I'm supposed to tell you about that, for security reasons,' he went on hesitantly, 'but I'd have thought you lot were all right.'

The expressions of utter boredom had now left the faces of some of his listeners.

'Would you repeat that, young man? Did you actually say that you've found a form of treatment that is an effective cure for drug addiction?' The voice of the burly red-faced chief constable of the Cambridgeshire Constabulary boomed from the front row of those facing the speaker.

Wade blinked and scratched at his nose. 'Well, yes, I suppose I did say that,' he replied. 'There is still a lot more work to be done, of course, but we are rather pleased with our progress.'

'Be more specific then,' the same chief constable demanded, his bushy eyebrows drawn almost together in a frown of deep concentration. 'Does it work, this cure of yours? Has it been approved for general use? If not, how long will that take?'

'I'd rather just say at this stage that it's statistically effective—under laboratory conditions. It's a long way yet from being ready for testing on humans, and with this kind of research, it's impossible to say when that will be. It might be months—or years.' Wade's hands came up in a helpless palm-upwards gesture. 'We know of some possible side effects already: a few of our test animals developed a form of anorexia. Lost their appetite, so to speak. That could be a problem, but on the other hand, we've found that healthy non-addicted animals treated with the blocking agent subsequently proved immune to the habit-forming effects of hard drugs, and even nicotine. So, perhaps it's to that aspect—the prevention, rather than the cure—that we ought to give the highest priority.'

Dr Wade's audience now seemed to have become fully wide-awake, and interested—very interested.

'Christ! That's even better. Immunise all the bloody kids while they're in infant school. That'd stop the flaming rot, and put the drug barons right out of business,' boomed an excited voice from a man with a weight problem, in the third row.

'Much of the petty crime in my area is done by addicts, to get the cash to buy more drugs,' someone else added, rather unnecessarily.

'If I didn't have a drug problem on my patch, I'd really be able to cut my crime figures,' yelled another excitedly.

The minister from the Home Office remained silent, but sat open-mouthed at the revelation of something he, and his colleagues in government, knew nothing about. Yet he was rapidly assimilating the advantages—political, medical and economic—if the problems of drug, tobacco and alcohol abuse were to disappear almost overnight.

Even chief constables occasionally display human emotions: like a riot situation, albeit on a small scale, the excited reactions of a few transmitted themselves to the many, and this collection of staid, hard-headed authoritarians got somewhat verbally out of hand.

The chairman had to shout to make himself heard, but he eventually brought the meeting back to order by announcing

15

an immediate adjournment for lunch, and suggesting that the questioning of Dr Wade could continue on an informal basis in the bar, which was now open.

The chief constable of the Cambridgeshire Constabulary and his colleague took their drinks over to a table in the far corner, by a long window that faced out on to a forlorn-looking formal garden.

'You know, Sidney,' the CC muttered thoughtfully to his companion, Detective Chief Inspector Sidney James Walsh, after he'd downed a fair proportion of the liquid in his glass, 'this research chap may be a genius, but he's also bloody stupid. Why the hell did he blurt all that out in front of this lot? I wouldn't trust half of these twits here to keep a secret like that, not even if they were deaf, blind and bloody dumb. The drug barons are not going to be very happy if a cure is found for addiction, and, for that matter, neither are the tobacco companies. Cigarettes made a three billion dollar profit in the States last year, you know, and that'd all go up in smoke like their products if this venture ever gets off the ground.'

Detective Chief Inspector Sidney Walsh relaxed back in his chair. He was a six-foot, lean, fit and confident man, in his early fifties, but just now, as he nodded his agreement, his ruggedly handsome face was stern and thoughtful.

'If the merest whisper of this gets out,' he said seriously, 'we could have half the world's hitmen descending on Cambridge, with just one object in mind, to wipe that research team right off the map.'

The CC drummed his fingers on the table. 'Why the hell does it have to be on our patch?' he muttered irritably. 'Tomorrow you'd better go and see whoever's in charge of the university's security, Sidney. It's their problem really, not ours, but you'd better make sure they know what they're up to. If anything does go wrong, we'll be expected to clear up the mess. Do what you can, but don't breathe a word of this to anyone, do you hear? I can't do anything myself because I'll be away for a couple of days—wife's birthday, you know. I'm taking her to Paris, or I will if this bloody fog clears. We'll have a chat about it when I get back. Maybe we can get this research project moved to somewhere that's more secure—anywhere that's off our patch will do.'

Sidney Walsh looked dubious. 'On anything to do with university property I normally liaise with their chief security officer, but he's just retired, and the new one won't know what's going on. I'm not sure I know just who to talk to on something like this, especially if I can't say precisely what it's about.'

'I don't care who the devil you talk to,' the CC stated firmly. 'Just make certain that if anything does go wrong, no one can blame us. That's what's important. Right!'

2

The bitter winds from the icy wastes of northern Europe had swept ruthlessly into eastern England, blowing away the clammy foggy mists and causing the knobs of fires and thermostats to be moved up a few notches, and extra thick woollies to be dug out from bottom drawers.

The cold weather did not worry some, though.

Detective Chief Inspector Sidney James Walsh's rather bland but functional office in Cambridge's Parkside headquarters building was double-glazed, centrally heated, and comfortably warm.

It wasn't the cheeriest of places, but he sat contentedly enough at his desk, puffing at his pipe; near at hand, a cup of coffee was gradually cooling to the desired temperature.

Spread out before him were a number of neatly typed reports, which, when read, would end up in the various case files that were in piles on the far side of the desk top.

He could afford to feel relaxed and at ease, for none of those cases was

19

of a particularly serious nature, even though they were being investigated by his so-called Serious Crime team. Most of those cases were progressing quite satisfactorily too, as these reports of yesterday's interviews and other activities would no doubt confirm. They might even contain that little extra piece of information that would enable him, after due thought and consideration, to point an accusing finger at some minor criminal, or to deduce some new line of inquiry that might also result in the solution of a crime.

The mental activity required for that sort of work was not dissimilar to that needed by a crossword addict, or a jigsaw puzzler. The only difference was that the real clues, or pieces, first had to be sorted out from the far greater number of irrelevant facts. It was an exercise that Walsh enjoyed, and one that he was good at too. What he had before him would keep him happily and productively occupied for the rest of the morning, perhaps even longer.

Perhaps there is some unwritten Murphy-like law of human behaviour, which states that when one anticipates a period of relative pleasure, then something will occur to disturb it. If there isn't, then there ought to be, because it happens often enough.

In Walsh's case the interruption came in the form of a telephone message—to the effect that the chief constable wished to see him. Such a summons was not a rare event, of course, but this one had an unusual feature: the CC was not in his office on the top floor of the building, but at his home near the village of Barton, some way out from the city, and that was where Walsh was expected to meet him.

The CC's house was a spacious modern residence, standing secluded in its own well-wooded grounds. It might have warranted the description of being elegant and in the 'Queen Anne' style, were it not for the incongruous white-painted Corinthian columns that supported the low-pitched roof of the porch at the front of the building.

The sitting-room inside was equally spacious, with wide windows facing out to a long-lawned seasonally barren garden, but although it was expensively furnished, the general effect of the décor was rather colourless, and it lacked any specific feature to catch the eye and create interest.

'Sidney heads my Serious Crime team,' the chief constable explained, having introduced Walsh to the other visitor, who was already seated comfortably in one of the deeply cushioned armchairs.

'And I'm very pleased to meet you, too,' replied the dapper, brown-suited, thin-faced American, whose hair was much darker than it had any right to be at his age, as he reached forward to shake Walsh's hand.

'Julian is a member of one of the United States' intelligence services, Sidney,' the chief constable explained, beaming an unusually broad smile from his ruddy face. 'Think of him as CIA, FBI, or one of the others, if you know what they are. It doesn't matter, you'd be wrong. What he does is so secret that even he doesn't know who he works for sometimes,' he chuckled. 'Go on, Julian, tell us what's so important to us here in Cambridge that you can't come straight out and tell it to me on the phone.'

The American seemed quite unperturbed by the flippant manner of his introduction, but he pulled thoughtfully at his chin while he studied Walsh's face. It was an examination that went on in silence for quite some time, giving the unmistakable impression that he was not over-happy at having a third person present at this meeting, and was therefore intent on making his own assessment of that individual's character and reliability.

'All right, young man,' Julian said eventually, having apparently come to some satisfactory conclusions on those points. 'As you might expect, we Americans have a few people scattered about in various different countries, just keeping their eyes and ears open, and finding out anything interesting that's going on.' He paused to clear his throat. 'One of them works for me, in Columbia. That's not always a nice place to be, you know—it gets a bit rough there sometimes. Anyway, this agent of mine has lately been keeping an eye on a man named Ramon DaSilva. You won't have heard of him. I don't suppose it's his real name, but it's the one we know him by. He's what you might call a freelance trouble-shooter. He specialises in sorting out problems for international crime syndicates. Not little problems, mind you—big ones, ones that require brain power rather than physical aggression, though I don't suppose he's lacking in that area, if he needs it.' Julian paused to rub a finger on the side of his stubby nose, then he continued. 'He's a very clever man, and not wanted by any police force anywhere, not to my knowledge anyway. That shows how careful he is.'

'You mean he's a hired killer, and he's managed to get away with it every time?' demanded the CC incredulously.

'That's not what I said. This man deals with more businesslike things than mere assassinations. How can I put it? If a cartel are losing too many men, or their shipments are getting picked up a bit too often, and they can't put their own finger on the reason why, they might well call DaSilva in to sort it out. That's one example, but on the other hand, say there's a dispute between two organisations, and they can't agree things themselves, they might call on him to arbitrate. He'd investigate the facts, and make a judgement. I've never heard of his ruling ever being disputed. I'll give you an actual illustration, if you like. About five years ago there was a problem in Italy. One of the syndicates and a Mafia gang started having problems in an area where their borders were ill defined. It was a typical Al Capone situation, with the local guys starting to bump each other off. It could easily have blown up into something really nasty, and trouble eats into everyone's profits. So another syndicate, one that wasn't directly involved, called DaSilva in to sort it out, and they told the guilty parties what they'd done. Before DaSilva had even arrived in Rome the warring factions had ordered a cease-fire, and were sitting round a table redefining their borders. They sorted it out themselves, in fact, but that wasn't the end of it—no, sir. DaSilva fined each of them a hundred thousand dollars for causing the trouble in the first place—and they both paid up. Half of the money went to an orphanage in Milan and the rest to a mission of Irish nursing nuns in the Tigre region of Ethiopia. What do you think of that? It's one of our biggest problems nowadays, the way international crime has got itself organised and regulated. It's getting more like a mini United Nations, with the top boys meeting regularly, and even co-operating on projects. They're not wasting their time fighting amongst themselves as they used to, but do you see what I mean about DaSilva? He's got a hell of a personality, yet he's only a little short guy—middle-aged, about forty-five I'd say. I can't tell you much more about him, unfortunately. He keeps himself well out of the limelight usually, and we don't even know where his base is. All I can add is that he does like his women—he's not too old for that.' The American grinned wryly as he shrugged his shoulders. 'I've got some photos of him for you. They're not very good, but they're the best I can do. Anyway, there you are, he's all yours. When I saw the word Cambridge in our agent's report, I immediately thought of you. I've got to be in London this evening, that's why I'm here now.'

'What do you mean, he's all ours?' the CC growled, his strangely beatific smile having long since been replaced by a wrinkled frown. 'What are we supposed to do with him? He doesn't sound the type we want around here.'

'Tough luck, old friend,' Julian replied with a faintly ironic grin. 'DaSilva arrived in Paris, from Lisbon, yesterday morning, and that's where we lost him, but he's coming here, to Cambridge, England. Why? We don't know. Two nights ago he took a phone call, promptly packed his bags, and was off in a hurry. All our agent overheard was, "Cambridge, England", bless her pretty little heart. Now, maybe I could help you more, if I knew why he was coming here. Have you got some sort of trouble with the drug barons brewing? I don't envy you if you have.'

The chief constable stared at him with his jaw now set hard like a piece of granite, and he shook his balding head.

'No! We've no trouble that I know of,' he said blandly. 'We live a quiet life here, you know. Just the odd murder or two, and an occasional bit of rape and pillage to keep us on our toes.'

Sidney Walsh rubbed his chin thoughtfully and ventured a suggestion. 'Are you sure he's coming here on business? Could he not be having a holiday, or visiting friends for Christmas?'

The American sighed, held his hands up

26

in a helpless gesture and looked up at the white artexed ceiling in exasperation.

'For Christ's sake, man. No one in their right mind comes to England for a holiday in winter. Hell, you won't see the sun again for six months, and even then it'll be raining, and that east wind of yours'll be blowing—'

'You said he gave those fines to charity,' Walsh said, interrupting the American's ramblings. 'Does that mean he's a religious man, in spite of his line of business?'

Julian nodded his approval at that question. 'Now, that's a good point you're making there, son. We think he's a Catholic, but whether he can get absolutions for the kind of sins he gets involved in, I don't know. Whatever you do, don't you underestimate him. He prefers to act as a loner, but if he needs to, he can call on resources that are so vast they'd make your annual budget spends here look like loose change in a petty cash box.'

'He likes his women, you say? How does he like them? Does he take one round with him from country to country, hotel to hotel, or does he pick up new ones in different places?' Walsh wanted to know.

The American looked at him keenly, then shook his head. 'He never stays in a hotel. The times we've come across

27

him he's been in an out-of-the-way flat or apartment, with a local girl hired as cook, bottlewasher and live-in tart. When he disappears into the blue, the girl's paid off. We've talked with a couple of them, and they seemed to like him—our girl in Columbia certainly did. You'll be careful what you do with those photos, won't you? He ain't stupid, and if he gets wind you're after him, our agent in Bogotá might just end up with her throat cut. I wouldn't take too kindly to that. Now, I must be on my way.' He pushed himself up from his chair. 'It's been nice meeting you again, and I'm sorry I can't stay to meet your wife, but I have so much to do... You know how to get in touch with me if you need me. I'll be having our people over here look for DaSilva too. I want to know what he's up to, even if you don't.'

The chief constable motioned to Walsh to stay behind, then escorted his guest outside to his car. When he came back he was rubbing his chilled hands together.

'That was clever of you to divert him with that silly remark about DaSilva coming here for a holiday, Sidney. I was afraid you might say something about this "cure for addiction" business. We don't want the likes of Julian knowing anything about that. Now, what have you done about the security at the Medical Research Centre?'

Walsh smiled grimly. 'Absolutely nothing,' he said bluntly.

The CC's eyes narrowed and he banged his fist on the arm of his chair angrily. 'What the hell do you mean? I told you to—'

'Well, just listen, and I'll tell you about it,' Walsh retorted calmly. 'I found out that old Professor Hughes at Downing College was on the university's security committee, so I went to see him. After a lot of beating about the bush we did get talking about the medical research projects, but it all turned out to be a waste of time. While I was there someone rang to tell him that the Home Office had instructed Scotland Yard to take complete control of all security at the Medical Research Centre. They've the authority to do that under some subsection of the Prevention of Terrorism Act, apparently. The man who's got the job is Superintendent Anderson. I've met him once or twice, but I don't know much about him. Edwin Hughes nearly hit the roof. You can understand why—the university doesn't like outside interference from anyone—but there was nothing he could do about it. I didn't mind—I didn't fancy the job.'

'No, I bet you didn't.' The CC looked

better-tempered now. 'Well, it looks as though we might have to get involved, whether we like it or not. Clearly, what that scientist chap said at that conference has leaked out. What are we going to do? We don't want blokes like DaSilva on our patch causing trouble.'

'What are we going to do? We can't do anything until we've found him, and how can we do that if we can't show these photos about? They're not much good anyway,' Walsh replied, flicking through the glossy prints.

'You'd best have a photofit sketch done from them. We're always waving those things under people's noses. They never seem to do a lot of good, but you never know,' the CC suggested.

Walsh nodded reluctantly. It was only a little while ago that he'd felt relaxed and at ease; now he could feel himself tensing up. With all this talk of hitmen and international crime syndicates it was difficult to think clearly and logically, but he forced himself to make the effort. 'I think we should have surveillance teams watching the Research Centre, and the homes of those two scientists, Wade and Chambers. If they really are the reason why DaSilva is coming here, we may not need to go out looking for him, maybe he'll come to us. I'll need to tell my team what's going on, though.'

'Oh no, you won't,' the CC uttered firmly. 'Definitely not. There's only you and me who know what's really going on around here, and I want it kept that way. Your team will just have to carry out your orders without questioning them, They don't need to know. Right?'

Walsh nodded reluctantly. 'All right! I'll take these photos, and get on with it then,' he replied, starting to get up from his comfortable chair, but then he changed his mind, and sat back down again. 'There's something else that needs doing first,' he added, staring directly at the other's rugged features.

'I'll buy it. What's eating you now?'

'We're assuming that DaSilva's coming here because of what was said at that conference in Berkshire—'

'Of course we are,' the CC interrupted. 'You don't really believe that nonsense of yours about the fellow coming here on holiday, do you?'

'No! Let me finish.'

'Well, get to the point then. I should have been in my office hours ago. I'm way behind schedule as it is.'

'Well, someone at that conference must have passed on the information about the drug research project. That aspect needs following up straight away.'

31

The CC stared at Walsh's face and the middle finger of his right hand started to tap on the arm of his chair.

'You're quite right—and if that someone talked about the cure for addicts, then he would also have talked about the plans for combating drug imports. It's easy enough to avoid trouble, if you know where it is.' He scratched idly at the top of his head. 'There'll have to be an investigation—but we can't do it. How far do you think we'd get investigating the affairs of five chief constables and a Home Office minister, even if he is a junior one, and there's all the others who were there. The place could have been bugged, you know.'

Walsh nodded. 'It's possible, but even if it was, you wouldn't be able to prove it after all this time, so you've got no choice but to act as if there was an informer. Will your American friend have told London about DaSilva's movements?'

The CC shook his head vigorously. 'I doubt it. Julian controls a string of sleeper agents, I think. That's long-term, patient stuff, but the sections of their secret services don't work well with each other, so it's hardly likely that they'd pass relatively minor information like that to any of our lot. Julian's only told me because he knows Cambridge is my patch, and because I did him a favour once when I was in the army. He hasn't forgotten that yet, thank goodness. They're the best kind of friends to have, the ones that owe you something; but you heard him—I've got to be careful what I do with that information, or he won't come up with any more. Oh well, I suppose I'll have to go to the very top. I can't just do nothing about it.'

'What, the Prime Minister?' Walsh asked, raising his eyebrows in surprise.

'Good lord, no. The Home Secretary. He's a sensible enough bloke—for a politician. Let's see if he's in his office. It's a bit early for him to be in the House. You never know your luck.' He reached for the nearby telephone, thumbed through a small black notebook he'd taken from his inner jacket pocket, then dialled a number.

'Chief Constable, Cambridgeshire. I'd like a word with the Home Secretary if he's there... Yes, of course it's important—would I be ringing him on this number if it wasn't? No, I'm not going to tell you what it's about... So, you may be his personal private secretary—so what?...I'll wait.' He put his hand over the mouthpiece. 'He's there,' he whispered loudly to Walsh.

Then the conversation started.

The CC set out most of the facts, briefly but concisely.

'So! You think we've got a mole in high places, do you?' the Home Secretary said, after a few moments' consideration.

'A rat, more likely,' the CC suggested.

'Yes, very true. This hitman you say is coming—can you handle him, or would you like Scotland Y—'

'Not likely. Your minister's already sent a Superintendent Anderson up to the Medical Research Centre. God knows what stories are being spread round to account for that. I'm putting Sidney Walsh on to it... Yes, that's right. He was the one on that business in Brighton a while back. If it weren't for him you lot would all be banging your heads on the walls of padded cells right now.'

'It's brick walls I bang my head on most of the time. All right, you carry on, but if you do need any help, let me know. As for investigating the people at that conference—you'd better leave that with me. We, er, do have a department which exists specifically for things like this. I'll get them to liaise with you if they turn up anything useful. Goodbye for now. Thanks for ringing.'

'So that's that, Sidney,' the CC said smugly, as he put the receiver down. 'I've done my bit. Now, you find this fellow DaSilva, then we'll see about putting a spoke in his wheel.'

34

In Walsh's office the two other members of his Serious Crime team looked at him expectantly.

Detective Constable Brenda Phipps stood restlessly by the window, looking very slim and attractive in her tight blue jeans and white polo-necked sweater.

Detective Sergeant Reginald Finch, long and lanky, fair-haired and blue-eyed, sat on the chair at the far side of Walsh's desk, where he could stretch out his legs more comfortably.

'Well, what's up, Chief?' Brenda Phipps demanded impatiently, casually sweeping an unruly lock of brown hair from her forehead with the back of one hand.

Walsh laid several sketches and written descriptions of Ramon DaSilva on his desk.

'I want you both to leave whatever else you're doing, and find this man for me,' he announced.'There's not a lot to go on, I'm afraid. He's short, dark-haired, and probably has a swarthy complexion, and we believe he's a Catholic. So what I'd like you to do, Brenda, is list all the Catholic churches within a twenty-mile radius of Cambridge, and work out a manning plan so we can watch for him if he turns up at any of their services. Reg, I want you to organise a twenty-four hour surveillance of the university's Medical Research Centre, and the homes of these two chaps as well.' He then laid down photographs and details of the researchers, Dr Wade and Dr Chambers.

'Hell fire, Chief, that'll take all the manpower in our sections, and more,' Brenda Phipps protested. 'What's this fellow done to warrant this sort of treatment?'

'It isn't what he's done, it's what he might do. You find him for me, then maybe I'll be able to tell you. I can't at the moment. You just get cracking! When you've got your rosters and schedules worked out, come and see me with them. If we haven't got enough people in our own teams, we'll have to find some more from somewhere else, won't we?'

Left on his own again Walsh got up and went to stare out of the window.

It wasn't a big city out there, but it was a bustling, busy city—a university city—vibrant with activity. Many of those within its boundaries were intellectually brilliant, in a wide diversity of subjects. They probably formed the world's richest and most fertile concentration of brain-power, one that generated new thoughts and new ideas, many of which had benefited all mankind. Just as this 'cure for addiction' project might, if it ever existed long enough to get off the ground.

Now there was an impending threat to this intellectual excellence. Internationally organised crime was coming here with murderous intent, planning to disturb the academic peace.

The complacency he'd felt earlier that morning had now long gone. It had been replaced by an apprehensive doubt about his own abilities to cope with a situation that he'd never come up against before. Any number of unknown callous men might be following DaSilva here. Men who were experienced in all aspects of evil, from simple robbery to tortuous murder—and they were completely free from any of the restrictions of decency and fair play that society required its police force to observe. What was it Julian had said? 'Their resources are vast.' The resources he could fall back on were anything but that. He had a small team on which he could rely, plus a much larger number of officers specially trained and equipped to stop speeding motorists, find lost bikes and children, break up the odd pub fight, and generally act as peacemakers in local domestic squabbles. With resources such as these he would have to try to protect those people out there from this looming threat of mindless violence.

At that moment he felt himself no more

able to do that than could a Stone Age savage protect himself from a stream of modern bullets with a wooden shield—or, perhaps more appropriately, than he could tackle a swarm of angry hornets armed with only a feather duster.

The slim, red-haired young girl struggled up the second flight of stairs of the luxury block of flats in Huntingdon. She carried a small battered suitcase in one hand and a bulging duffel bag slung over her shoulder.

She stopped outside the door with a number four on it, hesitated, gripped her bottom lip firmly between her teeth, then resolutely pressed the door bell.

The dark-haired man who opened the door was only a few inches taller than her own five feet four. He was wearing brown corduroy trousers and a thick white sweater. His grey eyes seemed friendly enough, but his lightly tanned face looked tired.

'Good afternoon,' he said politely.

'Mr Silver? I'm Angela—you're expecting me, I believe,' she replied nervously.

'Am I? Good—well, you'd better come in out of the cold. Let me take your bag and your coat, or would you rather keep it on? I've got the heating going flat out, but it still doesn't seem to be getting very warm in here.' He shivered involuntarily as he spoke.

Angela looked curiously about her as she followed him through the small hallway into a spacious, comfortably furnished sitting-room. It seemed warm enough to her, over-warm in fact. The dark-haired man went to sit in an armchair pulled up close to a log-effect electric fire.

'Mr Marston sent me,' Angela added. She had remained standing by the door, a little bewildered by her casual reception.

The man's head turned, and the grey eyes looked at her impassively. 'And did Marston explain precisely what was required of you, if you're suitable?' he asked.

'Yes,' she replied shyly, her gaze moving from the man's face to the carpet on the floor in front of her.

The man rubbed his chin thoughtfully. His first impression had been that the girl was skinny, but on further reflection he changed his opinion. She was certainly slim, but there was flesh on her bones, and her tiny waist flowed into nicely rounded hips and down to slender supple legs.

The girl stirred nervously under his scrutiny.

'Will I do?' she said tentatively.

'Perhaps. Did Marston give you anything to bring with you?' he asked, tonelessly.

The girl's bottom lip was starting to flutter, and her eyes clearly betrayed her inner feelings—she was frightened, and very apprehensive. 'Yes! There's an envelope in my bag.' She turned away to fetch it, then stood watching while it was opened, and the contents read.

'So! You worked a computer system fraud to get yourself five thousand pounds; and you were careless enough to get caught, were you? What did you want that kind of money for? You're not very old, are you?' he asked with a suspicion of a smile on his lips.

Angela's big blue eyes were definitely watering; soon a tear would form if she couldn't blink it back.

'I'm nearly nineteen, and I wanted a newer car,' she blurted out. 'Mr Marston said that if I was suitable...and did what you wanted...it could all be forgotten, otherwise...I, er...I'll be sent to prison.'

The man's jaw hardened as he stared back at her. 'He said that, did he?'

He felt annoyed. He'd expected Marston to send someone worldly wise, someone confident and brazen, who would do a job willingly—for a fair price. Instead he'd been sent a blackmailed girl who was clearly terrified, and probably inexperienced as well. Marston was a London solicitor, and the syndicate's UK money launderer;

at that he may have been good, but at judging another man's taste in women, he was very naïve.

'Don't you want me? I don't want to go to prison. Won't I do—please?' Angela whispered fearfully. The tear escaped and ran slowly down her cheek.

The man saw that tear. The girl was scared, as much by him and what he wanted her for as by the prospect of appearing in court and a life-ruining prison sentence. Not a very nice position for anyone to find themselves in—having to face up to the devil or the deep blue sea—least of all for a pretty youngster like this one. He tried to maintain his stern gaze, but gradually a more sympathetic smile came into his eyes.

'All right, all right. Yes, you'll do,' he grunted reluctantly. 'Now, I'm cold, I'm tired and I'm hungry, and there's nothing edible in the fridge, so the first job we've got to do is to go out and do some shopping. You can cook, can't you? Good! You can rustle up something when we get back, then I want an early night. Oh yes, and Marston has sent these for you.' He handed her a cellophane-covered card. 'You'd better take the first one now, I think, and the doctor has given you a clean bill of health, too, if you didn't know,' he added, having now sorted through all the documents in the envelope. At least in that respect, Marston had been thorough.

Angela took the pills from him with a strange expression on her face. 'You mean I haven't got Aids or any other kind of disease, I suppose. Thank you! You don't seem to take any chances, do you, Mr Silver?'

'Ronald Silver—you may call me Ron— and no, I don't take unnecessary chances. Neither should you. You ought to ask me if you can see my blood donor's card, to make sure that I've no infections.'

Angela pressed out the first of the birth control pills and put it in her mouth with a look of disgust. 'And have you got one?' she asked.

'Oh yes, but I don't happen to have it with me at the moment.'

'So! This is what you spent your money on,' Silver said dubiously, opening the passenger door of the rusty twelve-year-old Mini. 'Personally, I don't think you had a bargain. I hope the heater works, it doesn't look as though much else will.'

'Of course it does,' Angela replied spiritedly. 'It's a very reliable car, and the rust's all artistically applied, so that no one will want to pinch it.'

'Very likely. See if you can drive it

into town without scratching any of your artistic rust.'

'Ordnance Survey maps, please,' Ronald Silver asked of the girl behind the bookshop counter, 'and a street map of Cambridge.'

'There's the Cambridge one. What area Ordnance Survey map do you want? Or you can buy a pack like this one. That's got the whole of East Anglia in it, from North Norfolk, right down to the London area. They work out cheaper that way.'

'They'll do nicely, thank you.'

Displayed in the window of the men's outfitters were waxed waterproof jackets, wellington boots, sheepskin coats, gloves, and a variety of warm clothes, suitable for an English winter.

'I'll pop in here while you go to the supermarket. If there's any money left over, get yourself some new undies or something. I'll meet you back at the car, but don't be too long, I'm half frozen as it is,' Silver said as he handed over a wad of notes.

Angela looked at the money in her hand and her blue eyes lit up in surprise. 'Maybe there's things about all this that I might get to like, after all,' she muttered to herself, as she turned to cross the road.

'I think you're English,' Angela said positively, taking yet another sip of red wine, when they were sitting down to dinner that evening.

'Why do you say that?' Silver asked conversationally, carefully cutting into the hot steak on his plate with a serrated knife that was not as sharp as it ought to be.

'You've got a well-educated voice. I might be wrong, of course, there is just a slight accent which I can't quite place. Do you do a lot of travelling abroad, or are you based in England?'

'Is your steak as nicely cooked as mine?' Silver asked, ignoring her question and topping up her glass of wine.

'Mine's fine, but if we're going to eat like this all the time, I'm going to get mighty fat,' she replied chattily.

'Does that worry you? What you look like, I mean? Whether you've got a nice figure, or not?'

Angela shrugged her slim shoulders. 'Not particularly. My figure's just the shape of the body that happens to move my brain around from place to place, but putting on weight will make me feel listless and sluggish. I wouldn't like that.'

'Good for you,' Silver smiled approvingly, apparently finding the young girl's conversation refreshingly direct and uncomplicated.

Angela smiled mistily back. Her face felt flushed, but this, her third glass of wine, was definitely helping to make the world seem just a little bit more rosy, and a little bit hazy as well.

'You've got a nice face when you smile, Ron,' she was rather surprised to hear herself say. 'I don't feel so frightened of you as I did. That horrible man Marston's dead scared of you. I know that. I could sense it when he told me to be careful not to upset you, or ask too many questions. Maybe he's right to be scared, there's an awfully cold glint in your eyes sometimes. Mind you, I think that's probably because you're lonely. I think that might explain it,' she confided thoughtfully.

Silver looked up in astonishment, frowned, and changed the subject.

'Now, this is a company's courtesy flat,' he said quietly. 'It's for the convenience of visiting customers, so the other residents here are used to different people coming and going. It would be better if you could avoid getting into conversation with them, but if you can't, I suggest you say I'm an American businessman, and that you're my secretary. Other than that, you may have your own key, and come and go much as you please. When you need more money for anything, just say so.'

Ronald Silver sat by the fire, in his dressing-gown, reading through the papers in a quite bulky file. Marston had done well to gather so much information in such a short time.

There were photographs of the two research scientists, Wade and Chambers, and maps showing where each of them lived, as well as sketched plan layouts of several laboratories, including the medical one. There was also a list of some local people in the syndicate's pay, who might possibly be of use.

He had yet to work out his strategic plan. There was a lot of deep thinking to be done before he was ready to commit himself to any form of action. Tentatively, though, he had in mind the planting of two or three bombs in suitably easy targets, and making them out to be the work of 'animal rights' activists. Then the real target of Wade's and Chambers' laboratory might appear to be merely one of a series. That would lessen the risk that suspicion might fall on the syndicate's valuable high-level informer.

Unfortunately, if one pursued that idea logically, it meant using a common explosive. Such amateur organisations would have no access to Semtex or the like, but, of course, in that respect, there were explosives lying around all over the place, if one knew where to look, and was prepared to take a risk. Old army firing ranges were the obvious places to start with. He put the file down, and opened out one of the Ordnance Survey maps. If he couldn't find one in them, he'd get Marston to ask his local employees.

It was a few moments later that Angela came out of the bathroom.

'I bought these with your money. Do you approve?' she asked shyly, as she pirouetted round to display herself in scanty black lacy underwear that contrasted dramatically with the bare white skin of her body. Then she knelt down on the rug by the fire to dry her hair. Presumably the quantity of wine she had consumed had helped overcome some of her earlier embarrassment, or else she was putting on a brave act, by behaving in a way she thought someone in her position ought.

Silver nodded his appreciation.

'Charming,' he replied. He laid the Ordnance Survey map of North Norfolk down on the floor, and relaxed back in his chair to watch her. If she was acting a part, it seemed only fair for her audience to give her some kind of encouraging attention. With all her clothes on he'd thought her skinny, but with them all just about off—well, there wasn't a lot to complain about.

He reached forward to twang the narrow back strap of her bra—that had always been a weakness of his, ever since he'd been a kid. He was rewarded with a shy grin, but by the time her hair was dry, and had been thoroughly brushed and combed, Angela's bottom lip was again gripped between her teeth, and a frown had reappeared on her forehead.

Clearly she wasn't looking forward to the next stage of their agreement, and under the circumstances, he wasn't too sure that he was either. The electric blanket had been on now for over an hour, so in a little while he'd better take her to bed. The more frightened she became the worse it would be for both of them. The sooner it was all sorted out, the better.

3

A narrow rutted track led to a spacious shingled car-park, laid out amongst scrubby bare hedges; already it contained several cars.

The nearby low red-brick building seemed to be the place where most of the visitors wished to congregate, but one particular driver seemed content to be alone.

Out of that car's boot came green wellingtons, a dark brown waxed jacket with many zips and pockets, and matching over-trousers. A hat was pulled firmly down on the head, and the flapping ear-pieces were strapped together under the chin. With thick gloves and tinted spectacles, there was little enough of the person within showing on the outside, and that was very wise—for anyone venturing out on to North Norfolk's Titchwell marshes during a particularly cold spell in the midst of winter. A large canvas haversack slung over a shoulder, and the straps of a camera and field glasses passed over the neck, completed the standard, common enough attire of the enthusiastic amateur ornithologist, now fully prepared to venture forth and spy on the private and social activities of the hundreds of birds for which the marshes are famous.

The small group of similarly clad people gathered by the entrance to the building, now with a leader or guide, moved slowly off in Indian file, down a low-lying well-used narrow path. It was duck-boarded in places where the mud lay really thick and glutinous, and it passed between high brambly hedges which confused any sense of direction.

The loner followed them, but some distance behind.

After a short while the hedges thinned out and it was necessary to climb boarded steps cut in the side of a low sea wall.

That sea wall had had a more specific purpose, back in the late 1940s, when the land to either side had been under cultivation; but that was before those fateful, memorable gales had whipped the North Sea into the raging fury that had battered and flooded most of England's east coast, destroying homes, drowning families, and tearing down those puny walls of earth and sand that had kept it at bay from low-lying areas.

Here, at Titchwell, the battle with the elements had not been continued. Nature's gauntlet still lay where it had fallen. Now the whole place was a memorial to a defeat, erected by the defeated, in the guise of a victory for wild-life conservation—a sanctuary for birds.

For someone who had just been hemmed in by hedges and had walked with eyes downcast, searching for safe footholds in the squelching mud, arriving at the top of that low wall was not unlike emerging from some dark manhole, be that unlikely manhole on top of a church tower—for the apparent vastness of the vista was astonishing. Low skies and scudding clouds merged with the grey drabness of land and sea to make indistinct horizons that seemed an infinite distance away.

There was another feature that drew immediate attention up there on that sea wall—the wind. Strong and steady, it blew from the east with an icy interminability that sought, and found, the hidden interstices in clothing claimed by its makers to be impenetrable.

The group adjusted collars and cuffs, and pulled up hoods, then commenced a slow plod to the north and the distant growling sea.

To the left the land consisted of a confusion of deep, muddy creeks that twisted and twined through the grey-green vegetation—the real salt marshes that were flooded and drained by each tide; but

51

on the right, the water was trapped in rush-bound lagoons, rippled by the wind and alive with the rustling movement of reeds.

Something in all that caught the attention of the guide, and his pointing arm brought the others of the group close around him to hear his words. Binoculars were raised and aimed in the direction of a far-distant patch of reed.

The loner, plodded on, and went passed them.

'...from Greenland. They come every year. Quite rare really...' the guide was saying.

The loner glanced in that direction, but saw nothing significant. In any case it seemed incredible that any sane bird with the strength and ability to navigate the odd few hundred miles from Greenland would be stupid enough to stop here, in this wind-blown inhospitable spot, rather than fly on to some warmer, sunnier land.

Further on, the concrete top of a wartime blockhouse showed above the water. Uneven subsidence had left the whole massive construction angled and askew in the mud.

The distant rumble of the sea now became the dominant sound, even above that of the wind whistling by the earpieces of the hat. The path led on into low sand dunes topped by tufts of waving marram grass, and thence to the beach.

The tide was well on its way out, and low waves turned and rolled into thin white lines, far away across the glittering expanse of flat muddy sand.

The loner turned to the left, and trudged along the bank of shingle, each step sinking in a few inches, testing out the muscles at the back of the legs. Nearer the sea another blockhouse lay in wrecked dismembered lumps, from which bent and rusty iron bars protruded grotesque shapes. A further reminder of the strength and fury of stormy seas.

It was a bleak and lonely shore, but with each step a distant, narrow, brick structure, surrounded by still-green vegetation, became more visible in the far dunes ahead. This was the spotter's post for the artillery firing range that had been here during the war, of which this area still contained so many poignant reminders.

Guns on the low hills inland had rained shells down on this beach, training operatives in the skills which would enable them to kill, maim and destroy—from a safe distance. Many of those shells, however, had not exploded on impact. They had merely penetrated the sand and mud to a depth of perhaps twenty feet or so, to a layer of preserving peat. There they had lain harmlessly, while the years had passed and foe had become uneasy friend, and the subtle pressures and vibrations of storm and tide had gradually eased them upwards to the surface.

The loner soon found one. It was a high-explosive, twenty-five pounder shell. The conical tip that had failed to detonate on impact protruded just above the surface. Bare hands eased away the mud and sand, until the heavy object, five inches or so in diameter and fifteen inches long, could be lifted clear. It was not alone; two yards away was the fin of a mortar bomb, and beyond, a lump of casing, which might be part or whole. Cautiously, and with the utmost care, the loner carried the shell to the deserted brick building, out of sight and out of the wind, and laid it gently down on the firm concrete floor. It was not wise to take it further, not with the detonator still in place, and the removal of that was a risky process. The army bomb disposal teams that patrolled the area every few weeks never even tried, they exploded them where they lay in the sand.

Nevertheless, with care, that removal was possible. A chisel from the haversack scraped away rust and exposed shiny brass where the detonator cap screwed into the steel of the casing, but it needed the small narrow blade of a knife, and the sharp point of a dart, to clear the head and slot of the grub screw in the casing that locked the brass threads. A squirt with WD40, both feet to hold the shell firm, then, pressing hard down with the screwdriver, a sudden anti-clockwise jerk, and the grub screw was loosened. Now the detonator could be unscrewed, if corrosion had not locked it all solid. Wide-jawed stetsons could clamp the casing, and mole grips the brass cone, and then a massive but controlled heave, to gain a movement of just a fraction of a turn. Another heave, and now it could be turned by hand, revealing puttied screw threads as brassy bright as the day they had come off some wartime Midlands factory lathe.

There was no need to carry away the heavy steel cylinder. The olive-coloured, toffee-like contents of the casing could be spooned out into a plastic food container. RDX, in military terms, or trinitrotoluene, in civilian scientific terminology, but more commonly called TNT; it was still active after all those years, but safe enough to handle, provided it wasn't hit hard or impacted with a bullet.

The loner threw the casing and detonator into the murky waters of the salt marsh, repacked the haversack, and set out on the long trudge back to the car-park.

Now the icy biting wind pressed on the loner's chest like a giant invisible hand, but an occasional welcome stop to peer through the binoculars at some blurred distant view would serve to convince any chance observer that here was yet another bird-watcher who had merely strayed further afield than usual.

The bitterly cold east wind had been blowing constantly every day for nearly a whole week, but now it was driving a fine sleety rain with such force that it easily penetrated into the bus-stop shelter where a rather bedraggled-looking Detective Constable Brenda Phipps stood waiting. Her hip-length parka was water-proof enough, but below that her jeans, particularly on her left side, were already soaked through. She was used to a certain amount of discomfort and periods of inactivity whilst on surveillance operations, but standing around outside in weather like this was quite miserable, even for someone as physically fit and mentally tough as she considered herself to be. There was little consolation in knowing that she wasn't suffering on her own. There were twenty or so other plain-clothes officers out and about that morning, watching the Catholic churches in Cambridge, and more in places like Ely, Huntingdon and Royston. That was a lot of the Constabulary's available manpower.

She looked at her watch. There was still another ten minutes before the service in the biggest of the churches, the one on the corner of Lensfield Road and Hills Road, would come to its scheduled end and allow its congregation to pass out through the arched doorway and disperse in all directions. On a day like today that dispersal would be quick—thoughts of warm homes and hot lunches would present an attraction that would far outweigh any desire to stand around and chatter to once-a-week friends and acquaintances. That meant there would be little time for the police surveillance team to study the leavers and pick out those whose physical and facial characteristics matched those of the unnamed man they were after. There were six officers to cover this church, just enough, based on the observations made of those people going into the service. She could actually see one of them. Detective Constable Arthur Bryant had been studying the balls of wool in the shop on the opposite side of the busy road junction for twenty minutes now. Two more officers were round the corner in Lensfield Road, and the other two were the lucky ones, warm and dry inside the church, celebrating Mass, and doing their secular duty at the same time.

A red double-decker bus drew up, *en route* to the railway station. Brenda stepped back out of the queue. Five minutes later the inner wooden doors of the church opened, and another bus, this one on its way to Addenbrooke's Hospital, arrived to block her view. When that had gone there were dozens of people milling about on the far pavement, buttoning coats and putting up umbrellas. One of them was her fellow police officer who had been stationed inside. He was walking purposefully, clearly following a lone shortish man in a grey overcoat and trilby. Several people were crossing over to her side of the road, to join the bus queue, and one of those was a bespectacled man, about five feet sevenish, wearing a brown waxed waterproof jacket with the wide collar turned up, and with a flat cloth cap pulled well down over his forehead.

Brenda's heart beat a trifle faster. It was difficult to see his features, but he was the right height and had the stocky stature of the man that she was looking for.

The next bus was also going to the hospital. Brenda stepped back to let others get on, but since the man she was interested in was one of those, she got on too, and went to a seat at the rear of the lower deck, where she could watch him.

Rather surprisingly, he alighted two or three stops before the hospital, in an area of highly desirable residences set well back from the road and secluded by trees and high hedges.

It was not good sleuthing to follow a suspect so closely, but Brenda had no choice but to get off as well. She would certainly lose him if she stayed on until the next stop and then ran back. Fortunately, he seemed quite unaware of her existence. He walked quickly along the pavement, keeping close to the thick laurel hedge which provided a little protection from the driving wind, and then turned a corner into a side street.

Brenda took the opportunity to use the radio in her pocket to report her whereabouts to the control room in headquarters. The man was to be observed, but not apprehended, and once she'd found out where he was going, there would be nothing else for her to do. Another team in headquarters would search the electoral registers to find the names of those residing at the suspect addresses, and think of innocent-sounding reasons to visit them in order to identify those short-statured men who were long-standing inhabitants of the city. When they had been eliminated from the lists, the wanted man might be among the remainder, if there were any. It was an expensive and time-consuming exercise, and one that, in her opinion, had all the hallmarks of desperation—a wild gamble, almost verging on the panic-stricken.

She slipped the radio back in her pocket, and hurried round the corner after her particular quarry. He should be sufficiently far ahead now for her to follow without it being quite so obvious what she was doing.

Perhaps the cold wind had numbed her mind, certainly she should not have been so close to the hedge when she turned that corner, because he was waiting for her.

For a moment they just stood there, staring at each other. His eyes were narrowed and confident, hers were still wide with shock and surprise as he made his move. One of his hands grabbed her left wrist, the other reached out for the hair at the back of her neck.

'I don't like being followed. What the hell do you think you're playing at?' he snarled angrily from between clenched teeth.

Brenda let out an involuntary gasp of alarm, and leapt back, ducking her head to avoid the hand grasping for her hair. She tried to wrench her arm free, but his grip was too strong, then her unarmed combat training switched itself on and got itself going. She spun quickly on her left heel and brought her right hand round in a swinging chopping blow that caught him just above his left ear. Just in case that wasn't enough, she brought her right knee up viciously into his groin. That effectively ended the action, for her assailant silently folded in the middle and sank slowly to the ground, quite *hors de combat.* Fortunately for him Brenda's first blow had been sufficiently stunning to anaesthetise him through the worst of his excruciating pain. Fortunately for Brenda, that first blow had landed just two inches above the point in the neck where it might have been fatal, and that saved her from getting into a whole load of trouble. It wasn't a thought to which she gave any consideration just then; it would be later that she would reflect on how dangerous such highly trained, even over-trained, reactions might be.

Instead, Brenda radioed police head-quarters.

'This could be the man you want, Chief,' she suggested a little breathlessly. 'He must have spotted me getting on the bus, because he was waiting round a corner, and tried to grab me.'

'Did he now? Is he still in one piece?' Walsh asked. His voice over the radio sounded flat and emotionless. Clearly he had no doubts of her ability to look after herself.

'He's having a quiet sit-down at the moment, and he's making some rather funny noises, but I think he's all right really.'

'Hang on to him. I'll get a car to you as soon as I can.'

Detective Constable Arthur Bryant had forsaken the study of balls of wool in shop windows, and had also gone after a suspect short-statured man. This man had walked through the city streets with quick jaunty steps, then he too turned a corner into a narrow side road. When Bryant cautiously followed he did not walk into a confrontation of violence—perhaps he would have preferred to do so. Instead he found his quarry standing by a front door, and holding it open.

'I like you,' the man called out with a broad sweet smile on his face. 'Come on in out of the cold. I've got enough lunch for two, then we can get to know each other.'

'Er, not today, thank you,' Bryant muttered hurriedly. He lengthened his stride almost into a run as he set off to make his way back to headquarters.

'How is he?' Walsh asked the police doctor.

'He'll survive. He had a knee in the privates, I gather,' the doctor replied with a wry smile. 'I offered to check things out for him, but he declined. I don't suppose he'll be feeling amorous for a while. The blow to the side of his head shook him up quite a bit too, but he's just about over that. Give him a cup of coffee, a couple of aspirins, and let him sit quietly for half an hour; then you can question him. I asked him his name, but he wouldn't tell me.'

'He wouldn't tell us either. Was there nothing in his pockets to tell us who he is, Reg?' Walsh asked.

'No. There was only some money and a small bunch of keys, boss,' Reg replied cheerfully, 'but one of those was a Rover badged car key, so I've sent a patrol car up to the hospital with them. That might be where he was heading before he spotted Brenda tailing him. It's worth a try. If that key fits one of the Rovers in the car-park there, it might well be his.'

That classic piece of detective reasoning proved to be correct; with the man's car found, it only took a few moments to interrogate Vehicle Registrations with its number, and find the name and address of the owner.

'Are you Kip Bush, of 10 Glendavon Drive, Mildenhall? Visiting someone in hospital after church, were you? You'll be a bit late now, I'm afraid,' Walsh said to the man sitting at the other side of the table in the interview room.

Having heard his name spoken, the man stopped studying his hands, and glanced up at Walsh's face momentarily; but he blinked twice, pursed his lips reluctantly, then carried on with an intent examination of the nail of his right index finger.

'I wish to make a telephone call,' he said eventually. 'In private. I have that right, I believe.'

'Yes, you have, and you may,' Walsh admitted, 'but then I shall expect some co-operation from you, otherwise you could face a charge of wasting police time, in addition to one of assaulting a police officer. Dial nine, then the number you want.' Walsh pushed the telephone to the other side of the desk and got up.

'Lock the door behind you, and keep your wits about you,' he said to the uniformed officer standing guard as he went out. 'He looks a slippery customer to me.'

However, having made his phone call, Kip Bush refused to answer any questions on the grounds that the blow to his head was far more serious than the doctor had acknowledged. He insisted on being given two more aspirins, and being allowed to rest quietly in a darkened room.

Walsh left him to it; he was busy enough in the briefing room, sorting out the results of the morning's surveillance of Catholic churchgoers, and that was where the chief constable found him when he strode purposefully in, barely an hour later.

'What the bloody hell's going on, Sidney? It's like a madhouse in here. I've never seen so many people on duty on a Sunday. Christ, the overtime alone is going to cost me a fortune,' the CC complained caustically, having drawn Walsh over to the window, out of earshot of the others in the room.

'You can't make an omelette without cracking eggs,' Walsh replied determinedly, his eyes narrowing at this unexpected verbal attack. 'We've been watching all the Catholic churches for DaSilva. I told you what we were planning to do, so you can't say you didn't know.'

'You can stuff your bloody omelettes where they hurt, Sidney. You also told me it was going to be a nice quiet operation—well, either someone's been listening in to our radio frequencies, or someone's tipped off the press. I've had two reporters phone me already, trying to find out what the hell's going on. You've messed it all up, if you ask me.'

'You reckon? We may have DaSilva

downstairs in a cell right now. If that's messing things up, then we could do with a few more messes around here,' Walsh retorted angrily.

To his surprise the CC's face slowly creased into a broad grin, and he started chuckling. 'DaSilva be buggered. Julian rang me a little while ago. The fellow you've pulled in is one of his not so bloody clever agents. Apparently he had the same bright idea as you did, to watch the churches for DaSilva, and all he got for his trouble was a knee in the goolies. You can set him free, and tell him to leave our women coppers alone in future. I'll let this operation of yours run its course, and I hope you find him, because if you think you're going to repeat all this chaos next Sunday, then you've got another think coming. Too many of my officers are going to be dead knackered by tonight. A fine start to the week that's going to give them.'

4

For the police and the fire service, the week got off to its fine start at about two o'clock, in the early hours of the morning.

A bomb exploded, not in the Medical Research Centre where trouble was anticipated, but in one of the laboratories near the School of Veterinary Medicine.

It wasn't a very big bomb. The noise it made came only as a muffled thump, barely loud enough to carry to those sleeping residents in the big houses that lined the main road some distance away. In fact, it might have passed unreported for quite some time, had it not started a small fire. It was that rosy glow in the otherwise gloomy blackness that caused the fire brigade and the police to be alerted.

By the time they arrived, the fire had nearly burnt itself out, but since it was pretty obvious that the conflagration had been caused by an explosion, the CID and the forensic section were quickly notified.

That dragged quite a few people out of their warm beds and into the cold night air.

'It rather looks as if someone bashed a hole through the roof and dropped the bomb down,' Detective Sergeant Reginald Finch suggested, pointing a finger upwards at the hole in the plasterboard ceiling and corrugated asbestos sheets above.

'That's likely enough,' Dr Richard Packstone, the dour, grey-haired leader of the forensic team acknowledged as he peered round the gloomy dank room, where wisps of smoke still rose from piles of blackened debris.

'Have I set up a surveillance team to watch the wrong laboratory, boss?' Reg Finch asked.

'No, I don't think so,' Walsh replied cautiously.

'Is this anything to do with the man we've been looking for all week, Chief?' Brenda Phipps demanded.

'Possibly,' Walsh admitted blandly, as he too peered around the room. The lights were powered by the portable generator in the forensic van, since the explosion had destroyed the laboratory circuits. It was a spacious building, but fairly old, built of brick, with metal window frames and a pitched roof of mossy corrugated asbestos. The remains of three rows of benches took up most of the floor space, but the most damaged area, close to the outer wall, seemed to have contained a desk, on which, judging from the pieces strewn around the floor, there had been a computer or some other kind of electronic equipment.

The windows were barred on the inside by heavy steel grilles and the doors were all metal. Clearly an attempt had been made to make the building secure against petty burglary and simple break-ins, but it was hardly proof against someone with pure destruction in mind. An agile person could easily clamber to the roof, with the aid of drainpipes and window ledges, and once there it would hardly have taken a minute to smash a hole through the brittle asbestos roof and the ceiling below, and drop in an explosive device. Was it good planning or just luck that this small bomb had destroyed the most expensive piece of equipment in the laboratory?

Walsh went outside.

The security patrol man, with a restless alsatian dog at the end of a short thick lead, was standing talking to the fire officer. Walsh interrupted their conversation.

'What time was your last patrol here?' he asked abruptly.

'About a quarter to two. Everything seemed all right. There couldn't have been no one hanging about inside the fence—Bill here would have gone barmy, wouldn't you, old chap?' the man replied, reaching down to lightly tug at one of the dog's ears.

'How many visits do you make here during the night?'

'I'm scheduled to do six. I'm supposed to vary the times as much as I can, but it isn't that easy, not with all the other sites I've got to go to. I'm not here very long. I walks round the buildings, checking the doors and windows, then I let Bill off while I walk round the fence, to make sure that's all right. We've never had no trouble before.'

'We'll need a statement from you, but that can wait until morning. You'd better get on with your patrols. Come on, you two,' Walsh said to Brenda Phipps and Reg Finch. 'Bring some torches and we'll go and see where this bomber got in through the perimeter fence.'

The wire mesh fencing was stretched taut between regularly set solid steel stanchions, and was at least eight feet high, topped by four rows of barbed wire. To get over it and back would have needed ladders; however, the person or persons who had entered the premises earlier had done so in a much easier fashion—a section of the wire had simply been cut away. Walsh clambered through the gap to the footpath on the other side, being careful where he placed his feet. Then he stood still for a moment

70

facing the laboratory. The wind was not quite so cold tonight, but it was blowing as steadily from the east as it had been all week—directly into his face. That alsatian would not have scented anyone hiding out here in the darkness, waiting for the patrol man to complete his round.

'That way the path leads to Caius College rugby ground, Chief,' Brenda said, peering at the street map which Reg was holding up to the light of her torch, and pointing with an outstretched arm towards the city.

'The other way goes to the village of Coton, boss,' Reg added.

Walsh nodded, but he was studying the ground by the gap in the fence. Close to the wire the grass had grown thick and long in soil that was firm. The bent stems showed where feet had been, but they had prevented any prints being made. He moved away and crouched to study the surface of the path where the grass had been worn away. It was still soft in places where the meagre warmth of the daytime sun had rested long enough to cause a minor thaw, but soon it would be as hard frozen as the rest of the area. It was obviously a well-used path, for there were many footprints, shoes as well as boots, but the predominant users were cyclists.

'Hold your torch so that it shines at an

71

angle, Brenda,' he asked, peering down, trying to work out which cycle tyre tracks in the soft patches overlaid all the others, and were therefore the last to have travelled that path.

'Oh lord, he's going to do his Red Indian act again, Reg. We could be here all night. We'll be icicles ourselves by morning,' Brenda whispered loudly. The chief had a well-known weakness for Boy Scout tracking, and that, in the past, had meant them all following the faint, almost indistinguishable signs left by someone's passing. A pleasant, harmless enough occupation, one might have thought, except when the tracks led through brambly hedges, thick woods and ploughed fields, and the only certain result was that they would all get thoroughly muddied and dishevelled.

Walsh heard Brenda's comment, but he made no reply. What he was doing had a purpose. On suitable ground, away from tarmac and concrete, people left tracks. It was as simple as that. If one could read those tracks properly, then one might get some ideas about the person who had made them. If one was very lucky, one might even find a clear footprint with some particular characteristics that might later give positive identification to the maker of those tracks. If one did not look, one would not find. It was all a matter of reasoned observation. That taciturn old aboriginal tracker with whom he'd spent a week out in the Australian desert many years ago would have gained a degree in reasoned logic at any university. A long bony finger had pointed out the features of a footprint in such a way that what he said seemed so obvious—once he'd made his explanations. He could deduce whether the maker of the tracks had been running in fear, or walking at leisure, when they had been made, how tall he was, and how much he weighed. What would that old fellow have made of the mess of tracks, here on this well-used path? Wellington boots and trainers had made most of the footprints, but they were overlaid by many cycle tracks. The very thin ones would be road racing machines, the really wide ones with heavy treads were mountain bikes, and the ones in the middle were the ordinary kind, cycles made at any time during the past fifty or sixty years. Cambridge had those sort by the hundred. Back wheel tyre tracks naturally followed and superimposed themselves over those of the front wheel, but unfortunately the riders did not always stay on the muddy areas, and there was no following their routes where there was ice and grass, not by the restricted light of these torches. It was all too confusing.

He sighed, and stood upright. 'I'll let you off tonight, Brenda,' he said quietly. 'We won't do our tracking now, we'll wait until first light, then we'll walk this path in both directions. Something might have fallen from the bomber's pocket, you never know.' One needed to be optimistic at times. He climbed through the fence again, and went back to the burned-out lab to see how Packstone and his team were getting on, sorting through the debris.

It occurred to him that this bomb attack might be a red herring, set up by DaSilva to mask his real target, the Medical Research Centre. If that were the case he must expect more of such incidents. Unfortunately there were dozens of targets like this in the city: he'd get Reg to make a list of them, but it would be impossible to watch them all. He would have to go through all the proper motions of investigating this bombing, in the hope that something might come of it, but it was depressing, knowing that he was really waiting for an attempt to be made to destroy the Medical Research Centre lab, and its two scientists, Wade and Chambers. Fortunately they wouldn't be such soft targets. He had his own men watching them, and in addition there would be whatever measures the superintendent from Scotland Yard had set up to improve the university's security systems and keep them on red alert.

There was little else he could do, he decided—he'd just have to wait for events to unfold.

He did not have to wait for very long.

It was a crisp and bright winter's morning when the second bomb of the day went off—inside the Medical Research Centre.

The sound of the explosion was not loud enough to carry very far, or have any dramatic effects on those few people out and about at the time, but when the screaming fire engines, ambulances and police cars turned up, there were suddenly dozens of curious spectators to throng those narrow streets.

To those researchers and employees not in Dr Wade's and Dr Chambers' neurological research laboratory on the first floor, it was as though they had experienced a major earthquake, and for a short while afterwards there was a stunned and eerie silence.

Inside that laboratory, however, after the sudden blinding flash and the deafening roar of the explosion, the scene was one of utter blitz-like devastation.

Dave Brewer, the lab assistant, found himself on the floor, sitting propped up against the wall where the blast had flung him. Wreaths of thick black smoke and dust swirled in the draught from the shattered windows, completely obscuring the far end of the room from view. Confusion made him shake his head, and that caused his eyes to focus, uncomprehendingly at first, on the very still body of the senior research assistant, Dr Maureen Connery, lying sprawled on her back on the floor, not very far from him. Her woollen tartan skirt and silky white slip had been rucked by the blast up round her waist, revealing white lacy briefs under brown tights, but those tights were torn on her left thigh and the blood that pulsed from the deep wound there added to an ever-widening pool beside her.

Brewer's brain slowly reasoned that that pulsating red flow meant a severed artery, bleeding that would prove fatal if not quickly staunched. His limbs seemed strangely reluctant to carry out his brain's instructions, but he forced himself to crawl to her, wincing and sobbing from the excruciating pain from his broken ankle. Once there, however, he thrust the thumbs of both hands viciously into the crease of her left groin, pressing down and flattening the artery against the bone. It was good to see the flow of blood cease its surging flood, and decline to a mere trickle.

The smoke was clearing a little, and

he had time to turn his head and look round, but of the third person who had been in that room, he could see no sign. Occupied as he was, there was nothing he could do to help anyway. It was as much as he could do to prevent the waves of dizziness and nausea overcoming him, but by concentrating hard he managed to do so, and he maintained that life-saving pressure on the woman's artery until anxious staff from the other laboratories in the building arrived to administer first aid.

Unfortunately, the parts of Dr Justin Chambers that those rescuers found at the far end of the room were like Humpty Dumpty's—they never would be put together again.

The laboratory was still a scene of chaos when Detective Chief Inspector Walsh arrived. Staff and firemen milled about in apparently aimless confusion, some merely curious, others distressed and in tears.

Once he was satisfied that the injured had been cared for, Walsh set his team to clear the area of such onlookers, then posted two uniformed policemen to guard both access doors and keep unwanted people out.

'Right,' Walsh said to Brenda Phipps and Reg Finch in the corridor outside. 'The first thing to do is to get a list of all the people who were here at work today. Then you can set young Bryant and Alison Knott taking statements from them. I'll want a detailed account from each person of what they did, and who they saw, right from the moment they got here this morning.'

Dr Richard Packstone, the leader of the forensic team, came over to interrupt. He was frowning deeply and his jaw was set firm.

'It's a bomb again, I'm told,' he remarked, blinking his eyes rapidly, as though bemused by the fact that he now had two such incidents to investigate. 'Is this what all the panic's been about lately?'

'Probably. One of the scientists is dead, I'm afraid, so this incident is much more serious than the other. We're going to need your help, Richard, and we're going to need it quick,' Walsh stated emphatically as he pushed the double doors open so that they could both enter the lab.

'The windows are all blown out, I see,' Packstone commented quietly, as he looked round. The exhortation of the need for speedy results affected him not at all. He'd heard such pleas from investigating officers far too often during his career for that to worry him. Forensic work was painstakingly methodical and precise; it did not go well with haste and speed. He'd act as quickly as he could, as always, but things would be done properly.

'I'll get these windows sealed up first, and check out the power sockets,' he decided. 'Then we'll be able to get some light on the scene. If you want speedy results, you can help by getting the staff here to make me up a plan of this room, and mark on it as best they can the exact positions of all the equipment. I might have to make a scale model,' he said, scratching at his head, but he was no longer talking to Walsh, he was working out a plan of action in his mind. He turned away to bark instructions to those of his team who had followed him in. 'Get polythene sheeting taped up over those windows. I want two of you outside. Organise all the uniformed men you can find to pick up every piece of glass and debris that was blown out of the windows. Photographers, video cameras, you can start your "pre-search" scanning. Ceiling and walls first, but mind where you put your feet.'

Packstone was as meticulous and effic-ient as any perfectionist could be, and Walsh knew that it might be many days before sufficient of the fragments could be sorted and identified to allow Packstone to pronounce on what kind of bomb it was, and how it had been detonated. That was information Walsh wanted quickly, but in the meantime, he had other things to occupy his mind. Whatever the bomb had been made of, DaSilva had managed to get it into this laboratory, in spite of the surveillance and security systems. Clearly there was a possibility, indeed a probability, that DaSilva had had the help of someone working in the lab; it must surely have been an 'insider' who had given him vital information about the security routine and the layout of the place. DaSilva might not have needed to plant the bomb himself, of course; his 'insider' might have done the job for him. Perhaps there were two shadowy figures to find, not just the one.

Still, either DaSilva or his 'insider' had gained access to that high security area, and in doing so they may have been seen by one of the other Medical Centre staff. That was the right place to start: the statements being taken from those employees might contain that vital piece of information. He went to find out how that task was progressing.

Brenda Phipps and Reg Finch had wasted no time. They had commandeered a lecture room a little way down the corridor on the same floor, and were there with the lab director and his personnel manager, writing names on roughly sketched layouts, when Walsh walked in. Reg Finch made polite introductions but Walsh did not stay after he'd given the conventional responses. Over by the window sat a lone figure, a man who was pale and trembling. He had the knuckle of a forefinger stuck in his mouth, like a child on the verge of tears. It was the man who had given the lecture on drug addiction at the conference in Berkshire.

'Dr Wade? I'm Chief Inspector Walsh. You weren't in the lab when the bomb went off, then?' he asked. It was an unnecessary question, but it served to start a conversation.

The other looked up at him with frightened eyes, shook his head and gulped. 'No, I was with the director in his office, but I'd only been out of the lab a few minutes,' he croaked hesitantly. 'Chambers was still there, and now he's dead. I was working right beside him when the director phoned for me. I'd be dead too if he hadn't. Oh God, it's so awful.' He put his head in his hands and his shoulders shook as emotion overcame him.

Walsh rubbed his chin in embarrassment. 'You were very fortunate, then,' he said gruffly, sitting down next to him on one of the red plastic chairs. 'It must all be a great shock to you, I understand that, but we're going to need your help. You must try to get a grip on yourself. Now, answer me a few simple questions. Were there any materials in your lab, any combinations of chemicals, that could have caused that explosion?'

Wade's face came suddenly out of his hands in some surprise. 'Good lord, no. There's no possibility of that. None whatever.'

'Good. Now, what about the equipment itself? I've heard of cathode-ray tubes blowing up?'

Wade blinked in puzzlement, then his blotchy face took on a scornful expression. 'No chance, Inspector.'

Walsh nodded; at least his questions had brought back some semblance of normality to the frightened man. 'Right then, who was there, in the laboratory, when you went to the director's office?'

'There were just the four of us. Myself, Chambers, Dr Connery, she's our senior assistant, and Brewer, our general dogsbody. We were getting ready to use the computer. What the others were doing at the far end of the lab, I can't remember.'

'I see. Had any other people come into your lab during the morning?'

'I can't remember anyone, but it's hardly likely the bomb was planted this morning, is it? Not with all four of us around. It must have been put there over the weekend. Oh God, that's even more horrible, it means the timer must have been deliberately set to go off when the lab was occupied, mustn't it? That means someone was out to kill us all.' Wade's face took on a fresh look of abject terror.

'We'll have another chat later, I think,' Walsh suggested. 'In the meantime I'd appreciate you doing a sketch of the layout of your lab, and marking on it all the equipment and apparatus you had in there. Will you do that for me? It will certainly be of the greatest help, I assure you.' It was also a kindness to find the shaken man something practical to do, to take his mind off things. Clearly, at the moment, he was not in full control of his emotions. For someone as obviously highly strung as he was, and who had missed a violent sudden death by only minutes, perhaps that was understandable.

Wade nodded, and blinked again several times as the purport of Walsh's request sank in. 'I'll go and get some paper,' he muttered hesitantly, and went off, rather unsteadily.

A new arrival came bursting into the room. A tall, thin-faced man, of about fifty years of age, with short dark hair and slightly reddened cheeks. He had an

83

anxious worried look in his eyes as he strode over to where Walsh was sitting.

'Right, Walsh. I'm here now. I'll take over,' Superintendent Anderson said, loudly and arrogantly enough to attract the attention of those others in the room.

Walsh got to his feet rather warily, but he held out his hand in a gesture of welcome. He smiled slightly, but his eyes didn't join in; they glinted ominously.

'No! I don't think you will take over, Superintendent. I'm not on your patch, you know. You're on mine,' he said positively, trying unsuccessfully to prevent a note of hostility coming into his voice. A confrontation with a senior-ranking officer, at this time, with all these people about, was not welcome, yet he was not going to relinquish command of this investigation, not here, not in his own city.

'I'll have no bloody insubordination from you, Walsh. I've been sent here by the Home Office,' Anderson spluttered aggressively.

Walsh shook his head defiantly. Attack was always the best form of verbal defence, so he attacked. 'You're merely an adviser on security procedures, Super-intendent—that's a private matter between the Home Office and the university, and that's where your authority ends. Whereas I'm here officially—in charge of a murder investigation. There's been no call for Scotland Yard's assistance, nor will there be.'

'I'll soon cut you down to size, Walsh. I outrank you, and you'll do what you're bloody told,' Anderson stuttered angrily. 'Murder inquiry, be buggered. This is bigger than you can handle—' He was cut short by a voice from behind him.

'Try cutting me down to size, Anderson,' boomed that voice. 'I outrank you by a million miles.'

Anderson turned sharply, and found himself facing the big, red-faced chief constable of the Cambridgeshire Constabulary, who was incongruously resplendent in his full beribboned uniform.

'Trying to pull rank on one of my officers, who happens to be acting with my full authority, are you, Anderson? Well, that won't get you anywhere. You're supposed to be responsible for the security of this place, aren't you? So where the hell were you earlier this morning and over the weekend? Don't tell me. At home with the wife, watching television, I'll bet. Well, while you were lounging around on your lazy arse goggling at the box someone got in here and planted a bomb. Just what you were supposed to prevent,' the CC went on remorselessly. 'Now, I'll tell you what you can do, before you go crawling back to London with your scraggy tail between your legs—you can write me a detailed report of all the security activity on this site since you took over. I want to know who came and went; where, why and what for. Every last detail, and you can hand it to Chief Inspector Walsh before you leave. Is that clear?'

Anderson's face was far redder now even than the CC's, and his eyes were wild with frustration, but discipline and the certain knowledge that he had no other choice forced a simple, 'Yes, sir,' from between gritted teeth, and he strode off, without looking back.

Even before he'd left the room the CC was chuckling aloud.

'I thought you might be needing me here, Sidney,' he said as he put a massive arm on Walsh's shoulder, drawing him over to the window, out of the hearing of the others in that room. 'It's a good idea of yours to say this is a simple murder inquiry,' he went on, speaking much more quietly. 'If we can avoid the use of words like bomber and terrorist, so much the better. You're getting things organised, are you? Well, since I'm here, you can take me round and show me what's going on. I spoke to the Home Office before I came out. They're going to leave everything to us, but we can call on outside help if we need to. You haven't found this fellow DaSilva yet, have you? Well, it looks as though he's found us, doesn't it? You're going to have to tell your team something about him now—how much, I'll leave to your own judgement. Keep absolutely quiet about Julian, though, not a word about him. Come on. Lead the way. I want to have a chat with Packstone. I'd imagine he might like some help from some of the other forensic laboratories when he's got himself sorted out, wouldn't you?'

The atmosphere in the small room in the corridor near the stairs seemed rather detached and mundane, compared with the excited feelings of tension in the rest of the building, but with the door closed, it was quiet, and a place where they could talk in private.

'The bomb must have been planted during the weekend then, Chief,' Brenda said positively, 'if what Dr Wade said is correct, and no one other than the four of them was in that lab this morning. I think I'd better get up to the hospital shortly and have words with Dave Brewer and Maureen Connery. We'll need them to confirm what Wade has told you.'

'I've got the weekend reports from our own surveillance crew to go through, boss,' Reg said quietly. 'We can compare their record of the people coming in and going out with Superintendent Anderson's, when we get it. Now, are you going to tell us what this is all about, or have we still got to work in the dark?'

Walsh leaned his elbows on the small table and looked thoughtfully at the two members of his team, who were apparently so eager to hear what he had to tell them. Of their trustworthiness and reliability there was no doubt; he had worked with them both for too long to have any concerns like that. Yet they made a strange pair. Reg Finch was intelligent and languidly efficient. He was married to a social worker, and his interests in history and a local home for crippled orphans left him with little spare time away from his police duties. Brenda Phipps, on the other hand, was always full of life and vigour, in spite of the amount of energy she expended keeping fit. Surprisingly in one so active, her off-duty hours were spent meticulously and patiently repairing and restoring chipped and broken pieces of porcelain and bone china. Recently though, an old and badly damaged violin had come within her orbit. No doubt, in time, that too would be resurrected to near perfect condition.

The common factor with them both was that their originality of thought went hand in hand with the ability to do meticulous research. A not too common combination. They also worked well together, and with him, and they had the confidence in each other that was so vitally important.

'No, you haven't got to work in the dark,' Walsh said eventually, 'but what I tell you is top secret, and must remain so. Is that clear?'

Two heads nodded emphatically.

'Right! Wade and Chambers were doing research on drug addiction. They've been developing a treatment that cuts out an addict's craving for narcotics, alcohol or anything like that. Wade was stupid enough to let the secret out at a conference recently. As you can imagine, the drug-peddling barons won't be happy if such a cure is found, and we believe that one of them has sent this man DaSilva here, to stop that research being finalised,' Walsh said, his face very serious.

'Hell fire, Chief,' Brenda exclaimed excitedly. 'It's all quite clear now. That first bomb this morning was claimed by an animal rights group—but that must be a red herring, to try to throw us off the scent. This is the real one. DaSilva must have planted the bomb here hoping to wipe out the whole research team, all in one go. If Dr Wade hadn't been called away to the director's office, he'd have been killed as well as Dr Chambers.'

'No wonder he looked scared, boss. That's probably the closest shave he's ever had,' Reg observed grimly. 'We'll need to watch Wade like a hawk from now on. They're bound to have another go at him. Was it just Chambers and Wade working on this project?'

'Those were the important ones, Reg. The other two in the lab were just assistants, helping as required and directed. We don't need to worry about them,' Walsh replied. 'Now, we've got to pursue a logical course of action. We must keep on searching for DaSilva, that's obvious, but our main priority must be to find out how the bomb was planted. That ought to lead us either to DaSilva, or his accomplice. The security screen was breached somehow, probably over the weekend or very early this morning. Reg, you concentrate on that aspect when you go through the security reports for the weekend. Then while Brenda's at the hospital talking to Brewer and Connery, I'll interview the lab director and have another word with Dr Wade. Hopefully he'll be more in control of himself by then. In the meantime, let's hope that Packstone comes up with something quickly about the type and construction of the bomb—that might help too. We'll meet up later and compare notes.'

90

5

The hospital ward was bright and cheerful, with a few Christmas decorations already hanging from the white-painted ceiling; vases on a table by the window contained a colourful display of flowers.

Brenda Phipps made her way to the fourth bed in the row, and introduced herself to its occupant.

'Are you feeling well enough to talk to me, or shall I come back later?' she asked, looking down at Dave Brewer, the laboratory assistant.

He was in his early thirties, with a face that was lean and craggy enough to be attractive to some women. He lay back against his pillows, clearly tired out by his recent experiences; but there were few men, however weary or near to death's door they might be, who would not readily scrape up some energy from somewhere, or even send the Grim Reaper back to sit in the waiting-room, rather than deny themselves time in the company of someone as attractive as Brenda Phipps.

'I'll give it a whirl; but don't expect any Mastermind answers. My brain's not working very well at the moment. Not that it ever does, really,' Brewer croaked hoarsely.

Brenda smiled at him encouragingly, and sat down on a nearby chair. 'Your brain was working all right back there in the laboratory. They tell me that Dr Connery would have died if you hadn't stopped her bleeding when you did.'

Brewer blinked, as though that incident had in fact slipped from his mind, and then his face creased into a faint grin of recollection. 'Maybe, but all I'll get from her is a slap round the face, for getting my hands up her skirts when she wasn't looking.'

'Possibly, but I think she'll be grateful to you just the same.'

Brewer gave a slight shrug and a shake of his head. 'I don't know about that. I went into X-ray as she came out, and the nurse there told me she'd got no broken bones, so she'll be up and about before me, very likely.'

Brenda nodded. 'Probably. You'll need crutches while that ankle knits together, that'll slow you down a bit,' she bantered with a grin.

'Us Brewers are tough nuts, but Maureen and me were lucky, being down the far end of the lab, I mean. Poor old Dr Chambers didn't stand a chance where he was. It's awful really. He was a decent sort of chap too.' Brewer was silent for a few moments, but he obviously wasn't one to dwell for too long on unpleasant thoughts. 'You're a copper, are you? I've never come across one who looks as pretty as you before.'

'Thank you. Detective Constable Phipps, at your service. Well, in the line of duty, at any rate.'

'Shame. Do you know who planted the bomb? It was a bomb, wasn't it? I can't think of what else it could have been. Nothing we use could have gone up like that,' Brewer said positively.

'I'm hoping you might have seen something that will give us a lead,' Brenda replied earnestly. It was time for this conversation to get down to business.

Brewer pursed his lips doubtfully and shook his head. 'I don't know that I can help you really. What would it have looked like?'

'It's difficult to say. A box or package probably. No, what I'd like you to do is to tell me everything that happened this morning, right from the moment you arrived at the lab.'

Brewer looked thoughtful, and eased himself more upright on the pile of pillows. 'Let me think. I got there just before nine. I parked round the corner, in Audley End

Road. Will someone look after my car, do you think? I wouldn't want it left where it is too long. The wheels'll get pinched.'

'Don't worry. Your personnel department will see to it.'

'Good. Now, when I got in the lab—'

'Just a moment. You had to go past the security guard at the gate first, didn't you?' Brenda interrupted.

'That's right, but the chap on the main gate knows me, so I didn't need to show my pass. I can't remember his name, but the guard they've recently put in that little room on our corridor was Smith—Brian Smith.'

'Did you speak to him?'

'No. I saw him through the doorway though. He was talking on the telephone. I don't know if he saw me, now I come to think of it.'

'Good,' Brenda said, writing rapidly in her notebook. 'Were you the first to arrive in the lab?'

'Lord, no. I'm never first. There's no point in me getting there early, I haven't got a key to the lab door. Everything seemed normal enough, as far as I can remember. Maureen had already started checking the computer print-outs. That's our usual job first thing on a Monday morning, checking and filing the print-outs of last week's inputs,' Brewer explained.

'What about Dr Chambers and Dr Wade?'

'Well, Dr Chambers was at the far end of the room, by the computer. Dr Wade came in after me, but he wasn't wearing a coat, so he must have just popped out to the loo, or something.'

'Good. It's all coming back to you nicely, isn't it? What happened after that?'

'Not a lot, frankly. Mondays always start quiet, if you know what I mean. We both just got on with our work.'

'And Dr Chambers and Dr Wade?'

'I heard them talking down the other end of the lab, but I don't know what they were up to. I remember the phone ringing just before Dr Wade went out. Then a little while after that, maybe ten minutes or so, the bloody bomb went off.'

'Yes, but are you saying that until Dr Wade went out, nobody else had come in or gone out of that room?' Brenda asked, while lightly tapping the top of her pen on her teeth.

'I suppose I am. If anyone did, I don't remember it,' Brewer replied positively.

'Right, when you arrived, can you recall whether the lab was cleaned as you'd expect it to be?'

'Oh yes, I'm sure it was.'

'Good, so the cleaners had been in there over the weekend. Was there any sign that anyone else might have been in there?'

Brewer rubbed his forehead as he concentrated. 'I see what you're driving at now. Yes, someone from the computer section must have been in. On Friday one of our input terminals was playing up, so I stuck a piece of paper on the screen saying, "Out of order", and reported it to the maintenance section. My bit of paper wasn't there this morning, so they must have fixed it over the weekend.'

A nurse came over with a glass of water and two pills for Brewer to take.

'One's a sleeping pill, so don't stay more than another five minutes,' she whispered to Brenda.

Brenda nodded.

'Right, Mr Brewer, we're doing well. Just one other question. You must get letters and parcels in the post, mustn't you? Someone brings that round, surely?'

'Good lord, that's right. Maybe the bomb was in a parcel. They sort the post out in the main office, and bring it round to the different labs. Usually that's about half-past nine. Do you know, I'm hanged if I can remember anyone coming this morning, but they must have done, there's always something for us, especially on a Monday. I must have been lost in my thoughts. I get a bit like that when I'm concentrating hard, particularly after a late night. Maybe Maureen dealt with it. I know I didn't.'

'Out on the town, were you, Sunday night?'

'London. I went to the Albert Hall. Itzhak Perlman was playing, with the Royal Phil.'

'Lucky you. I've got a CD of him playing all the Paganini caprices. Are you a violinist yourself?'

Brewer blushed. 'I play a bit,' he admitted.

Brenda smiled and closed her notebook. She expressed her thanks for his help, and her wish that he had a speedy recovery, then left him to begin that recovery by slipping into his pill-induced sleep.

'This is a terrible thing, Chief Inspector. Poor Chambers, and one of our brightest young men too. He had a brilliant future ahead of him, and now it's been wiped away—it's quite, quite tragic,' the white-haired, elderly lab director said despondently from behind the massive desk in his office on the top floor of the Medical Research Centre building. 'It's a mercy there wasn't more damage, or even a serious fire. The sprinkler system didn't come on, so they tell me. We must look into that. Even so, there might easily have been more fatalities, so I suppose we must be thankful for small mercies.'

'It was a relatively small device, fortunately,' Walsh commented, looking with interest at the other man's face. This director had the keen eye and pragmatic self-confidence to be expected in one who managed and motivated some of the university's more practical, but possibly unpredictable, intellectuals, yet even so, the happenings this morning had left him dazed and bewildered. It was hardly surprising, for bombs were not everyday occurrences, not within the confines of Cambridge University buildings, anyway.

'There had been some changes to your security systems recently,' Walsh continued. 'How did that affect the work in the labs, particularly the one Wade and Chambers worked in?'

The director rubbed at his chin thoughtfully. 'It didn't affect it at all, really. Security is only a peripheral sort of function for us, you see. All we've really had to concern ourselves with is the prevention of petty break-ins, theft, and unauthorised entry by people who just want to nose about. We've always managed to do that with a guard to check passes at the main gate during the day, and random security patrols at night, by men with dogs. Superintendent Anderson brought in extra guards from other places to work in shifts and give full security cover on site, for the whole twenty-four hours, and he tightened things up where we'd got a bit slack, by insisting that everyone should show their passes, and only allowing visitors in if they were accompanied by an authorised staff member. He also stationed a guard in that small room at the head of the corridor leading to Chambers' and Wade's laboratory, during the day. We didn't mind that. There're two other labs and a lecture room along there, so nobody really knew which particular room was being targeted by the extra security. As I say, after working hours, Anderson had two men on duty all through the night. One patrolled, while the other stayed at the main gate. I thought it was all a bit petty at the time, but as things have turned out, I was obviously wrong,' the director admitted as his fingers rapped nervously on the desk top. 'As far as our individual research projects were concerned, it made very little difference. Each laboratory is virtually self-contained, as you've no doubt seen. That's how we wanted it to be when we first set Wade and Chambers on their special project.'

'But those people who worked in the other two labs on that floor were free to wander into Wade's at any time they wished, weren't they?' Walsh asked.

'Indeed they were, but we couldn't

have the doors locked during the day, because of the fire regulations. Besides, the whole point of the exercise was to keep unauthorised people from gaining admittance, and the new system seemed to do that.'

Walsh nodded. 'Tell me what you know about Chambers,' he asked. 'I gather he lived on his own. A divorcee, I believe.'

'That's right. His marriage broke up a year or two ago. I don't know the details, whether he left her or she left him, that sort of thing's immaterial to me. It didn't seem to affect his work in any way. He probably adjusted quite quickly back into bachelor life. That's not difficult in a place like Cambridge, not if one's prepared to enter into the social side of the University. Justin was in his middle thirties, and a bit introverted. I suppose most researchers are, to tell the truth, but he had a wide circle of friends, I'm sure. He played golf very well too—a twelve handicap's not bad if you can only get a round in once a week. James Wade is a bit older than Justin, he's nearly forty, married to a really nice girl called Patricia. You mustn't call her Pat, though, if I remember rightly; she doesn't like her name being shortened, and she'll bite your head off if you do. They've no children, but there's plenty of time for that sort of thing later on, isn't there? Wade's father is Jonas Wade, you know? Perhaps the name doesn't ring a bell. He's quite a wealthy man—in engineering, in the Midlands. Wealth is an anachronism here, of course. We respect the power of a man's brain rather than the amount of money in his pocket. As a researcher, Wade is very good, there's no doubt about that, but, well, he sometimes comes across as...well, a bit detached from the real world, if you know what I mean.'

'He certainly seemed to be very upset this morning, but I put that down to shock,' Walsh observed drily.

'Well, yes, that's probably quite true, but I'm not being unkind to him if I say he's somewhat lacking in, er, physical aggression, shall we say,' the director suggested with a wry grin.

'It takes all types to make a world. You saved his life this morning by calling him away from his laboratory. What was it you wanted to see him about?' Walsh asked.

'It was nothing really important, but I've come in for some criticism from the university's Security Committee for letting him address a conference without my vetting what he was going to say. I'd drafted out a reply in which I stated that I did not see that it was part of my responsibilities to censor the speeches, lectures or correspondence of my staff.

That's what such criticism implies I should do, doesn't it? Of course I would have stopped Wade from saying what he did, if I had known what he was going to say. I called him up to my office so that he could read the letter before I sent it off.'

'So there's no way he could have known that you'd be phoning him, then?'

The director shook his head. 'There is no possible way he could have known that,' he replied emphatically.

'I didn't see any signs of any animals in Wade's lab,' Walsh said. 'Yet I understood he used them in experiments.'

The director looked a little embarrassed. 'Well, yes, there are occasions when we need to do that, but they're all kept in another area, in the building behind the car-park, as a matter of fact, where they can be looked after properly.'

Brenda Phipps made her way through the vast complex of Addenbrooke's Hospital to a quiet annexe room, off a main ward.

Dr Maureen Connery looked very pale, in spite of the large amount of other people's blood now mingling with hers and coursing through her veins and arteries. She was in her late twenties, with short dark hair, brown eyes, and usually a ready smile to lighten a rather serious face into acceptable prettiness, but today that smile was not forthcoming—it took too much effort.

'Yes, I suppose I can answer questions. I rather feel as though my head's floating two feet above my body, I've enough drugs in me to sink a battleship, I think,' she answered bravely.

'That's not surprising,' Brenda replied. 'At least you're still in one piece and you've no broken bones.'

'Yes, I was lucky. Poor Justin wasn't, was he? It's awful, he was such a nice man, too.'

'He wouldn't have known anything, or felt any pain. That's a blessing, I suppose,' Brenda said sympathetically.

'It doesn't bear thinking about. Why on earth would anyone want to do such a thing? I can't understand it, but they must have suspected something like this might happen when they put that new security guard on our corridor, mustn't they?'

Brenda shrugged her slim shoulders. 'Maybe... However, I've a message for you. I've just come from seeing Dave Brewer, and he hopes you're feeling all right.'

Now a faint smile did come to hover round Dr Connery's bluish lips. 'They tell me he saved my life, and he must have been in a great deal of pain himself, too. It's funny, that—he's not the kind of man you'd think of as being any good in a crisis. I've always thought he was too much of a dreamer.'

'Yes, I got that impression too, but you can never tell with the quiet types. Now, he said that you were in the lab before him this morning, and that you'd already started to sort out some computer print-outs.'

Dr Connery thought for a moment. 'Yes, that's right. Justin arrived before me, and Dr Wade came in just after.'

'Was the lab door locked or unlocked when you got there?'

'Unlocked, of course. I haven't a key.'

'You saw the security guard in the corridor when you came in, I suppose?' Brenda asked.

'Oh yes, he said "Good morning" from his room.'

'Good. Now Dave Brewer reckoned Dr Wade might have come into the lab earlier and gone out again, since he wasn't wearing a coat.'

'He might have, but it would be just like him to forget his coat, even if it was cold outside. He's a bit like that.'

'I see. What about the delivery of the post this morning? Brewer couldn't remember,' Brenda prompted.

'No, he'd got his head down. I don't know precisely when the girl from the

104

office brought it in, but I took it down to Dr Chambers. There were a few letters and leaflets, and a biggish jiffy bag, but it wasn't very heavy.'

'Had they been opened in the post room, or do they just sort them out?'

'They just sort them out, they don't open them.'

'Did anyone else come in?'

Dr Connery shook her head, and winced slightly from the effort. 'No one else came in, not before the bomb went off. I'm sure of that.'

6

It was late in the afternoon when Walsh and his team met up again in the small room on the first floor of the Medical Research Centre.

'Right, now let's clear up the points from Brenda's interviews with the two injured lab employees. Firstly, the incoming mail,' Walsh suggested, setting the flame of his lighter to the bowl of his pipe, and puffing out a few clouds of grey smoke.

'I've got the routine for that,' Reg said, reaching for his black document case and taking out a clipped wad of handwritten notes. 'The post office delivers the mail to the guard at the main gate about eight in the morning. One of the Admin girls then picks it up on her way to the office, where they open any letters and parcels that are not personally addressed,' Reg explained. 'Obviously most of it is admin stuff, bills, invoices and so on. The rest gets sorted out into the different laboratories, and one of the staff takes it round. This morning the girl said there was a brown jiffy bag, book size, addressed to Dr Chambers.'

'That confirms what I was told, Chief,'

Brenda interrupted. 'It was Dr Connery who took the post down to where Dr Chambers and Dr Wade were working.'

'Dr Wade saw the jiffy bag too,' Walsh added, 'and it hadn't been opened by the time he left. He's quite positive about that.'

'So that could have been the bomb, then,' Brenda said, clearly a little disappointed if it were all as simple as that.

'No chance, Brenda. Anderson had arranged with the post office for all the incoming mail to be screened for letter bombs. That jiffy bag couldn't have contained a bomb, or else the GPO would have spotted it. Their equipment's working perfectly too, I asked them to have it checked,' Reg informed them.

'Well, that's ruled out then. Unless the jiffy bag the GPO checked was switched later on for the one with the bomb. That's a possibility. What about the maintenance department, and the "out of order" computer terminal that had been repaired over the weekend, Reg?' Brenda asked.

Reg thumbed through Anderson's report, blinked when he came to the end, then went through it again. 'Now, that does throw a spanner in the works,' he said eventually, shaking his head reluctantly. 'There's nothing in here about any of the maintenance personnel having access to Wade's lab over the weekend, or any of the other labs for that matter. I'll have to follow that one up.'

'Then there's the cleaners. They definitely went into the lab, so what's the procedure with them?' Brenda inquired.

'They come in at six o'clock in the morning. They used to have their own keys and work in pairs, but Anderson changed that. Now they all work together, doing one lab at a time, with the security guard keeping an eye on them,' Reg reported.

'If they were together it would be difficult for one of them to bring a bomb in and hide it somewhere, but not impossible,' Walsh commented quietly.

'Brewer also said that the guard in the corridor was on the telephone this morning, and clearly didn't see him,' Brenda went on.

'Anything strange or unusual like that needs looking into. Would you do that too, Reg?' Walsh asked.

'Have we established which of the four arrived first at the lab this morning?' Brenda demanded.

'Oh yes. Chambers was first. The main gate guard and the corridor guard both confirm that. Next to arrive was Connery, followed by Wade. Brewer was last,' Reg announced quietly. 'But there are other ways the bomb might have been planted. Either Wade, Chambers, or one of the other two might have been forced to take that bomb into the lab themselves, if someone was threatening their wives or kids. It may sound unlikely, but it's possible.'

Brenda scratched her head thoughtfully. 'That's true, Reg, but Wade's the only one who's married, and he's got no children. The other three are single or divorced, so the possibility of hostages with them isn't very likely, but it's a good point.'

'There's Anderson, too, boss,' Reg went on. 'If there's a high-ranking police officer passing secret information to the drug cartels, it might be him.'

'Anderson wasn't at the conference where Wade let the cat out of the bag,' Walsh said, staring down at his fingers for no particular reason, 'but the man he works for at Scotland Yard was. It's damned complicated, this business of a top-level informer. Still, while you're questioning the security staff, Reg, see if you can piece together Anderson's movements while he was here, without making it too obvious what you're doing. He might have spent some time in Wade's lab on his own. I'll have words with this MI6 contact the CC's given me. Fortunately, investigating the people at that conference is their job, not ours,' he added with a slight grin. 'Now, the Animal Liberation Front is one of the groups who've claimed the bomb at the veterinary labs. The local BBC radio station had a phone call early this morning, but within half an hour of their first news programme, two other organisations phoned in to claim it as well: the Anti-Vivisection League and a new one on me called the SAS. That means Stop Animals Suffering, apparently. No one's claimed the bomb here yet, probably because the afternoon's news report merely stated that it was an accident, the cause of which was being investigated.'

'I don't think we need to waste much time looking into those claims, boss,' Reg Finch suggested. 'We know who we're looking for. It's just a matter of finding him.'

'This DaSilva doesn't know that we know about him, Chief. That ought to give us an advantage,' Brenda Phipps proposed.

'It's fairly easy to guess that he's planned a sequence of supposed animal rights attacks on laboratories to mask his real target, but I'm surprised that these first two bombs have been timed so closely together. You'd have thought he'd have strung them out over a longer period, but no doubt he had his reasons. I think we might get one or two more bombs yet, just to rub the point in,' Walsh observed gloomily.

'The veterinary lab was a soft target compared with the one here,' Reg Finch pointed out. 'Perhaps the timing was brought about by necessity. The security systems here had certainly been tightened up considerably, and were going to get tighter. Anderson had arranged for an explosives-trained sniffer dog to come up twice a day from the Customs and Excise place at Stanstead Airport. It was due to start regular patrols round the labs tomorrow. It's possible that the route DaSilva used to get in and plant that bomb would only remain open over the weekend, so he had to strike then, while the going was good.'

'But how would DaSilva know what Anderson's plans were, Reg?' Brenda asked sceptically.

'That's the million-dollar question, Brenda. He must have had inside knowledge. How else could he find a route through an apparently foolproof security system?' Reg replied promptly.

'I want that route found,' Walsh said doggedly. 'Certainly he must have had someone's help. One of the guards probably, and if we can find out which one, we might have a lead to DaSilva himself.'

'Yes, yes that's very true, Chief,' Brenda

said, frowning impatiently, 'but can't we spend a bit more time thinking about what DaSilva's next move might really be? If you're right, and there are going to be some more bombs, surely we ought to try and work out which his next target will be. Then perhaps we can set up an ambush, and catch him red-handed.' Brenda chopped her right hand karate-fashion into the palm of her left, to demonstrate just how effective her idea might turn out to be.

Reg looked doubtful. 'It's a nice thought. I made a list of possible targets this morning, but there's too many to do the kind of thing you've got in mind. With all our other commitments, I don't think we can do much more to tighten up the security at those places other than get our patrol cars to add to the security guards' visits.'

'But that's just what DaSilva will expect us to do, Reg,' Brenda declared enthusiastically. 'Let's assume DaSilva will be watching all the places on your list. As I say, he'll expect to see signs of increased activity, won't he? But if we were to deliberately ignore one of the less likely places, he might spot that, and make that one his next target. If we set up an ambush there, we might get him to walk straight into a trap.'

Walsh smiled broadly but nodded approvingly. 'I thought I was the one who was supposed to be ambush-mad. You must come a close second, Brenda. It might work. It's certainly worth trying, I think.' He took Reg's schedule of prospective targets from his file and glanced down it. 'How about the Cattle Breeding Centre, the Animal Research Station or the Genetics Station? Either one of them might do.'

'The Cattle Breeding and the Genetics are next to each other, so that would be a big area to cover. I suggest we set an ambush at the Animal Research Station, Chief. It's not really a place that would interest animal rights activists, but as far as DaSilva is concerned, it'd probably do as well as any,' Brenda announced.

'If I was DaSilva, I'd do the bomb here myself, certainly,' Walsh said thoughtfully, 'but I'm not sure if I'd risk my own neck on the other targets. I'd probably get some lesser mortal to do those for me. So don't get too excited about it—even if we are successful with an ambush, we might not get the man we really want. Right, Reg, cancel the extra patrols at the Animal Research Station. We'll need to reconnoitre the site properly first, before we can set it up, but I'm not sure if we ought to man it ourselves. We've a lot to do, and we can't afford to be losing sleep every night, not if we want our brains working one hundred and ten per cent.'

Brenda's eyebrows promptly came closer together in a deep frown. 'Oh come off it, Chief,' she protested scornfully. 'Catching this DaSilva fellow is our number one priority, and whatever you say, this may be our best chance of doing it quickly. What's a bit of lost sleep between friends? Anyway, some of us could get a bit of rest while the others are watching. It's so important, I don't like the idea of leaving it to anyone else.'

Reg gave a loud chuckle. 'She's right, boss. There are others who can do an ambush as well as we can, but there aren't any who can do it better.'

With two of his team so obviously set on the idea, Walsh felt he had little choice but to agree to it. That wasn't really true, because he was the boss and could choose to do whatever he liked, but that ethereal thing called team spirit came into play. If you wanted a team to act like a team, you had to take the whole team's views into account.

'Right, we'll do it ourselves, but I won't accept any relaxation of effort because of it, understood?' Walsh decreed positively.

'While we're talking about DaSilva's future plans, boss,' Reg interrupted, 'he's disposed of Chambers and all the written

114

notes in the desk, as well as the data stored in the laboratory computer, but Dr Wade escaped, so DaSilva's still got him to get rid of.'

Walsh nodded. 'He won't find that so easy. Wade's scared out of his wits, he won't wander far from home. There's an armed minder in his house with him and his wife, and the place is being watched from the outside. He's safe enough, provided he doesn't do anything stupid. Well, I think we've done enough talking for now. Brenda, since you're so keen on it, you can come with me up to the Animal Research Station and help set up this ambush. Reg, you've got plenty to do, but you've got Alison Knott and Arthur Bryant to give you a hand. We'll meet up again later, in my office,' Walsh said formally, reaching forward to put his files in his briefcase.

'How are you two getting on with taking the statements?' Reg Finch asked the two junior officers attached to the Serious Crime section.

'We're nearly finished,' Detective Constable Alison Knott replied, her cheerfully plump face eager and enthusiastic.

'Two more, and that's all the lab staff done,' Detective Constable Arthur Bryant added. 'What's next? More statements?'

'Yes,' Reg answered with a smile. 'Six

cleaners. You'll have to go and interview them at home. It's possible that one of them planted the bomb this morning while they were cleaning the lab. Find out just what each of them did, and try to get them to confirm the movements of the other five.'

'Cleaners?' Arthur said disgustedly. 'Lord, we are scraping the barrel. Couldn't we do them when they come in tomorrow morning?'

Reg shook his head. 'I doubt if you'll feel like interviewing anyone at six o'clock in the morning, Arthur, not after you've been on ambush duty all night.'

'Ambush duty? Great! Where?' Alison's eyes lit up excitedly.

'You'll find out later. Finish what you have to do here, and get these cleaners sorted out for me.'

'So what time did you come on duty this morning?' Reg Finch asked the security guard.

Brian Smith rubbed his stubby nose apprehensively. This was the second time he'd been questioned that day, and he wasn't enjoying the experience. He hadn't actually been accused of anything yet, but it rather looked as though they might be trying to trap him into giving different answers to the same questions. If he did that he could be in serious trouble. From what he'd seen on the television they'd put him on his own for hours in a cold bare cell, to soften him up. Then they'd stick him in a chair, with bright lights shining straight in his face, and fire questions at him so fast and furiously that it wouldn't be long before he wouldn't know what he was saying. They'd try and get him to sign a confession too, and if he didn't, he'd be beaten up in ways that left no marks or bruises.

'I was in here at a quarter to six,' Smith began, doggedly trying not to panic, 'and my shift's long over. I ain't supposed to be here now. Why can't I go home? I do have a private life, you know.'

'We won't keep you any longer than necessary, but when bombs go off and someone gets killed, it does rather put a strain on lots of people's lives. It's no good moaning about it,' Finch replied sternly. He felt no sympathy for Smith. This bombing would affect his own private life much more seriously than it would Smith's, and in his case it would go on and on, until DaSilva, or whoever the bomber was, was apprehended. In the meantime, this Smith fellow needed watching carefully. He had a twitchy, rather squashed-up face, almost as though someone had once punched his jaw up nearer his forehead. Such facial features were difficult to read, and it was important to try and assess whether he was telling the truth, or lying.

'You went round with the cleaners this morning, then?' Reg asked.

'That's right. I did that,' Smith replied cautiously.

'Could any of the cleaners have brought a package in with them, and planted it in that lab without you seeing them?'

'I dunno, mate. I ain't ever had orders to search them, have I? You reckon I should have looked up under their skirts, do you? I wouldn't fancy it with most of them—there is a little blonde bint I wouldn't mind having a go at, but she was wearing jeans.' Smith looked rather pleased with himself for that answer.

'You saw nothing suspicious, though? Is that what you mean to say?'

'Yup, and before you ask me, yes, I did lock the door behind me when we went out.'

'Where were the other guards while you were doing the rounds with the cleaners?'

'How the hell would I know? In the guard room by the main gate, having a cup of tea, probably,' Smith said, taking a cigarette from a packet and lighting it.

'So this room wasn't manned then?' Finch asked.

'Of course it wasn't. You only need someone here during working hours. The rest of the time everywhere's all locked up, see.'

'And you stayed with the cleaners as they did each individual corridor and lab?'

'That's right, and I locked the main entrance doors to the building behind me, so no one could get in while we were doing the labs. That Anderson fellow said we mustn't do that when the cleaners were in there, because of the fire regulations, but sod him I say, you ain't born with eyes in the back of your head, are you?' Smith replied frankly.

'Did you have much to do with Superintendent Anderson, when he was here?'

'Me? No. He had us all in the office last Tuesday, or was it Wednesday? That's when he told us we'd all have to work shifts from now on. That didn't go down well, I can tell you; and then he went on about how we'd all got to tighten up on security. "No one, but no one, gets in without a pass, not even if it's the Queen herself," he says. He's a stupid bugger, what the hell would the Queen want to come here for?' Smith asked, his face creasing into a scornful grimace.

'You never went round the premises with Anderson then? Did any of the other guards, do you know?'

'I didn't, I dunno about the others. You'd better ask them.'

'So, when the cleaners had finished, what did you do then?'

'I went and had a cup of tea, then at quarter to eight I come up here to watch who comes down this corridor.'

'Right, and people started to arrive for work from about eight o'clock onwards, according to your earlier report,' Finch said, tapping the document in question.

Smith nodded vigorously, then stubbed out his cigarette in an old chipped saucer and brushed ash from his trousers.

'But some people on this floor say that when they came in this morning you were on the telephone and facing away from the door. Is that right? If so, how long did that go on?'

Smith's face turned red. 'It ain't true,' he replied angrily. 'Sure I had a phone call, but that weren't my fault. I saw everyone who went along that corridor this morning, I'll swear to it. What bastard's been trying to get me into trouble?'

'So you can state categorically that no unauthorised person went past your door this morning, can you?'

There was a short silence while Smith stared suspiciously at Finch. 'You're trying to bloody well trap me, ain't you? Well, it won't work, mate, I didn't see no bloody unauthorised people go past my door.'

'You were on the phone to your wife for something like four minutes. The switchboard operator confirms that, and you were sitting down at this table facing away from the door. You didn't see everyone go past, because you weren't looking all the time. That's the real truth, isn't it?'

Smith glowered and bit at his thumbnail, but his head shook slowly.

'One of the computer input stations in Dr Wade's lab wasn't working properly on Friday afternoon,' Reg Finch stated bluntly to the tall lean middle-aged man in green overalls, who was in charge of the maintenance section. 'It was reported by a D. Brewer, and he wrote "Out of order" on a piece of paper and stuck it on the screen. That paper wasn't there this morning. Does that mean you'd repaired the fault?'

'I didn't. Computers aren't in my line. The man you want is O'Neil, Martin O'Neil. He's in charge of computers. I'm only responsible for the general stuff—all the interesting problems, like leaking roofs, blocked drains and dry rot, and before you ask, no, I don't know why the sprinkler system didn't work. I can't get into the lab to find out, because all your blokes are in there. You'll find Martin O'Neil through that door over there.'

'That's right, Brewer did ring down on Friday, about a problem with one of his input stations,' O'Neil replied, nodding his head, and looking at his questioner with some interest. 'I fixed that on Saturday morning,' he went on. 'Well I didn't exactly fix it, not if you want to be pedantic—I changed the faulty unit for another one. That's it over there, on that bench. I haven't had time to get the back off to see what's wrong with it, yet. Why? What about it?'

'The security guards have no record of anyone going into that particular lab over the weekend, so how did you get in without them knowing?' Reg asked suspiciously.

O'Neil looked surprised, and then bewildered. 'I don't understand. What have the security guards got to do with it? We've got keys to every room in the building here. We don't have to ask them if we want to go anywhere,' he replied blandly, his eyebrows slightly raised.

Reg blinked a couple of times. What O'Neil had just said had driven the proverbial bulldozer right through Anderson's security procedures. 'Are you telling me that you got into that lab over the weekend without the security staff knowing anything about it?' Reg said with barely disguised astonishment.

O'Neil went one better, he looked back in utter amazement, but he recovered quickly and shrugged his shoulders impassively. 'No one's told me I've got to tell them what I'm doing. They knew I was here. I had to come in through the main gate on Saturday morning like everyone else. They know I do maintenance. Why else would I be in on a Saturday?' O'Neil explained. 'Anyway, how can the security people possibly know what we're doing, where they are? That door at the far end of the room you've just come through, that opens on to the rear hall by the back stairs of the main building. On Saturday morning I went up to Brewer's lab, checked out that what he said was right, then I took the unit out and brought it down here. Then I took a spare one back up. I didn't see anyone else about, not that I can recall, anyway.'

'Did you leave the lab unlocked when you brought the old unit out?' Reg asked mildly.

O'Neil paused for a moment. 'Well, yes, I suppose I did. Those things aren't really heavy, but they're awkward, if you know what I mean; you need both hands to carry

123

them. I never gave it a thought at the time, but I definitely locked it when I'd finished. I'm certain of that.'

'What time did you work to, on Saturday?'

'Half-twelve, or thereabouts. It's in the signing-out book.'

Finch looked round the small room. A wide bench held a variety of equipment, meters, probes, dials, and the shelves on the walls were full of manuals and reference books. 'You understand how all this lot works?' Reg asked in a voice tinged with reluctant admiration.

O'Neil smiled. 'By and large, yes. I'm a programmer really, but I've done my electrics and electronics, and I've always loved getting a soldering iron in my hands. In this job I get the best of both worlds.'

'I understood that the lab where Drs Wade and Chambers worked had its own independent computer unit. Was I right? That looks like a big main-frame computer in that room?' Finch pointed a finger towards the window in the inner wall.

'Yes, Dr Wade's lab had a self-contained system, but many of the other labs still use old BGBB in there.'

'A BGBB? It's not an IBM then?' Reg asked, rather mystified.

O'Neil chuckled. 'That's a fourth generation computer. The first installation was called Bertha, the second, Big Bertha, the third, Great Big Bertha, and this one's Bloody Great Big Bertha—that's what BGBB stands for. Lord knows what we'll call the next one when we get it. Well, I suppose I do really, but it's not polite. Each new one was smaller in physical size than the one we threw out, but hundreds of times more powerful. Believe it or believe it not, the one Dr Wade and Dr Chambers had was nearly as powerful as this, even if it was no bigger than a normal-sized desk. The input consoles and keyboards are standard, though. They're interchangeable.'

'The unit you changed—if you took the back off, would there be enough room inside for a small package? Could a bomb have been planted inside it when you were out at lunch perhaps, and then the fault in the unit upstairs created later, knowing you'd do a swap?' Reg inquired.

O'Neil looked doubtful. 'How small a package?' he asked, then picked up a screwdriver. 'Do you want to see for yourself?'

'You found him all right, did you?' asked the man in charge of the general maintenance.

'Yes, thank you. Now, if you've got a minute, I'd like a list of all the people in your section who were working over the weekend, and what jobs they did about the place. Take your time. I want a minute-by-minute schedule,' Reg Finch asked, moving a couple of dirty radiator valves from the only spare chair before sitting down.

7

It was dark by the time Walsh and Brenda Phipps arrived at the Animal Research Station to plan their ambush.

A two-storey office block fronted the main road, and behind that were several rows of low buildings, one of which was a laboratory; the rest presumably housed animals.

The Animal Research Station was situated on the western outskirts of the city, in an area of land bordered on three of its four sides by dual carriageway roads. The M11, on a high wide embankment, enclosed the site to the south-east, the A45 to the north-west, and the appropriately named Huntingdon Road to the north-east. The site was not completely isolated on those three sides, however: there was a footpath subway under Huntingdon Road from the nearby village of Girton, and a farm track and footpath passed under the M11.

'Someone watching from that corner room, on the top floor of the main block, can cover all the way round the back and that side,' Walsh decided, waving an arm towards the orange glow from the motorway illuminations on the far side, 'and from the front windows you'd be able to see anyone trying to get in from Huntingdon Road. What we need now is a good place to watch the farm track to the south-east, and we'll be in business. The top room this side should do that nicely,' he went on confidently.

Brenda looked a little doubtful. 'It's got more outbuildings, and it's a lot bigger than I'd thought. We're going to be too spread out for my liking. It won't be that easy to spot intruders, not if we get one who knows anything about field craft, and is prepared to crawl about on his belly. Even if we do see him, will we be able to concentrate our force on the right spot quickly enough to collar him?'

'You'd need a small army to cover every possibility, Brenda,' Walsh explained. 'The more people we have, the easier it will be for someone to spot us. I think six will do. Three can be on duty, watching, and the other three can be resting, but they'll be our strike force if anyone's spotted. If we have some unmarked cars roaming around nearby, they ought to be able to home in and cut off all the exits, if we can't collar him inside the fence ourselves. We'll have to keep our eyes wide open while we're watching, that's obvious, but at least we can be pretty certain that the intruder will make his move soon after the visiting security patrol man has gone round with his dog, like he did before. That ought to make life easier for us. Right, so that's settled then. We haven't too much time, and I want to have a word with Packstone, and have a look round Dr Chambers' rooms, before we get ourselves settled down to a night's ambushing.'

Brenda did not appear to be convinced that this ambush set-up was quite as simple and straightforward as the chief seemed to think, but since she had no positive alternative suggestions to make, any criticisms would have been rather pointless.

Mrs Villiers was very plump. She took up most of the space on the two-seater settee, which itself took up most of the space in the tiny sitting-room of the council house. She had iron-grey hair, wore no make-up, and had close-set small brown eyes behind the large lenses of her multicolour-framed spectacles.

'How long have you worked as a cleaner at the lab, Mrs Villiers?' Detective Constable Arthur Bryant asked. It wasn't a question of any importance, but it was a nice way to start the interview off, or so he thought.

Mrs Villiers remained silent, gazing at her questioner with a bewildered expression on her face, then she started to shake her head slowly. 'You ain't my idea of a copper. You're too weedy and you're still only a nipper. Coppers should be big and tough—people you can rely on. Are you a local lad? You remind me of someone.' Mrs Villiers leaned back, causing the settee to groan a protest, and at the same time she managed to light a cigarette, without actually stopping talking. 'It were a long while ago. What was his name now? Bert, was it? You've got his eyes, and his nose too. He took me out to Grantchester Meadows one night, he did. I was only a kid at the time, but I let him give me a peck or two on the cheek, like you do, you know, just to get things going, but it didn't start nothing with him, it didn't. "I've got a right one here," I said to meself. I ended up having to put his hand up me jumper or else we'd have sat there all night like a right pair of bananas. Once he got going he was all right. Like a bloody octopus, he was, hands all over the place.' She gave a hoot of shrill laughter at the sight of Arthur Bryant's reddening face. 'He turned out to be a right randy devil in the end. Those were the days. You youngsters think you know it all, but we old'uns could teach you a thing or two—'

'Mrs Villiers! Please!' Arthur interrupted desperately. 'This is very important. A man got killed today. When you went to clean that lab on the first floor, did you see if any of the others were carrying a small parcel, or a box, for instance? Anything that might have been a bomb?'

'Don't be so bloody daft, boy,' Mrs Villiers snapped irritably. 'You ain't got no hands to spare when you're out cleaning, you know. Brooms, dustpans, vacuum cleaners, polishers, bags of rubbish and God knows what else. Of course no one was carrying parcels. What a damned silly question.'

'I was twenty-five years in the army, Sergeant,' William Hardcastle explained to Reg Finch. The fuzzy hairs of his grey-white beard grew healthily enough on his chin, but had given up trying on the top of his head, except in long tufts round his ears.

'Logistics it was called when I came out, though it was only stores and procurement when I went in. But there's no call for army-trained men in civvy street, logistics or no logistics. I tried for a caretaker's job at a school, but didn't get it. Then this came up with the university. It's all right, it suits me. Six years I've been here, and now I'm one of the longest-serving men in security. Anderson? It was me who took him round and showed him where everything was. Oh yes, of course I took him into the maintenance area, and through the door and up the back stairs. He was a cocky bugger though. He reckoned he knew it all after he'd been here only five minutes like, and when he started telling us we was doing this wrong, and that wrong, well, I let him get on with it. You needn't worry about them in maintenance. They're all right. They've been here as long as I have. You could trust them with the Crown Jewels, you could.'

Walsh found Richard Packstone sitting at a bench in the forensic laboratory, peering through the lenses of a microscope.

'How are things going?' he asked quietly.

Packstone's eyes glinted with annoyance at being disturbed, then he glanced down at his watch and blinked in surprise.

'Good lord, how time does fly. Come into my office, Sidney, we'll have a cup of coffee. I need one, I haven't had anything since breakfast.'

That was an admission that didn't surprise Walsh. After Packstone's wife had died some years previously, he'd tended to isolate himself from his friends and colleagues. The fact that his main home interests were cryptology and the music of Gilbert and Sullivan would hardly have helped him to develop a new social life, even if he'd shown any great inclination to do so. He had no great inclination for cooking, or washing and ironing clothes either, and he soon lost weight and his appearance became rather scruffy. At that point one of Packstone's staff intervened, and persuaded him to take on a part-time housekeeper, thus at least ensuring a tidy house and a supply of clean clothes; however, getting him to eat regular meals had proved much more difficult.

'You've certainly got plenty on your plate—other than food.' Walsh smiled sympathetically as he sat down on the chair by Packstone's desk.

Packstone's lean face creased into what nowadays passed for a grin. 'It's what we're here for, isn't it? We haven't had to deal with many internal bomb blasts in this lab before, but I've managed to get hold of a relatively new computer program that's been specifically designed for such explosions, and I'm rather keen to try it out. It could be interesting, if it works.'

'How do you mean?' Walsh asked.

'Never mind, I'll demonstrate it to you, when we've got it up and running. I'm going to concentrate on the second bomb, since you feel the first might be a red herring.' Packstone looked up as one of his staff came in with two cups of coffee on a tray, and a plate of biscuits. 'Thank you,' he said, reaching for a custard cream.

'Do you know what explosive was used?' Walsh asked.

'Yes, we've analysed the smoke stains. It was trinitrotoluene, Sidney. TNT, in other words.'

'Was it?' Walsh said, his eyebrows rising in surprise. 'Now why had I assumed it would have been a modern plastic explosive—Semtex or something like that? Trinitrotoluene's not the normal terrorist's choice, is it?'

Packstone shrugged and seemed more interested in devouring the rest of the biscuits before Walsh got at them.

'I don't know anything about that. It's not my job to tell you what goes on in the mind of a person who plants bombs, but I suppose they'd use whatever explosive they could get their hands on.'

'Any idea of the detonator used?'

'No.'

'TNT, though,' Walsh persisted. 'It wasn't a simple military grenade, was it? You'll have found bits of shrapnel if it was, I suppose?'

Packstone leaned back in his chair, still munching, and peered through his spectacles at his interrogator. 'All right, play question and answer games if that's what you want, but I've no real facts to work on at this stage. All you'll get is gut feelings and reasoned possibilities. If it was a military-type hand grenade, then we've found none of the metal casing, as yet—and before you ask, no, it wasn't a mortar bomb lobbed in through a window either, the glass fragments are mostly outside. Any more suggestions?'

'I'm afraid so, we've several hypothetical scenarios. Firstly, the brown jiffy bag that lay on the computer desk. It was book-size and didn't weigh much?'

'It's possible, but unlikely. Bits of that desk went upwards and out through the nearest window. If it had gone off while it was being opened over the desk, that wouldn't have happened, would it? Mind you, Chambers might have dropped the jiffy bag on the floor and set it off that way, that's possible. Next?'

'There was a computer input station a bit further down the lab which had developed a fault on the Friday afternoon, and was replaced on the Saturday morning. Could the bomb have been in that?'

Packstone thought for a moment, then shook his head. 'Again it's unlikely. The centre of the explosion was the main computer station where Chambers was working. There were bits of him all over the place.'

'Right! What about the briefcases? Both Dr Wade and Dr Chambers took briefcases in with them—could the bomb have been in one of those?'

'It's possible. Wade's case was on the floor by the wooden coat stand, near the window, and was nearly undamaged, so it couldn't have been in that. Chambers apparently put his on the floor by the side of the desk. That's more likely where the bomb was, but you're not suggesting that Chambers was daft enough to bring it in with him, and even dafter to be around when it went off?'

Walsh shrugged his shoulders. 'Chambers might have been forced to carry the bomb, if some loved one was being held hostage.'

'It's a possibility,' Packstone said, shaking his grey-haired head reluctantly. So far Walsh was only posing sensible scenarios, and that was perfectly understandable, but his own job was to deal in facts, and there was a danger that too much speculation could lead to him getting false premises in his mind, and that could lead to mistakes.

'Look, Sidney, you'll have to be more patient,' Packstone said determinedly. 'It'll be several days before we can be certain just where the bomb was placed, and even longer before we can reconstruct the detonator, but in that respect, I might be able to give you a clue. I was looking at it under the microscope when you came in. It's just a fragment of brass, but it might be part of the case of a small bullet—it's certainly got a rim. It's a lucky find, this early on, with still so much debris to sort through, but that might be what set the bomb off. If it was, I've no idea how it might have been fired.'

'Dr Chambers certainly had good taste in furniture, Chief,' Brenda said, looking round the spacious living-room in the ground-floor apartment of the large Victorian house. The carved rosewood desk was certainly a highly desirable antique, as was the tall grandfather clock with its enamelled and painted face. Side tables and bookcases came into the same category.

'Envy is a sin, remember,' Reg Finch warned, as Brenda took a hand-painted Imari vase from between a pair of old brass carriage clocks on the mantelpiece with far more tender care than she would probably have used to handle a new-born baby.

'Sarcasm's no virtue either, Reg. This stuff just glows with...words fail me... beauty, I suppose. The insurance premiums on all this must have cost him a packet.'

'I wouldn't mind a few of these books myself either,' Reg said, peering at the titles of the volumes in the bookcase. 'Some of these are archaeologists' published site reports. They're hard reading, but you don't come across them very often. He was obviously interested in Celtic history too, from the look of things.'

'Very likely, but that isn't getting us anywhere,' Walsh interrupted. 'Look for anything that strikes you as being out of the ordinary, or anything that might indicate a relationship with somebody who DaSilva might be holding hostage. Reg, you do the garage and the kitchen. I'll check out the bedrooms. You search in here, Brenda, but be careful with all this bone china. I know you'd enjoy sticking the bits back together again, but I'd rather it wasn't broken in the first place—not by us anyway.'

The garage was cold and gloomy. Ladders and hosepipes on the walls; brooms, spades, and a lawn mower in one corner; the usual accumulation of bric-à-brac, Finch thought, with barely enough room left for a car. At the far end a door led through a partition wall into a small but comfortable workshop. A convector heater and draught excluder round the door and windows indicated that the room might be usable however Siberian the temperature outside. An old, padded office chair stood by the work bench under the window which looked out over the rear garden. On that bench was an Anglepoise lamp, and the dismantled parts of what appeared to be several small clocks or watches. There were empty cases on the nearby shelves. Brass carriage clocks with glass backs, sturdy old marble, carved wood; a wide variety of the timepieces made during the past hundred and fifty years. On the bench, around a pin vice, were filings of brass and steel.

Reg Finch spent some time opening drawers containing sets of tiny screwdrivers, files and drills, more watches and pieces of brass plate. There was a small intricate watchmaker's lathe to study, then he went back into the apartment to browse through the far more dull and mundane contents of the kitchen.

Walsh found that the contents of the bedrooms generally conformed with what he considered to be normality for an intelligent, healthy, well-balanced, reconstituted bachelor. He carried out a thorough search of drawers and wardrobes, bedside cabinets and coat pockets, but having found nothing of interest, he went back into the living-room.

Brenda knelt on the floor before a

walnut-veneered bureau, slowly turning the pages of a photograph album. She looked round as Walsh came in, then pointed at the bureau.

'It's got a secret drawer, Chief,' she announced casually, as though such things were commonplace. 'Just like the one that was demonstrated last year on the *Antiques Roadshow*. They're poems, but whether they're important or not, I don't know. Some of the words are double-Dutch to me.'

Walsh picked up the narrow box of the not-so-secret drawer. It had a polished walnut veneer on its outer edge, where it matched with the internal fittings. Secret the drawer may once have been, but even so there was an early nineteenth-century double bluff. It had been made with a false bottom, concealing a gap of perhaps less than half an inch, but adequate enough to contain quite a number of gold coins, or, as in this case, papers.

Walsh spread out the folded sheets.

There was nothing old about them. They were photocopies, on standard A4 paper. The originals had been handwritten in bold, looping letters that gave the impression they had been crafted with care.

The heading on the first page read, 'Cato ap Tiri', and under that, 'Tir na n'Og'.

What followed was verse, in English.

Neath constant blue, in summer's light,
I wait on grassy knoll.
The aeons pass like birds in flight
While time doth take no toll.
Yet do I stir and writhe with inner pain
Till you are with me once again.

Your lips were soft and warm and red
And you gave such loving sighs.
While the sun smiled down,
We shared the friendship of the thighs.
Yet do I stir and writhe with inner pain
Till you are with me once again.

'It gets a bit warmer, if you read on, Chief,' Brenda said, getting to her feet. 'There's no question of that poet's love being unrequited. All that seems to concern him is...well, when he can have it again.'

Walsh rubbed his chin thoughtfully. 'If Chambers wrote this stuff, then there is someone he cared about, someone who could have been held a hostage for his good behaviour.'

His musing was interrupted as Reg Finch came in from the kitchen.

'Boss!' he said soberly. 'Chambers was into horology. There's a workshop in the garage with all sorts of bits of clocks and watches lying about. If that bomb had a

141

timing device, then friend Chambers could easily have made it.'

'That truck had been used for shifting manure. It didn't half stink,' Arthur Bryant protested in a hushed voice, as Brenda Phipps led the way up the stairs of the Animal Research Station's main building.

'Get down on your knees as you go past these windows, Arthur, or you'll be in the stuff that truck shifts, right up to your neck,' Brenda snapped caustically. 'There's enough light coming in from outside for anyone watching to see you. As for the truck, if you can think of a better way to get six people and their gear into this place without anyone seeing us, you tell the chief. He'll be pleased to know. Now, the room you're watching from is the second one down here on the right. The door is open—leave it that way. There's a chair for you to sit on. It's well back from the window. See! You've a good clear view of the M11 embankment, and if you lean forward and turn your head you can keep watch on the filter lane from the A45 as well. Don't forget how we've split up the whole place into different sectors. If you report an intruder, you must say which sector, so that the three of us downstairs can home in on him.'

'This is going to be a doddle,' Arthur

said confidently, laying his binoculars, radio, and the two chocolate bars that he obviously considered necessary to sustain his energy and strength during his night's vigil, carefully on the floor. Then he settled himself comfortably in the chair. 'How long have we got to watch, each of us, did you say?'

'Two hours on and two hours off. We'll finish at six in the morning, when the people who look after the animals come in. They're part-time, they work until the permanent staff come in at nine, then they come back at seven in the evening and work until ten. We'll be going out in the same truck as we came in. If you don't like the stink you'll just have to hold your nose. Right, I'll leave you to it. Don't go to sleep. If the bomber comes and you miss him, I'll personally stuff you head first in the biggest pile of manure I can find.'

With such exhortations in mind, Arthur Bryant dutifully maintained his vigilance during his first two-hour period, and his second, but neither he nor any other of the police surveillance team saw an intruder that night, and no bombs went off, either there, or anywhere else in the city.

8

Angela drove out of Huntingdon in her rusty Mini, and headed south, towards London.

Today was her grandmother's birthday, and the presents she had bought—a pair of fleece-lined slippers and a white fluffy muff—should be very welcome, since of late her grandmother had been complaining of having chilly feet and hands. Those purchases lay duly wrapped in pretty paper, on the car seat beside her.

She had not gone very far when she realised that she'd forgotten the birthday card. That, her memory now smugly reminded her, lay where she had left it, on the chest of drawers in the bedroom.

She was a lady of leisure now, and in no hurry. Time was of no great importance, so she drove all the way round the next roundabout, and went back for it.

The apartment seemed quiet and deserted, and so it came as something of a shock when she pushed open the door of the bedroom and found Ronald Silver sitting at the dressing-table, staring intently at his face in the mirror. Surprisingly, he looked a lot different now than he had when she had left him earlier. His eyebrows were darker and more bushy, his cheeks seemed drawn in and hollow, and the skin of his face much less tanned. Instead of being in comfortable, casual clothes, he now wore a grey suit, which although it was still neat, had clearly seen better days, for the knees were creased and the elbows shiny, as though its original owner had spent much of his time sitting in and driving a car.

Silver had been startled by her sudden appearance, and he looked rather annoyed, and not at all pleased to see her.

'I'm sorry, Ron,' Angela gasped out, trying to hide her astonishment at his changed appearance, 'but I forgot my grandmother's birthday card.' She pointed to the chest of drawers, on which now stood two shiny bottles with unusual and colourful labels. One of the bottles actually stood on the birthday card. She reached out to move it.

'Don't touch!' Silver said sharply, and he went to lift the bottle himself. Surprisingly, he did that in the way one might pick up something that was searing hot, by using a handkerchief to protect the skin of his fingers.

'There you are,' he said curtly, handing Angela the card.

She gulped. 'Thanks, Ron. I'd better be off now, or I'll be late,' she said hurriedly, and quickly made her way out of the apartment and back to her car.

That awful man Marston had warned her not to ask questions, or pry into what did not concern her. That she certainly did not intend to do, but it did not stop her wondering just what Ronald Silver was up to.

The CC was certainly looking more grumpy than usual this morning. The slight shrug and the grimace his secretary had made as Walsh went into the office indicated that perhaps earlier visitors had found her employer in no peaceful pleasant mood. Walsh soon found out that he'd read all the signs correctly.

'Are you out of your tiny mind, Sidney?' the chief constable snapped angrily. 'Don't you realise you're up against a bunch of ruthless killers? And you tell me that you spent last night on a surveillance operation that even the most simple-minded rookie could have done in your place. God give me strength. How many times have I told you, you're a general commanding the battlefield. You've loads of people to do the running around and mucky jobs. How are you going to keep your brain cool and detached if you get yourself involved in petty little skirmishes?'

'Last night wasn't a petty skirmish,' Walsh replied icily. He may have had doubts about the wisdom of getting himself or his team directly involved in the plan to ambush DaSilva, but having committed himself to it, the last thing he was prepared to do was admit he might have been wrong. He'd involved himself because it was a team plan, and he was the leader of that team, and it was teamwork that won battles, wasn't it?

'You want your bread buttered on both sides all the time,' he went on in a growling tone. 'It's like the watch on the Catholic churches—because nothing came of it, you say it's all wrong, but if we'd caught DaSilva then or last night, you'd have sung a different tune. Can you really see me lying around snoozing in bed when there's a chance of winding this whole thing up quickly? No, you can't, because you wouldn't do things any differently, if you were me.'

The CC's eyes glinted ominously and his jaw hardened, but for some reason he didn't press home his attack on that front. Rather surprisingly for someone so well versed in battle tactics, his next sally had about as much venom in it as a punctured tennis ball being lobbed at the enemy, instead of a hand grenade.

'It isn't good for your marriage, Sidney, you being out all night too often. That wife of yours will take so much, and then there'll be trouble. I've seen it before, and I don't want it to happen to you,' he muttered sulkily.

'You leave Gwen out of this. She knows when things are important. She wouldn't have me chicken out of my responsibilities,' Walsh said confidently. That was true—but it was something he'd better bear in mind if this surveillance exercise went on too long. Gwen might think he was taking her too much for granted, and no woman liked that.

'Have you worked out how DaSilva got in to plant the bomb at the Medical Centre, yet?' the CC demanded, tentatively trying an outflanking move.

'We don't know that DaSilva did plant the bomb himself. We haven't ruled out the possibility that Superintendent Anderson planted it, as could any of the maintenance or security staff,' Walsh replied calmly and with a confident smile. 'There's also an outside chance that Chambers took that bomb in. It sounds unlikely but we can't rule out the possibility, not until Packstone's worked out just where the bomb was placed.'

'I gather you've been putting him under a bit of pressure.'

148

'It's no more than he expects. I want to know what I'm up against.'

'Of course you do, but Packstone's a wily old bird, and he won't say much until he's sure of his facts,' the CC announced glumly.

'He may have a clue to the detonator. He's found what he thinks is the casing of a .22 rifle bullet.'

'That's not a lot of help. If DaSilva wants us to think these bombings were done by animal rights activists, he wouldn't use sophisticated explosives and detonators, would he? You're making a mistake if you suppose you can outguess him by trying to think like a clever professional killer, because this professional killer is obviously trying to make himself think like an amateur. You've got to make the necessary allowances.' The CC leaned back in his chair and scowled down at his hands for some moments. When he spoke again his voice was quiet and serious. 'Now listen to me carefully, Sidney. Last night I had two fellows from MI6 at my place, grilling me about this damned leak business. Unfortunately, you and I are the only ones at that bloody conference who they can come out in the open and get their teeth into. They gave me some stick, I can tell you. They kept asking me why I was allowing you to run the

149

investigation, and where did I get my information about DaSilva? I haven't had to put up with anything like that since I did my counter-espionage course, twenty-odd years ago. Still, I stuck to my guns, and that's what you've got to do, Sidney, because they'll be after you next. You've got to say nothing about Julian. You don't know anything anyway, but the least said the better. I've said I'm giving you my full backing on this investigation, because you're the best man for the job. I've stuck my head squarely on the chopping block, but I'm not going to face the music on my own. Your head's on the block next to mine. If the axe falls, matey, it'll get you too. So you'd better get this DaSilva business all sorted out, pronto.'

Walsh's mouth twisted into a wry grin. MI6 officers were no respecters of persons, and the CC's ego must have been severely shaken to account for his unusual mixture of meekness and aggression this morning, but it wouldn't last long—he was a tough old character.

'Take that damned grin off your face, Sidney. It isn't bloody funny. I'm relying on you to sort this mess out,' the CC snapped irritably.

That was more like the CC he was used to. Walsh's grin broadened. 'Isn't that just what I'm trying to do?' he said soothingly.

Martin O'Neil, the computer technician at the Medical Research Centre, and his friend Bert Winters walked down the narrow lane and pushed open the door to the saloon bar of the Black Cat Inn.

They could have taken advantage of the subsidised meals at the university staff club canteen in Mill Lane, but because they would both eat cooked evening meals later, at home with their respective wives, they preferred to spend their lunch hour having a quiet drink and a game of darts in this little out-of-the-way pub.

'Hello there, John. Back here again? You'll become one of us regulars if you don't watch it,' Bert Winters said cheerfully to the stocky man perched on the stool by the bar.

'It's as good a place as any to sink a pint, Bert. I use Cambridge as a base when I'm doing East Anglia, and I thought I knew all the pubs in town, but I've only just found this one. What'll you both have?'

'A lager would suit me fine, thanks,' Martin O'Neil said, rubbing his chilly hands together. 'Its not quite so cold this morning, but it's still damned parky. Roll on summer, I say.'

'My usual, please.' Bert spoke more to the waiting barman than to the man he knew as John Long. 'The weather forecast this morning said this cold spell could last at least another week. At least we haven't got six inches of that white stuff, like they've got up north. I wouldn't fancy your job, John, being on the road at this time of year.'

'It's not so bad. The Christmas orders are all taken and delivered. All I'm doing now are courtesy calls, but it's just an excuse to dish them out their free bottle of seasonal greetings. It's funny how some of them are too busy to see me when I call during the year, but they can always find the time when it's nearly Christmas,' John Long said with a broad grin.

'I'll bet they do, but have you got any spare bottles of seasonal greetings? That's what we want to know,' Martin asked hopefully.

John looked round to see if the barman was out of hearing. 'It's funny you should ask that. I do have a couple over. They're the very finest malt whisky, you won't find a better, not even up in the Highlands. Trade price, seven quid each to you, since I know you,' he replied confidentially, in a lowered voice.

'Jeepers, that's cheap. I'll have one. It won't get you into trouble, will it?' Bert grinned conspiratorially.

John shook his head. 'No, but talking about trouble, I gather you've had a bit of that in your laboratories. What happened?'

Martin bit his lip and looked away. 'We're not supposed to talk about it.'

Bert's face showed embarrassment at his friend's over-curt reply. 'It was just a minor explosion in one of the labs, John. An occupational hazard, you might say,' Bert responded, glaring at Martin. His friend could be over-dramatic at times, and that was a bit unkind, particularly to someone who'd just done them a favour. This John was only a rep, and reps were often lonely people, being away from home for days at a time. Naturally they liked a bit of company, and the trouble at the lab was bound to be a topic of conversation.

'Oh dear! No one hurt, I hope? I didn't actually read what the papers said,' John admitted, not appearing to notice the coolness in Martin's reply.

'I'm afraid there was, John. One of the research chaps. He was too close to it.'

'Good lord. It didn't damage your computers though, did it, Martin?'

'That lab had its own self-contained unit, but there wasn't much of it left afterwards, I can tell you,' Martin replied with a half-smile. He felt a little guilty, after seeing Bert's glare of reproof.

'Self-contained? Oh dear, then all that lab's stored research data will have been destroyed. What a waste. They should have linked it into your main-frame, so you could duplicate the back-up copies. My firm keeps its back-up discs safely in a special fireproof cabinet, but I suppose everyone does that,' John Long said, taking another sip from his glass.

'Fireproof cabinets?' Bert chuckled, scornfully. 'They're only made of thin steel. That lab's back-up discs would have all gone up in smoke, unless you had a centralised feed link that no one knew about, Martin.'

Martin's face reddened, and his lips came together in a mulish look. He said nothing, but shook his head slightly and glanced away.

John Long broke the short silence that followed.

'Is one of you going to give me a game, then?' he asked, reaching for the darts from the corner of the bar counter, and getting to his feet.

'I'll take you on,' Martin replied, obviously glad to have the subject changed, but he grimaced when he saw Long's throw for nearest to the middle just clip the wire of the bull itself. 'I'll give you that. You go off,' he muttered.

'I'm away. Fifty-two.' Long plucked the darts from the board with one hand and gave them to Martin. 'You said the other

154

day that you did computer maintenance. Can you fix faults on any type of computer, or just what you've got in the lab?'

'It depends what's wrong, John. Why, have you got a problem?'

'My laptop PC. I keep my orders and customer records and things on it. It works all right most of the time, but if it gets knocked, it sometimes goes dead and I lose everything I've just put in. It's a damned nuisance, but it's mine, you see, not the firm's, and it's out of guarantee too.'

'It sounds as though there's a loose connection somewhere. I can't look at it during the week, there's too many people around in the department. I have to do things like that on Saturday mornings. I can't promise I'll fix it, but I can try,' Martin offered, then he surprised himself by throwing double top with his first dart, and the next two went straight into the treble twenty.

'Hell's bells,' muttered John Long, blinking at the sight. 'I haven't seen that done for years. I can't make it this Friday. Would next week be all right?'

'Sorry, John. We'll be off on our Christmas holidays then. Not that we're actually going away anywhere, unfortunately. We're back at work the second

155

week of the New Year. Can it wait until then?'

'I'm sorry about the bomb at the Medical Research Centre, Professor,' Sidney Walsh said, sitting himself down in one of the high-backed leather-upholstered chairs by the ornate fireplace.

The professor's college sitting-room was sumptuously and richly furnished. Some of the oil paintings hanging on the wall had been changed since his last visit here, and he would dearly have liked to spend some time studying the new ones, but it would hardly be polite to do that, under the circumstances.

Professor Edwin Hughes reached forward with the tongs to place another piece of coal on the already well banked-up and glowing fire. He was a portly, nearly bald man, of short stature, wearing baggy brown corduroys and a thick brightly coloured Fair Isle sweater. His face was friendly and cheerful, yet it was also shrewd and intelligent, as befitted one of the university's foremost academicians.

'It was no fault of yours, Inspector,' he said quietly, putting down the tongs so that he could pour his visitor a cup of coffee. 'You did try and warn us of a possible danger. Fortunately the bomb did no structural damage to the building.

It was built in the sixties, you know, to a much higher specification than we might use today.'

'Good,' Walsh observed drily. 'Now, one of the more remote possibilities is that Chambers might have been the carrier of the bomb. Under duress, of course, while a hostage was being held prisoner to ensure that he complied with his instructions.' Walsh put his cup down on the polished table beside him, and looked directly at the professor's round chubby face. 'Now, in Chambers' apartment we found some papers concealed in an intricate little secret drawer in a bureau. They're love poems, of a sort, but who they're about isn't stated. It might be someone who could have been held hostage. It's a long shot, I know, but I feel we have to check it out. Would you mind glancing through them? Reg Finch had come across "Tir na n'Og" before, but the other heading words, "Cato ap Tiri", made no sense to him, except that he thought they looked Welsh.'

Hughes had a wry, somewhat super-cilious smile on his face as he took the proffered papers, but he spread them out on his lap and read them carefully. Then he rubbed his fleshy chin thoughtfully. 'The handwriting looks very much like Dr Chambers'. I've had occasion to become reasonably familiar with it over the last few days. Now, this first word that your sergeant thinks might be Welsh—Cato. Well, the most famous Cato was Cato Marcus Porcius, but he was the Roman who fought against Hannibal in around 200 BC. He also wrote a treatise on agriculture, if that's of any interest. Next, the "ap". Yes indeed, that's Welsh or Celtic for "son of", so if this is a person's name, that person ought to be a male, which is confusing, because I hardly think Chambers would be writing love poems to a man. Lastly, "Tiri". Well the only Tiri I've ever heard of is that New Zealand opera singer, who did the World Cup rugby song a few years ago, but I can't see how she—'

'Kiri! Her name's Kiri, not Tiri, Professor,' Walsh interrupted.

'So it is. I'm sorry. I'm not being very helpful, am I? Perhaps its some nickname that Chambers had. Now the "Tir na n'Og", I can tell you more about. That's from Celtic mythology. It means the Land of Eternal Youth, the most desirable of all paradises. Chambers expresses it well, if he actually composed these poems, with his "constant blue in summer's light". Imagine an endless summer's afternoon to romp with a lovely companion on some grassy knoll. Yes, indeed, that's what Oisin did with Manannan's daughter Niamh—that's in the Irish stories, not the Welsh ones. Paradise—but it has its snags, as you'd expect in stories of gods and heroes. Once in the Land of Eternal Youth mere mortals lose all sense of time, and if they are ever foolish enough to leave—to go back to the real world—then they'd discover that time had been passing in their absence, and all they'd find would be the crumbling ruins of their previous life. The study of these Celtic myths can provide an interesting insight into the minds of those ancient people, Inspector, if you can ever spare the time. They had a genuine belief in the reality of the supernatural. Not just in their ability to communicate with it, but also to travel to and from it. Pliny the Elder linked the Celtic Druids with the Persians, by calling them "magicians", which is derived from the Persian word "Magi", of course, but, there you are, Indian Brahmins and Shamanism; they're all involved with the supernatural, and all interlinked in many ways. I wasn't aware that Dr Chambers had any interest in the subject, but he obviously did have. It's possible that these are only copies of ancient verses. The poetry is only mediocre, although something is always lost in translation, of course, but it certainly is in the ancient Irish style, with some of the standard phraseology. That "friendship of the thighs", for instance, was the ancients' way of saying that they were having an affair—a sexual relationship. "Nooky", they call it these days, I believe. Still, that doesn't help you in your hostage quest, does it? May I keep these copies? I'd like to reread them a few times at my leisure, and have a chat about them to some of my more learned colleagues. You never know, something might come out of mulling them over.'

'Have you got a Hutchinson there, Brenda?' Reg Finch inquired. 'Room three, on the ground floor. That's right, that one.'

Brenda Phipps sorted through the neatly arranged piles of statements spread out on Reg's desk. 'Wayne Hutchinson? Is that the one?' she asked.

'That's it. Mary Maloney went to get a drink at the vending machine in the corridor. Wayne Hutchinson was there too, she says, at about nine twenty. Is that what he says?'

'Yes.'

'Right, tick that bit with the red pencil,' Reg directed, then he leaned back in his chair. 'Well, that's about it, Brenda. All the research teams are accounted for during the period from eight o'clock on Monday, until the bomb went off. If they weren't in their laboratories, they were seen by others in the loos or by the vending machines,' he went on. 'I suppose that exercise was a bit pointless, really, since Wade and the other two both say no one except the post girl came into their lab during that period, but at least this confirms all their stories. There were also people in the office where the mail was sorted, so the jiffy bag, if that was the bomb, couldn't have been switched there.'

'So, where does that leave us, Reg?'

'The girl who took the post might have switched jiffy bags, but other than her and the cleaners, the only people who could have got into that lab, from knocking-off time on Friday until eight thirty Monday, were Anderson, the security guards, and the maintenance staff.'

'That's pretty well what we suspected, but you've done a good job here,' Brenda observed, looking at the piles of the lab employees' statements, whose movements had been so methodically compared, confirmed and cross-referenced. 'You'd have made a damned good accountant or auditor, you know, Reg.'

'I did think about it once, but I reckoned looking for fiddled expense claims, fingers in petty cash tins and dodgy share transactions would get a bit boring after the first ten minutes. At least we can't say that about the jobs we've got, can we?'

Dr James Wade lived in a large detached house in the Newnham area of the city. That in itself was a measure of a considerable degree of affluence. Such properties did not come cheap, thought Walsh, as he walked up the gravel drive to the front door, and rang the bell.

After a few moments the door was opened, but only the two or three inches allowed by the hardened steel chain on the inside. The face that peered out at him was female, and definitely not that of the member of the Cambridgeshire Constabulary specifically detailed to provide 'minder' protection for the Wade family.

Walsh frowned, dug his hand in his pocket for his warrant card, and held it up so that it could be seen.

'I'm Detective Chief Inspector Walsh. I'd like to come in and have a few words with your husband, if I may?' he said, making the not unreasonable assumption that the woman inside was James Wade's wife.

The door was pulled to while the chain was unclipped, then opened wide.

'Do come in, Inspector. The man you've stationed here is in the loo, so that's why I opened the door. I put the chain on, so I'm sure there was no risk. Tell me off, if you must, but don't let on to James, he's still a bit edgy at the moment.'

'You were taking unnecessary chances, all the same. You didn't know who I was, and that chain wouldn't have been much protection if I'd put my shoulder to the door,' Walsh replied sternly as he stepped inside, then he paused to study the slim woman standing before him. She was probably in her early thirties and she was dressed comfortably and casually in maroon designer jeans and a thick white sweater, both of which fitted well and emphasised the curves of a very neat figure. She was barely of medium height, with shoulder-length dark hair and even darker, very attractive eyes that glowed brightly, and a little wildly, in a rather plain face that looked tired and worried.

Walsh racked his brains to try and remember her name. The lab director had mentioned it. 'You must be Patricia Wade,' he said eventually.

'You've got it absolutely right. I'm Patricia. Don't call me Pat or Tricia though, I hate those names,' she told him with an attempt at a smile. 'Come through into the lounge. James! Inspector Walsh is here to see you, dear.'

'Hello, Dr Wade. I trust you're feeling a little better than when I last saw you?' Walsh inquired, but there was very little sign of an improvement—rather the reverse, in fact. Dr Wade slumped rather than sat in one of the beige armchairs. His naturally sallow skin now had a yellowish tinge; his eyes seemed to have sunk further into darkened sockets, but they glistened with some sort of emotion as Walsh came over.

'Have you got whoever did it yet, Inspector?' he croaked anxiously.

Walsh shook his head.

'Why not, for Christ's sake? It's your job to protect me. It's what I pay my taxes for. They're out to get me, just like they did poor Justin. It's all right for you to stand there with that smug expression on your face, you're all right, no one's trying to blow you to bits,' James Wade protested in a slurred voice as he struggled to sit himself more upright, then he reached for the half-full brandy glass on the nearby coffee table and drained it empty in one desperate gulp.

Walsh looked down at him, and his frown deepened. He'd gained the impression from his previous meeting that James Wade was, to put it mildly, a somewhat weak and spineless character; however, the depths to which this whimpering wreck had sunk were surprising, although the quarter-full bottle of brandy on the side table gave some clue as to how it might

164

have been achieved.

'Oh James, don't drink any more, please,' Patricia Wade pleaded. 'It would be so much better if you had one of those pills the doctor gave you.'

Wade turned his head to face his wife. His eyes were wide and bleary. 'Tranquillisers? Get stuffed. No way.'

Mrs Wade's hand reached out tentatively to touch Walsh's arm. 'I'm afraid he's not really in a fit state to answer questions, you know,' she said softly. Her face showed signs of distress and concern, and she probably wasn't very far from tears or a mental breakdown herself. 'Well, not if you want sensible replies, that is,' she went on. 'I really don't know what to do. He's been like this since he came home after that bomb went off. That's the second bottle of brandy since yesterday too. I couldn't even get him to go to bed last night. He slept where he was, with just a blanket over him. I know he's highly strung, he always has been, but I do wish he'd at least try and get a grip of himself. He just doesn't realise what a strain it puts on other people.'

'He's had nearly half a bottle today? Good lord!' Walsh exclaimed sympathetically. 'It's shock, of course. It affects different people in different ways. If I were you I'd try and get him off the hard spirits, or at least water the bottle down when he's not looking. It'd be ironic if he became an alcoholic, wouldn't it? Well, I wanted to talk to him about Dr Chambers, but there's obviously not much point, at the moment.'

'Can I help? We'd better go next door into the dining-room, we can talk in there. James'll be all right on his own. Mind you, in the state he's in it's about as much as he can do to make it to the loo in time. I've been dreading him having a calamity. That's the last thing I need.' She laughed nervously.

Walsh looked over at Wade, whose eyelids had drooped closed, and nodded. 'Yes, perhaps you can help.'

He followed Patricia Wade into the other room.

'What is it you wish to know?' she said, looking up at Walsh's face with those wide fathomless dark eyes.

Female eyes like that were dangerous. They had a strange power to hypnotise men caught in their beam—but not a man as old and wise as Walsh. He could look safely into their depths and brave the heady whirlpools they spun in his mind. The faintest of subtle perfumes, mixed with an air of feminine body warmth, wafted to Walsh's nostrils, and suddenly stirred senses and thoughts in his brain that were far, far removed from his search for the bomber who had killed one person and nearly maimed two others. It would be so easy to reach out a hand and to touch the soft warm flesh of this woman who was alone with him and so near.

He looked away, cleared his throat and moved to turn one of the dining-chairs for Mrs Wade to sit on. It seemed a wise thing to do.

'I wanted to ask about Dr Chambers' private life,' he said rather lamely. 'More particularly to find out if there was anyone, since his wife left him, with whom he was, well, more than usually intimate.'

Patricia Wade gave a light nervous laugh and hesitated a moment before replying. 'What's "more than usually intimate" mean? Surely you are, or you're not, but I suppose you mean, did Justin have a lover, don't you? Well, James hasn't mentioned anything specific to me, but I did get the feeling, from some of the things he said, that perhaps Justin was rather keen on that young research assistant of theirs. Maureen, I think her name is. We've had Justin and friends here to dinner several times, and we've met him at social functions, but he was always alone on those occasions.'

Sidney had weighty matters on his mind again, Gwen decided, as they sat in the dining-room having their evening meal. Being the wife of a conscientious and active police officer required a great deal of patience and understanding—if one was happy with the relationship, that is, and wanted it to continue. It meant having a heightened awareness of the other's moods, although moods was not the right word—states of mind expressed it more accurately.

Sometimes the mere act of changing into casual clothes when he came home enabled him to put some of his work problems to one side, but she'd noticed that the bigger the problem, the older and more tatty the clothes he changed into. Tonight he wore a favourite pair of old baggy brown corduroys, the knees of which were going thin, and the turquoise green sweater she'd knitted years ago, that had gone all loose and saggy after a couple of washes. Homely and comfortable, maybe, but a long way from the neatness of his attire while on duty.

She would have preferred it if he had confided in her, but she knew that there were many things he was not at liberty to discuss. She did not resent the fact—it would be a bit late to do so now, after all these years.

One thing he had mentioned, and that was about the man who had been killed by the bomb at the medical laboratory. Apparently Sidney was concerned that the man might have been forced to take the bomb into the lab himself, because of threats to an unknown lover. She had commented that a good-looking divorced university lecturer would have no problem finding a few female students who were ready and willing to be tutored in more exciting extra-curricular activities. That opinion obviously only confirmed what he had already considered, for he had merely nodded and said that so far he hadn't been able to find any such girls.

'That was a smashing meal, love,' Sidney Walsh said as he dutifully pulled up the sleeves of his baggy green sweater, prepared to do the washing up.

'It would have been better if you'd come home when you said you would. The parsnips were over-roasted. They were like bits of rubber,' Gwen chided amiably.

'I like them chewy,' Sidney replied absentmindedly. The beef had been tough and stringy too, but it would not be wise to mention that. He'd been aware of Gwen's glances during the meal. She seemed sensitive to some of his moods, but the reasons for this one he dared not tell her. Would any sensible husband tell his wife that that afternoon he'd felt such a sexual attraction for another woman that

169

he'd been sorely tempted to reach out and embrace her? That moment with Mrs Wade had been hellishly dangerous. What if he had touched her? What might that have led to? An ignominious rejection, most likely; but what if the slim Mrs Patricia Wade had responded? He gulped at the thought as he ran the hot water into the kitchen sink. That would have led to a frantic kissing session while her slender body was held close to his. Inevitably his hands would have wandered under that white sweater to caress the smooth flesh of her breasts; then they would have worked their way downwards, to venture into an area of lacy briefs and satin-skinned thighs.

What the hell was he doing, thinking like this? He was a mature sensible male, not some adolescent, stirred by a naked Page Three beauty. Mrs Wade was no such beauty anyway; Gwen was far more attractive. So what the devil was going on in his head? Had his hormone balance gone wrong all of a sudden? Was he slowly turning into some sex-mad dirty old man? How could it be normal to suddenly want to ravish a complete stranger? He'd always found women attractive, but there was no harm in that, that was just artistic appreciation, wasn't it?

He rubbed so hard to clean a plate that the sleeve of his sweater slipped down his arm and got wet, but he'd nearly finished. He pulled the plug out of the sink, rinsed it round with clean water, and turned to dry his hands on the tea towel Gwen was using.

A faint subtle perfume wafted to him from Gwen's hair. Almost hesitantly his hand reached out to touch the clear cool skin of her face.

Gwen looked up at his frowning, perplexed expression, and then suddenly her eyes twinkled with understanding; it was no work problem that was bothering him. She put an arm round his waist and gave him a hug, then she whispered, 'You'll be all right tonight, darling, or you will before you go out on your surveillance operation. Just let me have a bath first.'

Was it all just as simple as that? Walsh wondered, holding her tightly and allowing his hand to roam over the backside of Gwen's tight jeans. Probably not, but all of a sudden there didn't seem any need to ponder the question further.

9

Rather surprisingly, although the surveillance exercise at the Animal Research Station had again proved uneventful, Sidney Walsh had slept so deeply and soundly during his off-duty periods that he'd found himself as nearly well refreshed as if he'd had a normal uninterrupted night's rest.

So it was that the next morning, when he strolled down the long corridor to the forensic laboratory with his two assistants, there was a suggestion of a youthful jauntiness to his stride.

Dr Richard Packstone, on the other hand, looked very tired indeed. Clearly he had been burning both ends of his candle intensively of late. His tall spare-framed body seemed to have acquired a looseness, a droopiness, rather like that of an under-inflated car tyre or a tent needing its guy-ropes tightening. However, in spite of the dark shadows under his eyes and a day's growth of glistening grey-white beard, his voice had the sharp ring of clarity which suggested that his mind was as keen and alert as ever.

'We've inputted enough data now to be getting some consistent results,' he said firmly, pointing at the computer display screen.

Brenda Phipps moved round to the left side of Packstone's chair, so that she could have a better view of what was going on. This application of computer technology was new to her, and it looked as though it might be interesting.

'Let me explain how the program works,' Packstone continued. 'It's called "The Bomb Blast", for obvious reasons, but it's quite simple, really. It's a development of one of the CAD systems. CAD stands for Computer Aided Design, if you didn't know. You'll have seen the principles demonstrated often enough on the television, with some of their graphic displays. Basically, it allows a three-dimensional picture to be built up within the computer itself, but with the facility to be able to rotate it in any combination of the three axis planes, so that it can be viewed from any position or angle. The picture we need to build up in the computer is, of course, the place where the bomb exploded—the Wade and Chambers laboratory in our case. So, firstly, we entered in the overall physical dimensions of the lab itself. That provides the outline shape, and gives us our reference points.'

He pressed some keys on the keyboard and, sure enough, a rectangular box-like structure came up on the screen. 'Then we enter other features, the windows, doors, power sockets, and so on.' He pressed another key, and more lines appeared within the box. 'That was the easy bit, now we have to put in position the equipment and furniture. Here we've been most fortunate. The manufacturers of the electron microscope and the computer unit both use a CAD program for the design of their products, which we've been able to make compatible with this one. That's saved us a tremendous amount of time. So they went in, thus.' Packstone stood back for a moment and waved casually at the screen with his left hand. 'There', he went on dramatically, 'you have a reconstruction of what the interior of that laboratory looked like, just prior to the explosion. We've left out things like chairs and so forth, because we can't be absolutely certain of their precise position, but the main pieces of equipment are all there, and in the right places too; well, within a centimetre or so—the cleaners swept round all the heavy stuff, so the marks where they'd stood on the floor were clear enough. It looks quite simple, doesn't it?' Packstone reached for a white plastic cup, and sipped at its cold contents before continuing. 'You can see only the outer surfaces of the equipment on the picture at the moment, but all the inner details, all the component parts, even the wiring and cable clips, are in there as well. You can see that if we magnify up this section of the microscope.' He moved a mouse on the desk and manoeuvred the flashing square cursor to the spot he wanted, and pressed a key. The screen then changed to display what was presumably part of a circuit board.

'So that's the first stage set-up. That's the "where things were before the bomb went off" stage,' Packstone repeated. 'The next step is to plot where bits ended up after the explosion. Now, much of the debris bounced off the walls and ceiling before coming to rest on the floor, so we're not really bothered with that, it's the bits that got embedded in the plaster that interest us. Take this piece of the computer console. It was found embedded in the wall near the first window, just here.' He pointed at the picture on the screen. 'We know how much this piece weighs, how deeply it was embedded in the plaster, and the penetrative resistance of the plaster itself; and we know precisely where it was before the bomb went off. Now there's an interesting exercise in practical dynamics for you. A typical ballistics problem of the "where will the cannon ball end up?" type. Only in this case we know where it ended up—what we don't know is how big, and where, the explosive charge was. No difficulty there, the computer's programmed to work out the impact velocity and to work back to calculate the particle flight-path, then, given a known explosive material, it works out how much and where that explosive must have been placed, in order for that piece of debris to have ended up where it did. Do you understand?'

The serious faces round him nodded.

'Good,' Packstone continued. 'Obviously it's a little more complicated than that. This particular piece broke away from the rest of the structure around it, so there are other calculations of stress factors and sheer strengths involved, but we don't need to go into those. Last night we plotted nearly a hundred of the particles found embedded in the laboratory walls.' He pressed a key on the computer, and a confused mass of different coloured curving lines appeared.

'There you are! Where the red ones meet is where the bomb was positioned,' he announced proudly, then manoeuvred the cursor square to sit over that area, and magnified the section. 'Behind the top right-hand drawer of the computer console desk. There's no doubt about it.' Packstone leaned confidently back in his swivel chair.

It was unexpected information to his listeners though, and it took a few moments to be mentally absorbed, and for questions to form in their minds.

Walsh's first reaction was rhetorical, merely thoughts spoken out loud.

'So, the bomb wasn't in Chambers' briefcase after all. We don't need to worry about a hostage being held somewhere then.'

Packstone turned his head in surprise. 'You've been following that up, have you?' he said wryly. 'Well, I suppose you had to.'

'The drawer must have been taken out and the bomb stuck on the back. That wouldn't have taken long,' Reg Finch pointed out.

'Well, it definitely wasn't in the drawer itself, Reg. See for yourself.' Packstone rotated the image on the screen so that it became a side-on view, and pointed with his finger. 'There's the back of the drawer and there's the back of the desk. By far the majority of red lines start from the space between. It was probably just taped in place—with sticky tape.'

'The size of the bomb, Richard?' Walsh asked.

'Give or take a bit, six inches by four by one and a half.'

'Any traces of the container used?'

'No, Sidney, and if the container was plastic, I wouldn't expect to. It would have vaporised in the explosion.'

'What about the detonator and timer, Mr Packstone?' Brenda asked. 'Dr Chambers played about with old clocks and watches, so was the timer a mechanical one, do you know?'

'I can't answer that at this stage. We can only reconstruct the detonator and timer from the fragments we've found that are not part of the original lab equipment, but having said that, we are beginning to form some ideas.' He stood up. 'Over on that bench, over there.

'All these fragments are unidentified, as yet,' Packstone explained, indicating the layout with a sweep of his hand, 'so they're the pieces we're particularly interested in. See this one? It looks just like flattened metal, but it was a piece of tube, and that tiny bit of wire sticking out of the end may have been a helix wound spring. Now, if you look closely, you can just see that there's a cross-hole drilled through it. It could possibly be a pin-mechanism for firing a bullet, though we haven't found the pin yet.'

'And there's nothing like that forming

part of the lab equipment?' Walsh asked thoughtfully.

'Not that we can trace,' Packstone replied.

'The chief said you'd found what you thought was a .22 bullet case?' Brenda inquired.

'That's right, and that's what it was.'

'Well, it seems pretty conclusive to me, then,' Finch stated positively. 'A firing pin was pushed up that tube, compressing the spring, and held there under tension by another pin in the cross-hole; then it was somehow lined up with the bullet. When that cross-pin was pulled out it would have been like pulling a trigger: the released pin would strike the bullet and it would go off. That would be quite enough to detonate the bomb, wouldn't it?'

'It would, Reg, but it's too early to be so positive. I could postulate a few more alternatives using some of the other bits and pieces we've got lying on here, but at the moment, I do favour this one,' Packstone admitted. 'Now, about a timer—'

'I know! It probably didn't have one,' Brenda interrupted excitedly, waving a forefinger in the air. 'I bet it was a booby-trap device. That's why it was positioned behind the drawer. There was probably a string attached to that pin in

179

the tube's cross-hole, with the other end fixed to the desk somewhere, so when that drawer was pulled open, out came the pin, and...whoomph,' she continued, waving both hands in an artistic dramatisation of a bomb exploding.

'I like the ballerina bit, Brenda. Do it again,' Reg taunted, smiling broadly.

'I don't know, but she might well be right,' Packstone observed drily, smiling at the girl's animated expression. 'It fits in with what we know, even though that's little enough at this stage, but I must emphasise that you're only guessing about the detonator. That's most unscientific. I just don't have enough facts yet.'

'If Brenda's right, and the bomb was detonated in that way, then it's got all the hallmarks of amateurishness about it, to try and fool us into thinking it wasn't planted by a professional killer. Very clever,' Walsh pointed out shrewdly.

'That's right, boss. There can be little doubt that it was intended to get both Chambers and Wade, and at the same time wipe out the computer and its accumulated store of research data. Either Wade or Chambers could have opened that drawer at any time during the day. That's what DaSilva must have hoped, anyway.'

'I don't think you should let Dr Wade know how the bomb might have been set off,' Brenda suggested. 'He lacks the bulldog spirit, doesn't he? Well, if he's trying to make up for that by drinking brandy, he'll need more than one bottle a day if he finds he was even closer to death than he thought he was.'

'Quite possibly,' Walsh mused, 'but DaSilva will want to finish what he's already started, and it's our job to prevent that. Dr Wade's life is in danger, and possibly that of his wife, too. Well, at least we've ruled out the possibility that the bomb was in a switched jiffy bag, or Chambers' briefcase, that's something. If it was a booby-trap device it couldn't have been rigged up while Wade and Chambers were in the lab on the Monday morning, neither could it have been in place on the Friday afternoon, or it would have gone off then.'

'That tells us it must have been planted over the weekend, Chief, and that means it must have been done by someone on Reg's short-list. One of those must have been DaSilva's accomplice,' Brenda announced firmly.

Detective Constable Alison Knott stirred uneasily in the padded swivel chair in the top-floor room of the Animal Research Station. It wasn't that she was too comfortable, or even not comfortable enough, but the muscles of her legs were protesting at being inactive. Had she been at home in her flat, that muscle tension would have been dealt with by ten or fifteen minutes' activity with a skipping rope, on the square yard of space just in front of the fireplace in her tiny lounge, which was the only part of the floor solid enough not to resonate like a springboard and disturb the occupants of the flat beneath. Ten minutes of two-footed skipping jumps, followed by five of light, on-the-spot running, would suffice to make her legs ache, and leave her gasping for breath. It would prepare her body for sleep, certainly, but it also helped to regulate the weight problem that the almost rigidly adhered-to diet failed to control properly. Life was unfair in that respect. The chief inspector, Reg, Brenda, and even Arthur Bryant, all seemed to expend no effort on controlling what they ate, yet they remained fit and lean, while she, who did worry about her diet, remained fleshy, and a stone heavier than she wanted to be. She sighed regretfully. It was all to do with one's metabolism—wasn't it?

A tiny flash of light in the murky distance caught her eye, but by the time she'd concentrated on the spot, it had gone. A chance reflection on a puddle, or a strand of wire, perhaps. Then it came again, but not quite in the same place. It was in the low-lying area of darkness that escaped the back glow of light from the motorway beyond. There was a steep-sided brook there, and the footpath from Girton village, which followed outside the wire perimeter fence. She picked up the light intensifier binoculars and focused them on that darker area. It was like entering a submarine world where shapes were a hazy green, a mere half-shade lighter than the distant background. There was a shape that was moving, a vague shape, that was more gorilla-like than human, and it was wheeling—a bike? Yes, that sudden flash again, from shiny spokes. She blinked her eyes and stared again. It wasn't one shape after all, but two. There were two people out there, with two bikes.

'Arthur?' she said softly into her radio. 'You'd better wake everyone up. I think we have visitors. Outside the wire at the moment, in sector three. Arthur? Arthur? Are you there, Arthur?'

'Of course I'm here, Alison. Where else do you think I'd be? What's the matter?'

'There's two people on foot, but they've got bikes. They're outside the wire at the moment, in sector three.'

'I'd better wake everyone up then,' Arthur Bryant said excitedly from the downstairs room where the resting non-watchers formed the action task force.

'Right, Alison, what are these people doing?' Thankfully that was the chief inspector's calm voice.

'Nothing at the moment, sir. They're just going into sector four. Now they've stopped. They're just standing there watching, I think. No, one of them's bending down. I think he's cutting the fence wire. Yes, that's what they've done, they're inside now, moving towards sector eight.'

'Arthur, you go first. Go out wide to the right and get to the fence behind them. Cut them off so they can't get out the way they came in,' Alison heard Walsh say.

'They've gone behind the first row of sheds in sector eight,' Alison interrupted. 'I've lost them for the moment. No, I haven't. They've come round the side. I think they're heading for that big building in sector nine. That's the laboratory, isn't it? I can't see them any more, they're out of sight again.'

'Reg, you get behind them, between them and the fence. Brenda, you go round that building from the right-hand side, and I'll come in from the left. We'll have them trapped then. Alison! Get the patrol cars closing in, and keep your eyes skinned. Let me know if anything changes.'

Reg and Brenda ran off into the

184

darkness, but Walsh stayed where he was for a few more seconds—he had less distance to travel. There was time to adjust the ear-piece of his radio in his right ear, then he walked quickly down the tarmacked roadway towards the low, single-storey laboratory building.

'It's me, sir—Arthur. I'm down at the fence now. They've cut a real big hole in it,' a breathless voice crackled in the radio.

'Reg here, boss. I'm in position, too.'

'Ready when you are, Chief,' Brenda announced.

Walsh reached a hand up to the yard light switches on the side wall of the building.

'All ready? Right! Here we go,' he said as he flicked the switches down, and stepped quickly round the corner, feeling as he did so like some modern Wyatt Earp involved in a shoot-out in a lawless prairie town.

The whole area between the low buildings was now as bright as day, in the light of the powerful white arc lights.

One dark-clothed figure was on the roof, reaching down to take something from the other person, who was still on the ground. Both froze momentarily as the blinding lights enveloped them, then Walsh heard a shout, but could not make out what was said. The figure on the roof turned suddenly and ran up to the ridge, hurled a package out into the far darkness, then disappeared over the other side. Almost immediately there came a loud bang and a flash of light from the far side of the building. Walsh sighed with relief, none of his team should be anywhere near that explosion.

In the meantime the figure on the ground spun round, saw Brenda advancing from one way, and probably also caught a glimpse of Reg coming across the yard, for it turned again and sprinted away from both of them. Perhaps the figure hadn't seen Walsh in the way, but there was no subsequent faltering or hesitation when it did. It was definitely prepared to take him on, and it was coming at speed.

Walsh's heart beat faster. It looked as though the success of this part of their surveillance operation was going to be down to him personally. If he muffed this and let the team down, he was going to feel pretty stupid, but he blotted such thoughts of potential failure out of his mind, and moved forward positively. Obviously the black figure wouldn't run straight into his outstretched arms, it would veer suddenly to one side, to dodge round him; but which way would it go? To the left or the right? There would be a false move first, a feint in one direction or another, but he mustn't be fooled by it, he mustn't commit himself too soon. Suddenly he felt as if he was back on the rugby fields of his youth. There was no oval ball in the hands of this runner, but that made no difference, his job was to tackle, to tackle low and hard. That person must not be allowed to get past.

The feint came when the figure was only a few feet away. Its body leaned suddenly to the left. Walsh transferred a fraction of his weight that same way. The figure saw his movement and instantly jigged to the right. Walsh was fully committed now. He dived, arms outstretched to envelop that flying body just below the waist; but his legs had not the speed or power of spring that they once had. Failure stared him in the face, but sheer desperation gained him extra inches; his wildly flailing fingers caught an ankle and miraculously gripped tight. The figure came crashing to the ground with a cry of anguish and frustration, but by then Walsh was already scrambling himself sideways on his free hand and knees. He threw his whole weight on the writhing figure, and quickly got his strong arms round the black torso in a bear-like grip.

He became aware that this person could not be his quarry, DaSilva. There was a faint sense of perfume, for one thing, and for another, the certainty that his left hand was now solidly placed over the firm breast of a woman. That realisation, however, did not make him ease his grip, not until Brenda Phipps had come running up to make the capture certain.

Arthur Bryant had been warned by Reg Finch that the second intruder had evaded capture by running up and over the laboratory roof, and was presumably heading back towards the break in the wire. His eyes glinted with excitement. It was his job to bar this exit to all comers.

The explosion of the bomb brought him the fear of death or injury to his comrades, but it also made him angry. That anger, and the flow of adrenaline into his bloodstream, gave him an extraordinary feeling of strength, of merciless viciousness and of being ten feet tall. He stood himself squarely before the gap in the fence with his feet apart, crouching like a goalkeeper, peering into the gloom. The yard lights on the far side of the nearest building were of no help to him; in fact, they made matters worse by spoiling his night vision and intensifying the blackness. He would need his ears to detect the approaching intruder, so he moved his head slowly from side to side like an airfield radar scanner, and waited for a frontal attack.

However, the intruder had lost his

bearings and had come to the fence in the wrong place, and so he had to turn, to run alongside it, looking for the gap.

Arthur heard the sounds from the side too late to alter his stance significantly, and the resulting shoulder-charging flank attack sent him reeling. He recovered quickly, though, and came back to throw a salvo of punches at the black-garbed figure. The result was a short and frenzied fist-flying battle, until one of those flying fists caught Arthur a blow on the side of his head with such force that he was momentarily stunned, and he dropped to his knees. The intruder turned to the gap in the fence and dived through. Arthur leaped after him, tripped, dived forward headlong, and unwittingly executed an almost perfect rugby tackle. He hit the intruder thigh-high, driving him right across the footpath outside the wire, to the very edge of the brook. There the intruder grabbed frantically at Arthur, trying to regain his balance, but he didn't succeed. He slowly teetered over the edge of the steep-sided Washpit Brook, and the two of them together fell, down through the thin ice, and into two feet of bitterly cold and muddy water.

10

'Those two seem to think it's all one big joke,' Walsh muttered angrily. He looked down at his watch; it was seven o'clock in the morning, and he was feeling desperately tired now. The grey-painted interview room was bland and cheerless at the best of times, now it seemed even more dank and depressing.

'I'm afraid they'd worked out what they were going to do if they got caught, Chief,' Brenda announced brightly. Being up nearly all night did not seem to be affecting her. 'We're lucky that fellow didn't fancy changing into the clothes we'd got here and insisted on someone going to get some of his own; it does mean we now know their names and where they live.'

Reg Finch came in with a sheet of paper in his hand. 'The Bonn police didn't take long to come back on the girl, boss, and they've even faxed her picture. It's her all right, so that is her real name. She's got a record over there. She was caught at a rave party with marijuana in her pocket, but they let her off with a caution, because she was only eighteen. Zena Mueller, now

190

aged twenty-two, German national, born in a little place just outside Hamburg. She's been over here for two years, studying English, French and Russian at one of the language schools.'

'What about the boy, the Swede?' Walsh asked.

'They'll get back to us as soon as they can, but Svenson is a pretty common name there, so it might be some time.'

'How are forensic getting on, searching Mueller's apartment, Reg?' Brenda wanted to know.

'Not too good, apparently. The place has been made absolutely spotless, and it's been done by professionals. Every surface has been wiped over with an aniseed-scented spirit cleaner. No sniffer dog could get a whiff of drugs or explosives in there now,' Reg explained.

'Blast,' Walsh exclaimed despondently. 'It looks as though DaSilva had plans for all eventualities. He may not have risked his own neck with his decoy bombs, but he's made damn sure his two accomplices came to no harm if they were caught. All we'll be able to pin on them is a failed animal rights demonstration. They'll be put on probation, no doubt, and when that's over, the drug cartel which employs them will give them a bonus, and move them on somewhere else.'

'Cheer up, boss. If Svenson had heaved that bomb in our direction things wouldn't have turned out as well as they have. At least the ambush worked, at the expense of Arthur getting a ducking in the brook. That woke him up a bit, I've no doubts,' Reg said with a grin.

'The boy ought to go on another self-defence course, Chief. He's got more enthusiasm than skill at the moment,' Brenda observed with a hint of sarcasm.

'He did all right,' Walsh commented. 'Anyway, there's not much more we can do here, so I suggest we take a break. I want a shower and some breakfast. Mueller's and Svenson's solicitor will get here from London at ten thirty, so we can do a formal interrogation of the pair then. After that, I want to press on with an in-depth investigation of all the Medical Research Centre employees on our short-list. That seems our only hope of getting anywhere, at the moment.'

Ronald Silver heard the front door open and looked up from his chair by the electric fire where he sat reading. Angela came into the room.

He returned a simple nod in greeting and observed that her face held a serious expression. There were other subtle messages being conveyed too, by the set of

192

her jaw, the angle of her eyebrows and her measured step as she strode through towards the bedroom. This was quite unlike the lively jauntiness he'd become used to these past few days; but he turned his attention back to his book, and said nothing. There was a mood, undoubtedly there was a mood, and likely enough that meant a period of sulky silence, or even a verbally aggressive bombardment of whoever happened to be around at the time, innocent or otherwise.

A slight smile of amusement appeared at the corners of his mouth. He could easily play the part of a solid rock on which the crashing waves of her bad temper could dissipate their energy in harmless fury, but all the same, his mental preparation to do that presented him with a mild shock. There was no earthly reason why he should put up with the tantrums of anyone, least of all from a mere girl hired to attend to his creature comforts. Yet he had to admit that this mere girl had turned out to be quite different from what he'd expected. For one thing, she had no idea how a fawning, complacent concubine should behave. Clearly she had been forced into an arrangement that may, at the time, have seemed the lesser of two evils, yet once her fears of violence and pain had been dispelled, she had become like a healthy young lover, and had set about exploring her way into the maturity of full womanhood with an innocent enthusiasm. For him that had been a refreshing experience, and the fact that at other, more appropriate, times her conversation was both intelligent and lively resulted in her being a very enjoyable companion, and he hadn't felt like that about a woman for a very long time.

Angela came out of the bedroom, now dressed in a long flowered quilted cotton housecoat.

'Are you hungry? Do you want to eat out tonight, or would you like me to cook something?' she demanded aggressively, standing in front of Silver with her hands on her hips.

Silver looked up at her face. It was completely lacking makeup, and her eyes looked slightly red and puffy, as though there had been tears, or perhaps tears were imminent.

'It's cold and raw outside,' he said impassively. 'I'd prefer to eat here. Would you mind cooking something?'

Angela swung round without another word, and went into the kitchen. Through the half-open door Silver could hear the fridge door being opened and then a clatter of pots and pans. He smiled again, and turned a page. He did not doubt his ability to talk her out of her sulkiness, but he would do that in his own good time. However, after a few moments he rose and quietly laid the table in the dining annexe, setting out the cutlery neatly and also opening a bottle of wine, then he went back to his book.

He heard Angela come in to do that same job a little later, then go back to the kitchen. She seemed more composed when she next appeared.

'I've done corn-on-the-cob for starters, then I've a Marks and Spencer's sea-food platter. You seemed to like it when we had one the other day. Is that all right?' she asked, with a rueful attempt at a smile.

'Your talents seem never-ending, my dear,' Silver said smoothly, as he poured wine into glasses, and sat down at the table. 'I suggest we eat this while it's hot, but when we've finished I intend to ask you what you've been doing today, and then I expect you to tell me what has happened to upset you. In the meantime, think about what you were planning to do over Christmas. I am not yet certain, but it rather looks as though my stay here might be a little longer than I expected. Would an extension to our arrangement be acceptable to you? I had in mind that some of the time we could spend in London, to do some shows or concerts.'

Angela looked at him wide-eyed in surprise.

'You're asking me? As though I'd any choice in the matter?' Her lower lip fluttered, something she obviously didn't like it doing, for she promptly clamped it between her teeth, and looked down at her plate.

'I believe that by asking you, I am giving you a choice,' Silver said blandly, then set about the steaming, buttery corn-on-the-cob.

'I'm sorry, Ron,' Angela said contritely. 'I didn't mean to be rude. I'd need to spend a bit of time with my dad, but other than that, I rather like the idea. It surprises me, me saying that. When I came up here I was so terribly afraid of you, but, well, you treat me like a lady, both in and out of bed, and I'm not afraid any more—in fact,' she peeped up at him with eyes that twinkled through long fair lashes, 'to be absolutely honest, now I know what it's all about, I'm really quite enjoying myself, and I'm getting used to the idea that I won't have to go to prison now. You can't believe how wonderful that is. I'll always be grateful to you, Ron. It's been a constant worry on my mind, ever since I was stupid enough to take that money.'

'Well, that seems settled then, although, as I've said, my plans are somewhat uncertain. I must say I don't quite see you in the role of a hardened criminal, Angela. I hope you'll put that behind you. Myself, I think you should pursue your original plan; to train to become a nurse, I mean. You've microwaved this sea-food stuff to such perfection that whatever you do, I see a great future ahead for you.'

Angela's eyes brightened and her face showed more animation now that her mind had been diverted.

'I'd love to be a nurse, Ron. There's so much evil, pain and suffering in the world, and I'd really like to do something to help people.'

'Good for you. Yes, doctors and nurses can help to ease the pain and suffering, but the evil in this world is a different matter. The best any one person can do on his own is to try to blunt the sharp edges,' Silver said quietly.

Angela looked up at his face. His voice just then had been serious and thoughtful, but his expression was wellnigh impossible to read. She would have liked to ask him just what blunting the sharp edges had meant, but she decided not to—there was so much about him that she did not understand.

'Unfortunately I need a job that'll bring in good money now, Ron. Would I make a success as a woman of easy virtue, do you think?' she asked flippantly.

'I hope that won't be necessary,' Silver smiled as he reached over to take her empty plate. 'I'll give you a hand with the washing up, later.'

'Thanks, a hand of Silver could be quite valuable. Maybe I could sell it and get some money that way.' Angela joked, but more lightheartedly than she really felt. Money and her future were not things she wanted to face up to at the moment.

'A silver hand? There was a man with one of those once, in the Celtic myths,' Silver mused thoughtfully. 'Nuada it was, who had the silver hand.'

'We only touched on the Celts at school, but I don't remember a Nuada. There was a Lleu, or something like that,' Angela replied, wrinkling her freckled snubby nose in an effort of memory recall.

'Not Lieu—Llud. In the British or Welsh versions of the legends he's Llud—in the Irish, he's Nuada, but it's the same fellow. He was a king in the good old days of magic, witches and fairies. He lost his hand in a battle—they were always fighting in Ireland even then, so it's nothing new. Anyway, the loss of his hand forced him to give up his crown, because a monarch had to be perfect in those days—or at least without any physical defects. However, being a man of influence, he had the local magician, physician or Druid, call him what you will, make him a replacement hand out of pure silver. That's something you won't learn on your nursing course: Nuada or Llud, the first recorded person ever to be fitted with an artificial limb. Mind you, his other claim to fame wasn't so good, not from the medical point of view, because he also owned a sword, the wounds from which would never heal, and thus always proved fatal,' he added soberly.

'You know about lots of different things, don't you? You're very well educated. I still haven't worked out yet what country you come from. Sometimes I think you're a Scot, then you say something that sounds Irish. This Llud, was he the Lud of Ludgate and the Lud of Luddon that became London?'

'That I'm not sure. The Celts weren't great ones for towns, but the addition of the Don is right. Don, Dun or Dunnum was the Celtic word for fort or a fortified place. Hence Dundee, Dunbar and a whole host of other places, some of which were later Latinised with a Caster or Chester replacing the Dun. Take Brancaster, for instance, up on the North Norfolk coast, near the bird sanctuary. Branodunnum, its name was once, and like Llud, Bran was another character of the Celtic myths. With your blue eyes and red hair, Angela, you've a fair bit of the ancient blood flowing through your veins, I shouldn't wonder.'

'Finn mac Cool was another of the old heroes, wasn't he? I'll have to get a book from the library and read up on them.'

Silver smiled and nodded. 'You should. They're a link with a different culture, in a different age. The only time machine Man is ever going to have is his own mind. Those old myths and stories provide an insight into how people thought and behaved, three or four thousand years ago. Now, I've been doing too much talking. It's your turn. Tell me what you've been doing today, and what it was that had so upset you when you came in this evening.'

Angela pinched her bottom lip thoughtfully between thumb and forefinger.

'Was it that obvious?' she murmured softly, but the question was only to give herself time to think and find the right words. 'Well, I went to visit my grandmother again today, Ron. She's my dad's mum. She's eighty-six now, and getting very frail, although her mind is still pretty active. We had her living with us until about eighteen months ago, but it wasn't working very well. With dad and me out at work, she was left on her own too much. One day I came home and found her on the kitchen floor. She'd had a fall and couldn't get up. She'd been there all afternoon. It was awful. Dad doesn't get a lot at his job and there's the mortgage to find each month, so neither of us could give up work and stay at home to look after her. It was her idea to go into a home. "It's the best thing really," she said, "and I'll have some company of my own age." I didn't like it. It's not the right way to treat people, just because they're getting old, but we had no choice by then, because she'd made her mind up. You know how stubborn old people can get, once they get a bee in their bonnet. She refused to go into any of the council homes, not once we'd taken her to see them, and I can't say I blame her either. They weren't very cheerful places. The nearest one she liked was privately run, not far from Bedford.' She shook her head. 'It's wicked what places like that charge, Ron, far more than the allowance the government was prepared to pay. She'd got no money of her own, except her pension and that was reduced as soon as she went in, so dad and me said we'd make up the difference. What else could we do?'

'So you and your father found it tough going financially. I rather suspected something like that, but go on. What you've said so far is not an uncommon situation, not in the more affluent areas of the world, anyway,' Silver remarked seriously.

'I suppose not, but that doesn't make it any easier. Anyway, grandma was happy enough to start with, but the management of the home changed a few months ago, and the man in charge now, well, he's made it into a horrible place. The people there are treated more like half-witted children than adult human beings. I get so upset every time I visit her. I've had a go at the nurses, but it's done no good. Now grandma's got glaucoma, and can hardly see what she's doing. Which is a terrible thing for her, because she loved reading, and to crown it all the woman she shares a room with has become incontinent, so the place smells. She's not being looked after properly, Ron, and there's a waiting list for eye operations of a year or more. There's no way we can afford to pay for the operation privately. I don't know what to do about it, really I don't. It makes me so mad when I go there and see my grandmother being treated like that.' Angela's small fist clenched up tight in the anger of her frustration.

She looked up at Ronald Silver's face and gave a sudden gasp of fear and surprise. His eyes seemed to stare past her into an infinite distance, and they were moist, as though he was fighting back tears, but they also glowed with a terrifying light and his jaw muscles had hardened into rigid bars of restrained anger.

His voice was barely audible from behind his clenched teeth, but what he said was clear enough.

'I must find the time to visit the people who can treat our mothers and fathers in such a way,' and the accent was, without a doubt, the smoothly undulating lilt of the southern Irish.

The lab director's spacious office was warm, particularly to someone coming straight in from facing the bitingly cold wind outside.

Walsh took off his coat and hung it on the back of his chair, then sat down and smiled at both the lab director and Mrs Raymond, the head of the university security section.

'I need your help,' Walsh explained simply. 'We want to build up a profile, a dossier, on the lives of each of your security and maintenance staff, and we need to do it quickly—very quickly.'

'I've been expecting you to say that, Inspector,' Mrs Raymond admitted, idly scratching at the back of her head and studying the face of the chief inspector intently. To her he seemed a pleasant enough individual, better educated and certainly more well spoken than many of the senior police officers she had met in the past, but there was something about him, perhaps it was his shrewd eyes, or that indefinable aura of confidence that some men had, that disturbed her.

'You're convinced the bomb was planted by, or with the help of, someone working at the lab?' she continued, concentrating on the matter in hand. 'To be absolutely honest, I've come to the same conclusion myself. I hate to say it, but logically the security and the maintenance staff must be at the top of the list of suspects.'

'Precisely,' Walsh acknowledged with an approving smile. 'Among them is one who has probably been got at; bribed or blackmailed into helping the killer. Our first interviews were with the specific purpose of checking out the effectiveness of the routines—looking for a gap, a space through which the bomber could move. Well, we're past that stage now. There is no space or gap, so one of them is lying. We need to reinterview them with a different perspective to find the liar. We must delve into their personal lives, I'm afraid, and into their families, their friends, their past, their financial stability, and so on. That can take time, so to speed the process up, what I'd like from you both is a dossier on each person, with whatever information you know about him, or can find out. Hire purchase agreements, marital relationships, extra-marital relationships—anything against which we can compare the answers they give to our questions.'

'Personal private details? How very unethical we must all become when there's a killer in our midst,' Mrs Raymond observed reluctantly.

The lab director shook his head expressively. 'I don't think the question of morality applies. Civilised standards of normality only apply when each member of society is prepared to abide by the same principles. If anyone steps outside those standards, particularly if in doing so they take an innocent life, then they lose any right to the respect of privacy from the rest of us.'

'That would be all very well if you could apply the withdrawal of human rights specifically to the guilty person, but if I understand you correctly, what you're saying is that others—innocent others—must also suffer along with the guilty one. I'm not sure that's an ethically tenable position to hold,' Mrs Raymond proposed.

Walsh shrugged his shoulders and interrupted what might have become a lengthy discussion. 'Honest people have nothing to fear. Anyway, the situation isn't one in which personal opinions have any say. Society has passed specific laws which require individuals to give whatever assistance they can to the police, when acting in pursuance of their inquiries.'

'Maybe so, Inspector. Maybe so,' Mrs Raymond said reluctantly.

'Maybe so—nothing,' the lab director protested with great feeling. 'Someone killed one of my best researchers, and has driven another into what looks like becoming a serious mental breakdown; as well as injuring two other members of my staff. And why? Because they were involved in a research project that might eventually benefit all mankind. I've no feelings of sympathy for the guilty person at all, and I'll sympathise with the innocent people caught up in this trauma only when this assassin and his accomplices are safely behind bars.'

'We all feel like that,' Mrs Raymond said quickly, 'and you may rely on me to do my best to help. Unfortunately, I haven't been here long, so I don't know much about the private lives of those I'm actually responsible for, but I'll do my best. You want this done very quickly? I have another meeting planned for this morning, but I can put that off.'

'If you would. I'd like us to get started as soon as we can.'

'Don't worry, Inspector,' the lab director said confidently. 'Leave it to us. We'll get down to it straight away, and I've thought of a good way of doing it too. We'll get my secretary involved. She's perfectly trustworthy, but she's got that Marje Proops type of face that makes people tell her all sorts of things; things they wouldn't even dare tell their doctors. She'll probably end up doing most of it for us, once she realises the urgency.'

Walsh found the irony of the situation somewhat amusing. His meeting with the lab director and Mrs Raymond had been to acquire information which he could then use to put a number of other people's lives under close scrutiny. Then he'd gone back to headquarters to find two members of MI6 waiting to do just the same exercise—to him. The irony wasn't something one could actually laugh about, but it did put him in a relaxed mood, which was an ideal one for taking on a barrage of questions. The fact that he himself had a sound knowledge of the psychological techniques involved was also an advantage. Switching questions quickly from one topic to another, hoping to confuse the mind, was one ploy they used. He countered that by slowing things down, by filling his pipe, or asking them if they would like more coffee. Always they were trying to niggle him, to raise his blood pressure and his temper, hoping he'd contradict what he'd already said, but he could actually laugh aloud when one of them mentioned that the only person at that conference known to have contacts with international agents was Walsh's chief constable. Anyway, as long as he kept cool and calm he could parry the questions until the cows came home, and for the next hour and a half, that was precisely what he did.

11

Reg Finch glanced round the sitting-room before he sat down. It was tastefully but not expensively furnished, with all the colours of suite, carpets and curtains blending nicely together. A small artificial Christmas tree stood in the corner by the window, twinkling with tiny lights that sheened the coloured baubles and silvery streamers. Christmas was still a week or so away, yet several wrapped presents had already been laid beneath the needled branches.

'Why do I want to talk to you again? Well, I'm afraid you've got to face facts, Mr O'Neil,' he said seriously, running a hand through his overlong fair hair. 'As far as we are concerned, you're the only one we know who actually went into that lab between the Friday evening and the Monday morning—other than the cleaners, of course, and the guard was with them all the time. So, you can't blame us for being interested in you.'

Martin O'Neil, the medical research computer expert, frowned anxiously at his dark-haired, pretty wife, seated in the armchair on the other side of the hearth and the glowing gas fire. 'Well, yes, I do see that, I suppose,' he admitted reluctantly, but his mouth twisted into a grimace. It was all very well for this police sergeant to say that, but being a suspect in a case that was effectively murder was absolutely frightening. If it wasn't murder it was unlawful killing, and that sounded only marginally better. It was one thing to glibly say that British justice was the best in the world, but everyone knew that mistakes were made. Judges and juries were only human. If those mistakes didn't affect you personally, then you could be sympathetically offhand about it, but if they did, then the situation became positively dangerous. He hadn't given much thought to such things before, but now he felt scared, and it showed.

'That's all very well, but I know I didn't plant any bombs anywhere,' he protested nervously. 'No more did I help anyone else do it either, so I know I'm innocent.'

'Well, help convince me by answering my questions. Do you own this house?'

'Yes, Sergeant. We bought it four years ago through the Halifax. Our repayments are four hundred and twenty-five pounds a month, and they're up to date,' Mrs O'Neil volunteered.

'What about hire purchase agreements?'

'No! When we want to borrow any

210

money, we go and see our friendly bank manager,' Martin O'Neil replied with an attempt at a smile. 'We've got a separate loan account, and they transfer sixty pounds to that from our current account each month. I know that doesn't leave a lot out of my salary, but we manage all right, don't we, dear? At least Ann does, she's good with money. I generally leave all that to her.'

'I don't mind,' Ann O'Neil added with a genuine smile. She thought that this detective sergeant seemed a nice person, with such a friendly smile, and such blue eyes. 'I've a suggestion to make, Sergeant,' she went on. 'Obviously you're interested in our finances—wouldn't it be better if you had a look at our bank statements? I'll get them for you. We've got nothing to hide,' but as she got up, a baby started crying in the next room. They were short little squalls at first, but they grew louder and more insistent of attention. 'Oh lord,' she said ruefully, 'just look at the time. He's hungry and he wants his supper. I'm sorry but I'll have to deal with him. He's just like his dad, once he gets going he won't ever stop, not until he gets his own way. Martin, you get the bank statements, they're in the bottom drawer of the bureau.'

Finch moved his briefcase and notepad

from his lap on to the cushions of the settee beside him, and slowly turned the pages of the hardbacked bank statement file. Occasionally he made notes. The O'Neils seemed a normal enough couple, on the face of it, but it would do no good to let such thoughts cloud his judgement. Nice people turned out to be villains almost as often as unpleasant ones, unfortunately.

Martin O'Neil moved restlessly, watching Finch's impassive face and trying to slow the beating of his heart by telling himself there was nothing to be afraid of.

Ann O'Neil came back from the other room with her whimpering three-month-old son in her arms. 'You don't mind me feeding him here where it's warm, do you, Sergeant?' she asked as she sat down.

'Of course not,' Finch replied, looking up from the papers on his lap with a smile. Then he blinked and reddened slightly as the girl unzipped the front of her dress, casually pushed the strap of her bra off her shoulder and put the eager mouth of her child to the swollen nipple of her bulging breast.

Reg found it difficult to turn his gaze away. He and his wife were childless, and this sight of a nursing mother filled him with a deep longing, and a strange regretful envy. O'Neil junior, however, ceased his whimpering, and set about the task in

212

mouth with evident enthusiasm.

'I see here that you've had a few deposits to your account other than your salary. There's a couple of two hundreds in August and a three hundred in October. What were they for?' Reg Finch asked, having cleared his throat noisily.

'The two hundreds were what that Mr Poulter round the corner gave you for sorting out his firm's new computer system, weren't they, Martin?' Mrs O'Neil said, looking up momentarily.

'Yes, that's right. A typical sort of thing—you know, going harebrained into a first computer installation without thinking it all out properly. He hadn't done any staff training, and even if he had, they were so busy they didn't have time to input all the basic data to set the system up as it should be. So they got their knickers in a twist; a muddle wasn't the word for it. Anyway, I got him sorted out eventually.'

Finch wrote more notes. 'He paid you in cash, did he? What about the three hundred in October?'

Martin O'Neil pulled at his chin and took a sudden interest in the flowered curtains. 'That other three hundred was when I sold my motor bike.'

Reg Finch looked steadily at Martin's face, then turned his gaze on Ann O'Neil, but he couldn't see her expression; she had her head bent and was intent on her baby as she turned him to feed from her other nipple. 'That's your car outside on the drive, is it?' he asked.

They both nodded. 'It's barely a year old. You financed that through your bank loan, did you?' Finch inquired, finding it easier to watch the nursing mother now—she was so relaxed and everything seemed so normal and commonplace.

There was a short silence, then the girl answered. 'My dad helped us with that. He had an insurance policy mature; so he gave us a late sort of wedding present. We still had to find a bit more on top of the trade-in on our old car. We got that from the bank.'

Martin O'Neil nodded his head, vigorously. 'That's right,' he confirmed.

Finch rested his pen on the notebook and used that hand to rub his eyes. If O'Neil were a regular employee of a drug cartel he would have expected this bank account to have shown him to be more affluent than he was; however, if O'Neil had only recently been bribed by DaSilva, he would undoubtedly have been paid in cash, and warned not to flash his extra wealth about. Assuming the latter to be the case, then there must have been some contact between the two, probably on more than one occasion. He made that aspect his next line of questioning.

'Right, now what do you do in the evenings? Do you go out much? Take me through each day, from last Tuesday,' Reg asked.

The response to that was prompt and short. Martin O'Neil's main hobby was cricket, and that was, of course, in seasonal abeyance. So, except for attending his club's Christmas dinner, held the previous Friday evening, Martin had been at home each evening.

'I asked you, when I spoke to you before, if you'd seen any strangers hanging round the lab, or had any people ask you questions about the lab procedures or what you do. You said then that you hadn't, but you've had plenty of time to think about it now. Are you still of the same mind?'

Martin's forehead furrowed into a frown. 'I couldn't think of anyone then, but since—since, mark you—there has been a fellow who may have been asking questions. If he was, he was doing it in a very subtle way. I met him in the pub where I sometimes go in our lunch break. The Black Cat. It's not far from the lab. Long John, he said his name was. No, I've got that wrong. His name was John Long. He said he was a rep for one of the Scottish distilleries. He was a good darts player, too. I thought he was a decent

215

enough sort of bloke. We got talking, and in the conversation he did ask questions, but that was after the bomb went off, not before.' Martin suddenly got up from his chair and went over to a teak-veneered drinks cabinet, from which he took a bottle. 'I bought this from him, for seven quid, if you're interested,' Martin went on, raising his eyebrows questioningly. 'I'll be seeing him again after Christmas. He's got a laptop computer with a fault, and I said I'd have a look at it for him.'

Reg Finch's eyes had brightened considerably, and were now alive with interest. 'Long, John? Was he a stocky sort of fellow, about five eight or five nine, a bit swarthy, with a moustache?'

'I don't know about him being swarthy. He was a bit brown, as though he'd been in the sun recently, but, yes, stocky—I suppose you could say that, and about five eight or so, with dark hair.'

Finch rummaged in his briefcase and pulled out a sketch of DaSilva. 'Is that him?' he asked hopefully, passing it over.

O'Neil looked at it doubtfully, but studied it closely. 'He didn't wear specs, and he didn't have a moustache. I don't know really. Honestly, I can't say. It might look like him if you took them away, but I wouldn't swear to it at the moment.'

Finch drummed his fingers lightly on his

leather briefcase. 'I'd like to take this bottle of yours away with me. You can have it back, of course, when we've done some tests on it, and I'll get our artist fellow to do some sketches of that chap, but without the moustache and glasses, then I'd like you to have a look at it again.'

Martin gulped. 'Good lord, you want to test the bottle for fingerprints. Bert Winters, my mate, was with me that day, and he bought one too—maybe he'd recognise the chap in the sketch. But seriously, Long was a nice bloke, I can't see him as a killer, really I can't.'

'Maybe he isn't, but I think we'll check him out, if we can. I'll have a word with this friend of yours, Winters. He works at the labs too, doesn't he? Then I've got his address in my file. Can you remember anything else this Long said? Where he was staying, perhaps? You didn't see his car, by any chance?' Finch asked eagerly.

'I didn't see his car, I'm afraid, and he never said where he was staying, but I got the impression that it wasn't far from the Black Cat. Perhaps you could have a talk with him when he brings me his computer, in the New Year,' he suggested.

Ann O'Neil was kneeling, spreading a towel on the hearth rug before the fire. 'Pass me a clean nappy, Martin,' she asked. 'This little chap's tired out. He's had a busy, busy day, haven't you, darling? We'll soon have you ready for your beddy-byes.'

Finch quickly turned his gaze away from the sight of the soiled and dirty nappy. That was a less appealing aspect of babies. 'Just one more question to ask, Martin. O'Neil is a good old Irish name, but you've got no accent that I can detect. Have you any relatives over there, or have your family always lived in England?' he asked as he put his notebook away in his briefcase.

'Good lord, I don't know,' Martin replied, unsure whether to be amused or annoyed. 'One of my ancestors was a rifleman in Wellington's army, and fought at Waterloo, and my great great grandad died on the Somme, they say. As far as I'm concerned I'm as English as you are, and definitely a lot more English than Farmer George was when he became king in seventeen hundred and something or other.'

The faint sounds of a violin became louder as Brenda Phipps made her way up the flight of stairs to the top-floor flat in the weathered, grey Peterborough brick Edwardian house.

On the landing she hesitated before the white-painted, panelled door, to listen.

The player was attempting the adagio of Bruch's first violin concerto, but the timing wasn't quite right, and the bowing lacked those subtle changes in pressure that contrive mood and tension.

Brenda rang the door bell.

The playing stopped abruptly, and after a few moments the door was opened by Dave Brewer, the lab assistant. He wore a thick braided and frogged brown dressing-gown, over blue striped pyjamas, and he was leaning, heavily on an under-the-armpit aluminium crutch, for his right foot, or rather his ankle, was in plaster. He looked genuinely surprised when he recognised his visitor.

'This is a surprise! Do come in,' he said with a welcoming smile; and he rather clumsily manoeuvred himself out of the way.

'I should have brought a parrot with me. If you get really handy with that crutch, you could be in for a big part in *Treasure Island,* when they film it again,' Brenda suggested humorously as she turned to close the door behind her.

'True,' Brewer chuckled cheerfully. 'All I'd have to do is drink myself one-legless each night singing "Ho ho ho and a bottle of rum". Let me take your coat.'

'"Ho ho ho" is Father Christmas. The pirates sing "Yo ho ho",' Brenda corrected.

219

She slipped her arms out of her fur-collared suede coat and went through the hallway into the sitting-room.

'After a few rums, who'd notice?' Brewer replied.

The apartment was surprisingly bright and spacious, with a wide dormer window set into that part of the ceiling which was angled to the roof, and even though there were central heating radiators, a coal fire gave an extra cosy glow.

'This is very nice. I like your view.' Brenda spoke with a tinge of envy in her voice, for Brewer's dormer window looked out over the river, to the wide misty green expanse of Midsummer Common. Very nice indeed, for a town flat. 'Well, I'm glad to see you up and about, Mr Brewer,' she went on. 'I was surprised when the hospital said you'd been allowed home.'

'A tough lot, us old Brewers. Take a pew and make yourself comfortable. Would you like a coffee, or something stronger?'

'That's very kind, but no thanks. I've just a few questions to ask. I won't keep you for long.' She turned to sit on the wide soft-cushioned settee, and nearly sat on the violin bow. She picked it up and automatically set about turning the silver end screw to release the tension on the bow-hair. Impressed into the dark red wood, just above the ebony frog, was the name 'W. E. Hill'. She held the bow out at arm's length—there was just the faintest suspicion of a curve to the right.

'That's a very fine bow,' she announced absentmindedly. She put it down and picked up the violin which lay nearby. 'You won't mind me handling these? My father used to play in an orchestra—when he was alive. They'll come to no harm.'

Brewer's somewhat apprehensive look changed to one of smug pride of possession.

Brenda peered down the left-hand sound hole. The maker's label was faded and dirty, and the name she could not make out. There was a date though, possibly 1865. The shallow-arched one-piece back was of highly figured maple with the familiar narrow tripart band of purfling, just inside the flowing curves of the edges. The close-grained spruce front was neatly crafted too, although there was just a suspicion that the sound hole on the right might be a shade lower than the one on the left. The volutes of the scroll were deeply cut, crisp and boldly carved. She sighed; quality of workmanship glowed out to the appreciative eye. Even the varnish, worn thin and chipped in places, and a shade darker than ideal, still had a translucent depth that was not unlike the thin porcelain with which she was much more familiar.

'Very nice indeed.' She put the violin down with reverential care and struggled to bring her mind back to the real purpose of her visit.

'Yes, well, I've come to ask more questions, I'm afraid. This time of a more personal nature.'

Brewer grinned. 'Suits me,' he replied, shrugging his shoulders.

'How long have you had this violin and bow?' Brenda asked, searching for her notebook and pencil in her black leather shoulder bag. The notebook was easily found, the pencil needed some rummaging for.

'About a couple of years. My godmother left them to me when she died, which was very nice of her. The bow's a bit on the light side for me, really.'

'I heard you playing as I came upstairs. Max Bruch, wasn't it?'

That's right,' Dave Brewer said. 'I was trying to get some practice, but my fingers are stiff, and my shoulder's still sore, so I can't seem to get it comfortable under my chin. My vibrato's gone to pot too, and my bowing's all haywire.'

'That's hardly surprising, but it'll come back. Did you ever think of playing professionally?'

'Not really, you've got to be absolutely brilliant to make a living at it these days.'

Brenda nodded. 'Right, now let's get down to business. Personal questions. Have you any debts—mortgages, or otherwise?' she asked bluntly.

Brewer looked surprised and a little annoyed. 'No, I haven't, as a matter of fact,' he said flatly. 'I did have, when I first bought this flat five years ago, but my father left me enough to pay it off. That was three years ago. I'm not rich, not by a long chalk, but financially I'm comfortable. My salary, such as it is, is all my own, to do what I like with.'

'Do you own any shares?'

'British Telecom, and British Gas, and I've five thousand in the building society.'

'What's the violin insured for?'

'With the bow, six thousand.'

'Prior to the bomb going off, did anyone come to you asking questions about where you worked and how things were organised? I've asked you that before, but you've had a bit more time to think about it now.'

Brewer pursed his lips and looked thoughtful. 'No, I can't say anyone did. I haven't met any strangers for ages, except you and the nurses in the hospital.'

'Have you ever been approached by anyone who's offered you money to tell them about any of the research work that goes on in the lab?'

'No, never.'

'What was the name of your godmother, the one who left you the violin?'

'Mrs Amanda Sullivan. She lived in Bournemouth.'

'Irish, was she?'

'No, I don't think so, but her husband certainly was.'

There came sounds from the hallway, as if someone had just come in. Brenda turned to look over her shoulder, then stood up to face the newcomer.

'What are you doing here?' Dr Maureen Connery said sharply, surprise betraying the suspicion in her voice.

'She's on official business, Maureen,' Brewer announced rather hurriedly, 'and I'm being interrogated about my murky past.'

'Oh you are, are you?' Dr Connery said shortly, bending to put two bulging plastic bags of shopping on the floor. 'There you are. That's enough to keep you going for a while. Now, I deserve a cup of coffee after lugging all that lot up the stairs, or do I have to make it myself? My leg's aching.'

Brewer struggled to his one sound foot, his face reddening. 'You come in and sit down, Maureen. I'll make your coffee,' and he hobbled off to the kitchen.

'I was planning to visit you next, Dr Connery,' Brenda announced, her eyes bright with the humour of the situation. Clearly she was an intruder, trespassing on Maureen Connery's preserves. 'We could save some time and talk now, if you'd prefer. I've just a few questions.'

Maureen Connery half scowled, but then nodded. 'Why not indeed? We might as well get it over with.'

'It's very kind of you to do Mr Brewer's shopping for him. You can't be feeling all that well yourself,' Brenda suggested shrewdly.

'The hospital wouldn't have let him home if I hadn't said I'd keep an eye on him. It's the least I could do. He did save my life, didn't he?' Connery replied, in a somewhat more mollified tone, as she came to sit in an armchair by the fire.

'Not everyone would have thought so, all the same.'

'He can manage reasonably well on his own, but there's no way he can do any shopping or even make his bed properly. He had enough problems just getting up the stairs, but he's better off here than in the hospital,' Maureen Connery explained, smoothing down the skirt of her dress with one hand. 'I'm healing well, myself. What do you want to ask me?'

Brenda posed questions on Dr Connery's financial situation, all of which were answered simply and directly. A good salary and helpful parents ensured a comfortable standard of living, but it was the question of previous employment, since Maureen Connery had been a relatively new member of Dr Wade's research team, that brought a slight expression of concern and a longer period of reflection before replying. 'I spent a year with DuEstra in Somerset, in their research labs. Yes, that's right, it's part of DuEstra, the German drug company,' she replied, having seen Brenda's raised eyebrows and evident interest.

When Brenda left she had a very thoughtful expression on her face. Clearly there was something going between Connery and Brewer. Connery had let herself into the flat, and therefore she must have had her own key. The question as to whether that relationship had been flourishing before the bomb went off might well be important, for their statements regarding their actions on the morning of the explosion tended to support each other. If they were working together they might have been able to plant that bomb themselves, even if they had misjudged its power and got injured. In addition, they were both fairly affluent. Legacies and wealthy parents excepted, that might mean they had an income from surreptitious illegal activities. Brenda hadn't really thought so before, because these two had only been on the very fringe of the suspect list, but now, certainly, they made a good pair of suspects, as joint accomplices of the shadowy DaSilva.

Walsh rang the door bell of the pebble-dashed semi-detached council house for the third time, and still there was no answer. He stamped his chilled feet, and turned round on the doorstep to survey the frosty tussocky lawn and the round flower bed with its forlorn-looking stubby rose bushes. There was obviously no point just hanging about there, so he decided to go round the back to seek the house's inhabitants, if there were any at home who were not stone deaf.

There was a light on in the large rickety wooden garden shed. Walsh did not knock, he just pushed the door open.

'What the hell do you want? Oh Christ, not you lot again?' Brian Smith, the security guard, was clearly annoyed at being interrupted in his task of respraying the stripped-down bicycle frame that hung suspended on strings from the roof. Much of the space inside the shed was taken up by bicycles, of all varieties, a whole stack of them.

'What's all this, then?' Walsh asked quietly, in true television police fashion. 'Are you in the second-hand bike business?'

'You could say that,' Brian Smith admitted reluctantly. 'I does them up and sells them.'

'Making a few bob on the side, I suppose,' Walsh remarked casually. Probably they were all stolen, and Smith was merely switching saddles and mudguards, and giving a lick of paint here and there to prevent them being easily recognised by their real owners. Bikes were an inexpensive and easy form of transport for hundreds of undergraduates, so there was a ready market for a product that could be cheaply priced, assuming they'd cost nothing in the first place. The amount of police paperwork over lost or stolen bikes was colossal. Still, he hadn't come here with petty thieving in mind.

'I want to ask you some more questions, Mr Smith. Do you want to stay here, or go somewhere warmer?' Walsh asked.

'We'd better go in the house then,' Smith replied, putting the aerosol paint spray can down on the tiny bench and wiping his hands on his dirty dungarees.

'Right, Mr Smith, you've worked for the university for three years, I see, and prior to that you were unemployed for nigh on six months, and a long-distance lorry driver before that,' Walsh stated bluntly, reading from his file.

'That's right. I hurt me back unloading so I couldn't keep on driving, and I didn't get no industrial injuries compensation like what I ought. I had a bit of redundancy, but I was entitled to that, weren't I?' Brian Smith sounded truculent.

'You weren't entitled to help yourself from the stuff you were delivering. You were damned lucky that haulage firm made you redundant rather than go through all the hassle of a court action, weren't you?'

'That's a pack of damned lies. It was them crooks in the stores, they was the ones who short-loaded me. Everyone knew they were on the fiddle. They had to blame someone, so they picked on me, 'cos I couldn't fight back and make a stink,' he protested angrily.

'You might be right there—if you were pinching stuff and selling it, it didn't do you much good, did it? I see you were in court for rent arrears, and a hire purchase firm repossessed your car. You don't seem very good at running your finances, do you? What do you do with your wages? Do you booze it away, or do you have a flutter on the horses?'

'You ain't got no right to go nosing into my private business. I can barely make ends meet on the bleeding pittance the university pays me. What the hell's it got to do with you anyway? You can't pin this bomb thing on me. No chance. You're wasting your time there, mate, and it ain't no good you trying to make out someone's tipped me a handful of the readies to let them plant that there bomb, 'cos you can't do it, 'cos I didn't, see.' Smith looked directly at Walsh's face, and shook his head. 'Maybe I have done a bit of nicking in the past, but there ain't no way I'm getting involved with killing people. I don't hold with no violence, right? Not under no circumstances I don't. Even a bloke like me has got his principles, see?'

12

Bert Winters lived in one of the slate-roofed, grey Victorian terraced houses in the Mount Pleasant area of the city, not far from the Shire Hall, and the hill where once the medieval castle had stood—high, and no doubt proud, to dominate the town beneath and the river crossing. Reg Finch and Alison Knott had walked there, because braving the near-solid traffic congestion during the day in a car demanded infinite patience, and when one arrived at where one wanted to be, there would probably be no place to park.

'John Long?' Bert Winters repeated, taking the now spectacles-and-moustache-free sketch of Ramon DaSilva from Alison's outstretched hand. He leaned back in the armchair in his little front sitting-room and studied it, but more light was needed than that filtering through the thick net curtains which screened the small sash window from the street outside, so he switched on a reading lamp.

'It's not a bad sketch—I suppose. The general outline's all right and it's got some of the features, but—look, may I touch it up a bit?' he asked, and felt in his pocket for a pencil.

Reg's eyes brightened. 'Certainly. If you can make it a better likeness, go ahead.'

'His eyebrows need darkening up,' Bert muttered to himself as he set his pencil to work, 'and they're a bit thicker and they come a bit closer together. His nose is snubbier though, something like that. Now his eyes, they're always the difficult bit. Keen, they were. Serious, but with a hint of humour.' He pulled the cap off the pencil and lightly erased some of his shading with the rubber, then he held the paper at arm's length, and perused it with his head cocked to one side like a perky sparrow's. More lines and shading were still needed apparently, but then he was satisfied.

'That's more like John Long,' he said with a confident smile, and passed it to Reg Finch.

Reg looked at it, and blinked. 'Good lord!' he exclaimed. The face in the picture now appeared to stand out from the paper with a surprisingly three-dimensional reality, and the character of the man portrayed seemed to have been captured as well. Serious and determined, but sensitive, and the eyes—they reminded Reg Finch of old Professor Hughes's eyes, bright, alert, intelligent and humorous. A dangerous man as an enemy, but a welcome one as a friend.

'That's brilliant,' Alison said, leaning over to look. 'You're very good.'

Winters shrugged his shoulders without showing any embarrassment at such praise. 'I don't know,' he admitted lamely. 'I've always been able to do faces, ever since I was a kid. It just came naturally.'

'You've a good memory too. How many times did you actually meet up with this John Long?' Reg asked.

'Only twice. The first time we just got chatting, about the weather and things I suppose, you know how it is. The second time he played Martin at darts. He was damned good too.'

'That was after the bomb had gone off? What about before then?'

Winters pursed his lips, and shook his head. 'Definitely not before then.'

'Do you and Martin O'Neil go to that pub every lunch time?'

'Nearly always, unless one of us has got to go to the bank, or do a bit of shopping.'

'The week before the bomb, did you go to the bank, or do some shopping?' Reg asked seriously.

Bert Winters thought for a moment. 'Yes, I did. On the Thursday, as a matter of fact. I went to the bank to cash a cheque, and have a quick look round the shops for something to give the wife for Christmas.'

'So Martin went to the Black Cat on his own, then?'

'I don't know—probably.'

Finch nodded. 'The last time you met Long, Martin thought he was asking questions about the computer set-up in the labs. Did you get the same impression?'

'Not at the time,' Winters acknowledged readily, 'but now I do. I think he wanted to know if the bomb had destroyed all the back-up copy data discs, as well as the computer.'

'And had it?'

'I don't know. Martin obviously knew, but he didn't let on.'

'These bottles of whisky. There were only Martin's fingerprints on his. Long couldn't have been wearing gloves, not in the pub, so how did he hand them over without touching the glass surface?'

Bert thought for a moment, trying to recall the scene in his mind. 'They were rolled up in white plastic bags. He didn't touch the bottles at all. I've thrown my bag away, I'm afraid.'

'Where did they come from? Did Long have them with him, or did he have to go out to his car to fetch them?' Alison asked.

234

'He'd got a holdall, a brown leather holdall. They were in that,' Bert answered promptly.

'Martin said something about a faulty laptop computer that Long kept his customers' orders on. If he'd got a holdall full of give-away bottles, he'd obviously got more buyers to visit, yet he didn't have this computer with him. Didn't you think that a bit strange?'

'Not really. He'd said earlier that all his Christmas orders had been taken, all he was doing here were courtesy calls.'

'Well, thank you, Mr Winters,' Reg Finch said, getting to his feet. 'I wish all the people we interviewed were as helpful as you've been. We'll take this bottle of yours with us, just in case Long's prints are on that, but we'll let you have it back as soon as we can.'

'We really seem to be getting somewhere now,' Alison Knott said cheerfully, as they walked down the hill towards the traffic lights and Magdalene Street.

'You think so?' Reg replied cautiously, watching for a suitable gap in the traffic, so that they could cross the busy road.

'Well, yes. Surely this John Long was checking to find out whether his bomb had completely destroyed the computer and its data?'

'He might want us to think that. If we do, we must assume he didn't have any inside help to plant that bomb, mustn't we? Otherwise his accomplice would have told him whether it was successful or not,' Reg reasoned. 'This man looks after his helpers, so possibly this meeting in the pub was a set-up job, to make Bert Winters a witness to O'Neil rejecting Long's approaches. If O'Neil is Long's accomplice then his white plastic bag might have contained the balance of the pay-off money, as well as a bottle.'

'Oh lord, and I'd thought it was all quite simple,' Alison said regretfully, peering down at the dark waters of the River Cam as they crossed over Magdalene Bridge.

'Nothing's ever simple in a case like this, not until you know all the answers. It's then that you start kicking yourself for apparently not spotting the obvious.'

'What was all that about a laptop computer, then?'

'I don't know. Maybe they were talking in some pre-arranged code. Perhaps Long was asking, "Are you sure we don't need to do anything more?" In which case O'Neil's reply was, "Forget it, everything's all right." '

'So, all we've got out of this is a better picture of John Long,' Alison said ruefully, having to lengthen her stride to keep up with her longer-legged companion.

'We don't know for sure if Winters has improved it, yet,' Reg replied, maintaining his pessimistic attitude. 'Let's wait and see what the landlord of the Black Cat thinks. This way.'

They turned the corner by St John's College, and strode on down Trinity Street. On the other side of the road there were shops, lit up and glistening with Christmas tinsel, lights and fake snow to attract the shoppers, so Reg wisely stayed on the college side, otherwise Alison would be forever wanting to stop and look in the windows.

'Do slow down a bit, Reg. We're not on a route march, you know,' Alison protested, tugging at his elbow, and feeling rather nettled at having her enthusiasm so readily dampened. 'Don't you ever get excited about anything?' she went on to ask caustically.

Reg laughed. He turned his head to look at her, and promptly bumped into a well-wrapped-up crowd of Japanese tourists who were milling around on the pavement outside King's College, taking photographs.

'I'm so sorry,' he exclaimed, putting out a hand to steady the comparatively diminutive gentleman he'd nearly knocked off his feet. 'Well, yes, I suppose I do sometimes,' he admitted, striding on.

Alison frowned, and clung determinedly to his arm, to keep his pace down. They walked on in silence, passed the impassive stone lions guarding the Grecian frontage of the Fitzwilliam Museum, and then they crossed over Trumpington Street and Lensfield Road, into the area of narrow streets in which was the Black Cat pub.

The landlord had no hesitation in identifying the picture improved by Bert Winters. 'Oh yes. I remember him, all right,' he stated clearly. 'He was in here a few days ago with them two young lads from the labs round the corner. Played darts, he did. Held them funny too. In the palm of his hand, like a knife thrower does. You notice things like that in a job like mine. He ain't a regular. He's been in here, oh, I don't know, two or three times, maybe. No, I can't say for certain. I see too many different faces, but when he went out of the door he turned left, towards Hills Road and the Catholic church, if that's any help.'

It was in that direction that Reg Finch and Alison Knott walked, not to follow a long-cold trail, but because it was the shortest way back to police headquarters.

'I'm going to concentrate on Martin O'Neil, Alison,' Reg decided as he warmed his hands on the radiator of his office.

'These are rather petty details, but I'd like you to check them out for me, if you would. Go and see Mr Poulter, at Poulter's Office Supplies in Cherryhinton, and confirm that O'Neil did do some work on his new computer system. Then check whether O'Neil did sell his motor bike three months ago, I've got the registration number somewhere. Go and have a chat with his father-in-law—apparently he had an insurance policy mature and gave some of it to his daughter, to help them buy a car. Maybe Martin O'Neil is being honest with us, but I must admit, I rather hope he isn't.' Reg Finch paused while Alison scribbled feverishly in her notebook. 'But before you do all that, ring the Scottish distillery who produced that bottle of malt whisky O'Neil bought from the chap he met in the pub. If they sell their product solely through a wholesaler, ring that wholesaler and find out if they employ a rep named John Long. When you've done that, come and see me. The boss might well want this new picture of John Long shown round some of the small hotels or lodging houses that reps use. I have a feeling we're starting to get close to this fellow, but I'm not going to get too excited about it, not yet.'

'Oh come off it, Brenda. Surely we're

wasting our time investigating these two,' Arthur Bryant protested scornfully. 'Brewer and Connery nearly got blown to bits. They were damned lucky to come out of it with only minor injuries. You surely don't think that if one of them had planted that bomb they'd have stayed anywhere within a mile of it?'

Brenda frowned. 'The list of people known to have gone into that laboratory between the Friday evening and when the bomb went off has got those two on it, even if it is at the bottom. What you say sounds all right, but I could counter that by saying they might have risked it, if the price was right, and if they thought they'd be safe at the far end of the lab. Besides, perhaps the bomb was more powerful than they'd been led to believe.'

Arthur shook his head determinedly. 'No sane person hangs about where a bomb is going off, even if it is a small one. That bit of debris that cut Connery's leg open could easily have hit her in the head and killed her. No, the odds against this line of investigation are too high, it's not worth a bet.'

'If you don't place a bet, you might lose your money,' Brenda replied, irritation making her confuse her metaphors, but she recovered quickly. 'Work that out if you can. If you don't buy a lottery ticket, you can't expect to win.'

'True, but if you don't tread on thin ice you can't fall through, either,' Arthur retorted heatedly.

Brenda shrugged her shoulders, now quite calm. 'No doubt there's some deep philosophical message in there somewhere, or else your midnight dip in the Washpit Brook has affected your brain, wherever you keep it, but I'll tell you this, Arthur—if the chief hears you forming fixed opinions based solely on speculative judgements, your next dip won't be in an icy ditch, it'll be in really hot water. All those people who had the opportunity to plant that bomb must be investigated. That's what you're paid to do, and that's what you'll do. You can start by delving into the wishes of the dead—Somerset House, or wherever it is now. Brewer's godmother, Amanda Sullivan of Bournemouth, and Brewer senior, of Cambridge, both left him assets or money, which, he says, accounts for him being relatively affluent. Check their last wills and testaments. It won't help us a lot, not if he's telling the truth, but if he's lying—that's a different matter. You can do that all right, can't you?' Brenda asked sarcastically.

'I wouldn't be at all surprised,' Arthur replied sulkily.

There were no Christmas decorations to brighten up the CC's large office. It was never the cheeriest of places even at the best of times, and the few greetings cards spaced out on the windowsill did nothing to create a festive feeling.

'Do you think we're wrong, looking for this DaSilva fellow? This Zena girl and Svenson obviously work for one of the drug cartels—could they have planted the bomb in the medical research labs?' the CC asked, drumming his thick fingers on his desk top.

'It's possible. I don't know who they work for, and the solicitor who's come up from London to defend them was no help either. He was given instructions by an anonymous phone caller, and had two thousand in cash arrive at his office by post, with the promise of more when necessary,' Walsh replied. 'But I'm pretty certain DaSilva exists. Reg Finch phoned a little while ago to tell me that there's been a character hanging about in one of the pubs near the Medical Centre who fits DaSilva's description, and he was using the name John Long, too. Do you get it? Long John Silver.'

A flicker of satisfaction passed over the CC's ruddy countenance. 'Long John Silver, eh! So you think you might have got a good lead at last, do you?'

'I hope so. We're after a very clever individual, that's for certain. Someone working in that Research Centre was helping him, that's pretty obvious, but there are some other possibilities that are still valid.'

'Such as?'

'Anderson.'

'Did Anderson go walk-about alone on the Friday evening, before he left?'

'Apparently so.'

'Did he have a key to Wade's laboratory? How long would it have taken to set up the booby-trap?'

'I don't know about a key. It wouldn't have been difficult for him to get one, but we don't know for sure that the medical lab bomb was a booby-trap, that's only Packstone's speculation.'

'You're just bandying words, Sidney. Packstone's an expert, and he's giving a considered judgement.'

'So he may be, but all he actually said was that the detonator pin was possibly attached to the drawer. That pin could just as easily have been pulled out by a timing device of some sort, which has yet to come to light among the debris. Maybe the timer got stuck and only freed itself, activated itself, when Chambers moved the drawer. That's feasible, you know.'

The CC looked thoughtful. 'I hadn't

thought about the detonator having a stuck timer. If that was the case, then that bomb might have been planted at almost any time during the previous week. That would explain why you're finding it difficult to work out how the bomber got in.' He scratched his nose while he pondered. 'No. this isn't good enough. How can you be expected to work things out if you don't know whether the bomb was set off by a booby-trap or a timer? You and Packstone had better get your heads together and sort it out between you. I don't like two of my so-called experts holding conflicting opinions.'

Walsh nodded. 'All right, I'll go and have another chat with him. Now, have you learned anything about how MI6 are getting on with their investigations into the other people at that conference? I must say I was hoping they might give us some sort of lead,' Walsh asked, licking the inside of his lips because the cup of coffee usual at these briefing sessions had not been forthcoming this time.

'I wondered when you were going to get round to that.' The CC reached into a drawer and took out a file. 'I've got some extracts of their preliminary findings, and I had to do some sweet talking to get them, I can tell you. They're classified top top secret, so no one below the rank of assistant chief constable may see them.' He drummed his fingers on the desk again, then grinned broadly. 'You've got five minutes to enjoy the privileges of an acting assistant chief constable, to which I hereby promote you. When you've read that, I'm demoting you straight back to chief inspector.' He pushed the file across the desk.

Walsh read it through. Perhaps the situation deserved a smirk or a smile, but it didn't get one. Walsh frowned when he came to the end, and he promptly read it through again.

'It makes you flaming sick, don't it?' the chief constable observed, taking the file back from Walsh and putting it away in his drawer. 'These characters get themselves elected to Parliament while they're still wet behind their ears, with no idea what real life's all about. They do a bit of toadying, buttering-up and head-nodding till they get made a junior bloody minister, a PPS or some such nonsense, and then what happens? Success goes to their tiny minds, and morals, if they ever had any, go flying out of the window.' He grinned ruefully at Walsh and held his hands up in a helpless gesture.

'But this fellow got himself involved with two of these women. Surely he was warned what to expect when he took office?' Walsh said incredulously.

'God only knows. You'd have thought so, wouldn't you? Anyway, there you are. It don't help us at all, because there's nothing known that links either of these two girls to any drug cartel. Maybe they're just tarts climbing the social ladder, and collecting men on their "I've been done by" list, like er...like young Brenda Phipps collects bits of porcelain. Do you reckon having a junior minister roll you rates as high as finding a chipped piece of Meissen for only 50p in a car boot sale?' He chortled, then his face went serious again. 'On the other hand, those sort of girls do get planted in the big city, specifically to worm information out of the unwary. Anyway, down there in the Smoke they've got to take it seriously. Anderson's name's not mentioned, even though I specifically drew their attention to him.'

The silence in the forensic department was like that within a library, Walsh thought, when he'd pushed through the double swing entrance doors.

In spite of the noise the doors made before they came to rest, the concentration of those within appeared to be undisturbed. Obviously the occupants of the benches had become inured to those particular sounds. This was always a serious place.

Even the few festive paper-chains had been loosely draped across the ceiling in neat mathematical patterns. Humour was a rare emotion here, unless it expressed itself with the wry grin that a clever answer to a subtle cryptic crossword clue might bring. It needed a special kind of person to do their sort of work: testing and analysing, in microscopic detail, the apparently insignificant debris and traces collected from the scene of a crime. Stains, molecules, bits of skin, fluff or hair, magnified a thousand times or more, might just turn out to be a clue that could solve a crime—but, far more often, would not. These people had to accept a fruitless result from hours of concentrated work, with no more than a phlegmatic shrug. Did they have a secret yearning to stand up and cry out, 'Eureka, I've found it'? Would a tiny speck of gold in the sterile sands of comparative analysis ever have them jumping about in glee? Perhaps they were more like those bronzed young archaeologists on some sun-drenched ancient site, who patiently ease away the years with brush and trowel:

Maybe a midden;
Or a grave;
A sherd, a bone or just a stone;
Nought this day,
But finds galore—a scrape away.

247

Now why was his mind slipping into poetry? Walsh asked himself. The only poems that had come his way recently were those they'd found in Dr Chambers' rooms, about the fellow who was stirring and writhing with inner pain, until his secret lover was with him once again. Mrs Wade had thought that lover might have been Maureen Connery. Well, if Connery had been Chambers' lover, then his death had not filled her with much anguish. On the contrary, according to Brenda, Connery had been, or was now, involved in a romance with Brewer.

'Are you just sleep-walking, Sidney, or is it me you want?' The white-coated figure of Richard Packstone looked up from one of the microscopes at which he seemed to spend much of his time, and blinked vigorously to refocus his eyes.

'Yes, if you can spare me a moment?' Walsh replied, quickly refocusing his own mind on the reason for his being there. 'It's to do with the detonator on this bomb in the medical lab.'

'Oh, really?' Packstone muttered off-handedly. 'Come on in my office, then. What's the problem?'

'Well, it's this question of the detonator being a booby-trap. Because of it we're concentrating on the period from the

Friday evening until the Monday morning, for obvious reasons, but the suggestion's been made that perhaps there was a mechanical timer, one which failed to operate correctly, but was in fact set off by the vibrations made when Chambers opened that drawer. What do you think?' Walsh asked.

Packstone rubbed his chin thoughtfully. 'Just what kind of mechanical timer did you have in mind?' But he did not wait for a reply, and went on. 'There's the alarm clock or watch type. They're usually rigged up to make an electrical contact, but I suppose one could be made to wind up a string and pull the pin out that way. Well, we've found no clock parts at all, and we would have by now, if that had been used, and there are no batteries either. No, what's turned up since I last spoke to you does tend to confirm my original suggestion. We've found one of those small hooks, you know, the kind that are used with spring wires to hold up net curtains, only this one has a piece of string still tied round the thread end. Not the kind of thing you'd expect in a medical research laboratory, is it? It seems to me that this hook might have been attached to the trigger pin, and the bomber's last job, when he slid the drawer back, was to anchor that hook on something solid,

249

so then when the drawer was opened properly, the pin would have come out and the bomb would have gone off. The only thing that could have gone wrong with that scenario would have been if the string had broken, or the hook had come off, but if that had happened the pin wouldn't ever have come out, and the bomb wouldn't have gone off—so it'd still be there. I'm sorry, Sidney, everything points to it being a booby-trap bomb, and one that worked. You may be having problems finding out how the bomb was put into place between the Friday and the Monday, but you're stuck with that period. If the bomb was in place earlier than that, it would surely have been set off on the Friday afternoon, wouldn't it?'

13

'We've been thinking this fellow DaSilva is Mexican or Spanish—South American—well, John Long definitely isn't,' Reg explained when the Serious Crime team had met up again that evening in Walsh's office.

Decorative signs of the approaching festive season were as limited in this room as they were in the CC's office. However, on the small coffee table by the window stood a basket of dried flowers; its seed pods on stems, ears of wheat, berried holly and other things had been artistically arranged by Gwen, to add a little cheer for her husband when he was on duty.

'They've all said he spoke English as well as they did themselves,' Reg went on, 'and there's no sign that he'd just shaved off the moustache that was on the original photographs. He'd got a bit of a tan, it's true, but it was even, on his face at any rate. Myself, I think Long must be pretty good with the makeup box. He's definitely not a rep for the Scottish distillery, or its retailer. That doesn't help much, except to prove he's a suspicious character.'

'We must make the assumption that this Long is the man we're after, though,' Walsh said thoughtfully. 'He's probably using a private car, but he'd have to park it somewhere in the city. In the morning I think that the modified picture of Long should be shown to the drivers of the buses, particularly the ones on the Park and Ride service. We can do the railway station and taxis as well—and don't forget the attendants on the pay car-parks. Hopefully someone might have seen him. Organise Alison and Arthur into doing that, Reg. Now, what about your bottles of malt whisky? What have forensic come up with on them?'

'There's no unidentified prints, boss, and there are no traces of a price label having been stuck on them anywhere, so it's unlikely they came from a supermarket. In any case, that particular brand is relatively rare this side of the border. A dozen or so outlets carry it, London, Birmingham, Manchester, and so on. London's the nearest to us.'

'That's no help, then,' Walsh stated wryly. 'You're not happy with O'Neil, are you, Reg? But if we assume he is telling the truth then DaSilva obviously needed another source of information. That suggests his original source had either dried up or become unreliable.'

Brenda's eyes brightened. 'Dr Chambers is the only actor in this play who's suddenly disappeared off stage, but that doesn't make sense.'

Walsh shook his head reluctantly. 'Superintendent Anderson also got booted off the scene before he could find out how effective the bomb had been.'

'DaSilva must be worried about whether there's more copies of the computer data lying around. He's still got to deal with Wade yet, though. How is Wade getting on? Has he gone completely round the twist yet?' Brenda asked.

Walsh smiled and shook his head. 'Fortunately he's starting to pull himself together, but another shock like the other one might well tip him over the edge for good. He's lucky, his wife's taking the pressure well. She's managed to cut him down on the brandy, and she actually got him out for a short walk yesterday. You saw the other two who worked with Wade, Brenda. What did you find out about them?'

'They're both quite affluent. Arthur's checking out their stories for me. Connery is probably the dominant one of the two,' Brenda suggested. 'She's one of those people that weigh their words very carefully before they speak. That makes you think they're working out what's the best thing to say, rather than coming straight out with the truth.'

'The stories of the two general maintenance staff seem to check out all right, but I'm still suspicious about that security guard, Smith,' Walsh admitted. 'So, with O'Neil, that makes four people we've got who had the opportunity to plant that bomb and whose stories we're not happy with. I'm tempted to apply for search warrants and go through their places with a fine-tooth comb—we might be lucky and find something incriminating. Let's sleep on that tonight, though. We'll consider the situation tomorrow. You never know, something might turn up before then to save us the trouble.'

It was a damp and dismal morning, with a fine misty drizzle in the air, and still quite dark. Not a very promising start to the school holidays.

However, there were more important things to worry about at the moment, other than the weather. He needed more air in his front tyre. That last bump up the kerb had produced an ominous metallic thud, as if the wheel rim had hit the stone. If he did that again he might actually split the tyre.

Now that he'd got this paper round his mum had said he had to pay for things like that himself. That aspect of being a money earner had come as a bit of a shock. Until now bikes were for fun—for wheelies and frantic races through the woods and round the estate, with mud flying in all directions. The odd buckled wheel and bent handlebar had been part of the acceptable hazards of life itself. Despite the moans and the exhortations, the contents of his mother's purse had soon rectified the damage and put him back on the saddle, so that he could be off and do it all again. Now things were different. A simple puncture was no problem, but buying a new front tyre would hit his pocket hard, especially now, just before Christmas. Having a pump as an accessory would have been handy today, and, looking down at his jeans, clean on that morning, so too would mudguards, but mountain bikes like his scorned such sissy things, and so the problems their absence caused had to be borne with fortitude.

This part of his round was a bore and a bind. The houses down this road, and the next, were big posh ones, with their own drives. They took much longer to do, compared with the last part of his route, where the rows of terraced houses had front doors opening directly on to the pavement.

The next delivery was to The Pines.

A *Telegraph,* the *Mail,* and a women's magazine. He rode down the gravel drive, passed the eerily dripping green rhododendrons in the thick shrubbery, to the front door of the house, with its useless little porch and the wide, red-tiled step that made it so infuriatingly difficult to reach the letter-box without getting off his bike. The secret was to jump both wheels up on the step, mindless of the muddy tracks they left, but today, with a dicky front tyre, he dared not do that. So he stayed on the gravel, and putting his foot squarely on the tiles, leaned as far over to his left as he could. He just managed to push the rolled-up papers an inch or so into the letter-box. The *Telegraph* tore as it went in, but that didn't matter, that wasn't his problem.

A quick push with the left foot to get upright, and then he'd be away; but things didn't quite work out like that. The polished tiles were damp and his foot slipped. It missed the two full milk bottles by only a fraction of an inch, but the box of eggs there with them went flying.

'Oh Christ,' he muttered aloud. That meant trouble, and trouble like that was best dealt with by him getting the hell out of there. He jerked himself upright and put his weight on the pedals, and set off.

He'd gone barely four feet when the

explosion came from behind him. He felt a tremendous kick in the middle of his back and then, with all the eeriness of a slow-motion camera, he felt himself rise in the air and turn completely over, before crash-landing on his belly in a privet hedge; but he was unconscious when he slid from there to the ground.

The first to the scene, not that he'd ever been very far from it, was Police Sergeant Masters. He was six feet tall, fleshy and forty, and bleeding badly from a gash on the side of his head where a flying fragment of glass had found him, where he'd sat, in the easy chair that had been placed in the hallway specifically for the comfort of the minders provided by the Cambridgeshire Constabulary.

Masters was a tough and experienced man, and although his shoulder was hurting from the impact with the wall against which he'd been flung, and his shins were sore because the heavy mahogany door had landed on them when its hinges had given way, his first thought was to use his radio to summon help. Then he staggered outside, and found the body of the paper boy. He was joined there a few moments later by a frightened and wild-eyed Patricia Wade, with a filmy, flowered dressing-gown pulled tight at her waist to provide some vestige of modesty, and providing a sight that Masters would have given much more attention to had his mind not been preoccupied with other things. The boy was breathing, and there was no outward sign of bleeding.

'He's still alive, but we'd best not move him,' Masters muttered thickly to the crouching Mrs Wade. 'We'll put a blanket over him where he is. The ambulance will be along in a tick. They'll know what to do.'

Nearby was a pyjama-clad man who also ought to have known what to do, but Dr Wade just stood there, wringing his hands helplessly and staring down at the crater, and the damage the bomb had caused to the front of his house. His face showed an expression of sheer terror, and from his lips there came a childish whimpering sound. Masters looked at him steadily, then at the bewildered woman beside him, then ignored them both, and strode back through the debris into the house, to find a blanket, and a tea towel or something to hold to the side of his face, because the dripping blood was making a right mess down the front of his tunic.

'Hospital for you, Sarge,' Brenda said cheerfully, as she wound another bandage round Masters' head. 'This'll need stitches, and they'll give you a jab in your bum if your anti-tetanus isn't up to date.'

'I'll go when I'm good and ready,' Masters growled resentfully. 'No, Inspector, everything was quiet and peaceful all night. Nothing to do except read, and keep awake. No one can get to that front door over that loose gravel without you hearing them—besides, you can see who it is through the window as they come down the drive. It was just after seven when the milkman came. The usual one, I've seen him before.'

'Did you get the milk in when he'd gone?' Walsh asked.

Masters shook his head. 'No. It didn't seem worth it. I didn't want to make any noise, them two were still asleep upstairs, you see.'

'So what happened next?'

'Next was the paper boy. He rode up on his bike and stuffed the papers in the door. He'd hardly got going again when the bomb went off. I'm sorry. There's sweet F. A. else I can tell you. I haven't got a clue how that bomb got put outside there, I really haven't.' Masters rubbed his shoulder despondently.

'Brenda, go after the milkman, would you? We'd better have a word with him first,' Walsh asked.

'Sure, but I was thinking, Chief, someone could have got to the front door without crossing the gravel, if he came round the side of the house and kept on that narrow bit of grass along the flower beds under the windows,' she suggested.

Walsh nodded. 'I'll have a look, you just go and get the milkman.'

Outside, Walsh studied the ground round the shallow crater left by the bomb. The centre was a little way from the wide expanse of red tiles that formed the front step, part of which had now been blown away. He walked on the gravel path along the front of the house to study the narrow ridge of grass that edged the flower bed. Its surface was soft and would readily take an imprint—he found that out by pressing down with his fingers—but there were no marks that suggested the toe or heel prints of shoes. The flower bed itself was even softer, but equally barren of tracks. At the far side of the house a high boarded gate barred his progress. It was bolted, and the bolt was on the other side. He shook his head, regretfully—that line of thinking was definitely a blind alley.

Richard Packstone stood for some moments staring thoughtfully at the bomb damage, then turned to give instructions to those of his team who had arrived with him.

'Not a large amount of explosive, Sidney,' he said, as Walsh came over. 'It was intended for detonation close to the victim, I should imagine. A bit bigger than the usual letter bomb though. Was it the postman that brought it?'

Walsh shrugged his shoulders and shook his head, both at the same time. 'The postman hasn't been yet.'

'Oh! Well, never mind. I'll get on with the business of finding out what it consisted of.'

The milkman was a tall, well-built man, with a wrinkled rugged face not unlike that of the comedian Frankie Howerd, but confronted by so many very serious people, there was an anxious look in place of the usual blandly humorous expression.

'They used to have only one pint, but lately that's gone up to two, you see. Yes, oh yes, and half a dozen eggs on Tuesdays and Fridays. Oh dear, but, well, all I took them today was two pints of milk. I put them on that there step over there, you see, like I do every morning, and I took two empties away. That's all. For Christ's sake, I don't know nothing about any bomb. There weren't nothing there when I was here, honestly, and I didn't see no one lurking about, either. No, it weren't me that did it. I ask you, what would I be wanting to throw bombs about for, at my age?'

'The milkman must have put it there, boss. I know forensic have found no traces of explosive on the milkman's hands or on his clothing, but then, you wouldn't really expect them to, would you? DaSilva would have given him the bomb already made up. Money for old rope too. A nice cash sum for playing what the milkman probably thought was a practical joke. It's obvious.'

Walsh smiled, but with an effort. 'It may seem obvious to you, Reg, but short of thumb screws and the rack, we'll never get him to admit to it, and he didn't have any sizeable amount of cash on him either. We'll need to talk to the paper boy, if he survives. No, I'm afraid we're not getting anywhere very fast,' he muttered dejectedly.

'Cheer up, boss, we'll get there in the end. Now, there's something I should have asked yesterday, and I forgot. Margaret and me, we'd like to have a little dinner party on Saturday evening, and we respectfully request the pleasure of the company of both of you, with a friend or spouse each, of course,' Reg announced formally.

'That's very kind of you, Reg. Yes, I'm sure Gwen will be as delighted to accept as I am,' Walsh replied politely.

'Me, too, Reg, but if I'm on my own, that won't cause a problem, will it?' Brenda said, blushing slightly.

262

'Henry! The lady wants to ask you a few questions,' the grossly overweight, dark-haired mother of the newspaper boy announced dramatically, and noisily, at the bedside in the hospital. 'He's feeling a lot better now, especially since I told him his bike was insured with the house contents policy, so's he'll be able to get himself a new one. It's been worrying him, you see. It wasn't very old, the one he was riding. We paid half of it, the rest he had to save up out of his pocket money. As I said to my hubby, not that he's the boy's dad, you understand, that ended years ago, "No," I said to him, "it'll make the boy look after it properly if he has to pay some of it himself." Kids these days get given too much, and they don't appreciate it, do they?'

'Hello, Henry. You don't mind answering a few questions, do you?' Brenda Phipps said, smiling down reassuringly at the pale face of the young boy, who was obviously still shocked and bemused. 'What I'd like you to do is to tell me exactly what happened this morning, but take your time. There's no hurry.'

'Come on now, Henry. Do what the lady asks,' his mother instructed.

'Well, I don't know. There was this big bang behind me, and I sort of went flying.

263

I don't remember anything else,' he said hesitantly, eyeing his mother anxiously.

'Yes, that's all right. There's nothing to worry about.' Brenda said quickly. 'Now, you rode your bike up to the front door of the house, didn't you? Can you remember if there was anything on the doorstep?'

The boy closed his eyes in an effort to think, or to blot out the world around him. 'No, there weren't nothing there, honestly,' he said eventually.

'What about milk bottles?' Brenda prompted.

'Oh yer, there were milk bottles, of course. The milkman gets round before I does. Two, I think.'

'Anything else? It's important.'

'Only an egg box,' he replied reluctantly, 'and I knocked that with my foot as I went off. Them tiles were slippery, you see. It weren't my fault if I broke any, honestly. I couldn't help it.'

'How big an egg box? Was it a six or twelve?'

'Six.'

'When you knocked it, did it open up? Did you see the eggs in it?'

'No, I didn't see no eggs. It'd got a thick elastic band round the middle, hadn't it? Bloody hell, it ain't worth making all this bloody fuss over a few rotten eggs, is it?'

'Henry, don't you dare use words like

that,' his mother thundered. 'It must be the shock and all, him swearing like that. He ain't got it from our house, he ain't. He's been brought up proper, he has.'

He's been brought up proper, he has.

14

Ronald Silver came into the lounge after
having been for a brisk walk on his own
along the paths by the River Ouse. His
face was flushed pink, and he looked
much fitter and more healthy now than
when they had first met, Angela thought.

It was awful to recall those first few
hours they'd spent together, when terror
had gripped the inside of her stomach
with a cold and icy hand, but he'd treated
her so tenderly and with such unexpected
gentleness that she'd soon been able to
relax; and in no time at all, it had
seemed as if they'd known each other
for years. She'd come to terms with the
sexual side soon enough, but somehow
a mental relationship had developed too.
It was a strange sort of understanding
between their two minds, communicated
by the merest glance or a movement of
an eyelid. Like now, as he peeled off his
thick waxed jacket. The most fleeting of
smiles conveyed a lengthy message. A walk
enjoyed, pleased to be back in the warm,
and, nicest of all, was all well with her?
Her own response could probably be read

just as simply. Yes thank you, but all the better, now you're back. A black spectre did loom over her shoulder, warning her that this was a highly false situation, one that had no permanence or basis in reality. The future could be blinked away into temporary oblivion, most of the time, but these strangely happy limbo days were not really hers—they had been sold. She was just a plaything for a man of power, a vehicle to relieve Ron's lust, like any concubine of old. A one-man whore. Well, not exactly, for hers was only a short-term contract, with more than just a cash reward. Soon her past debts would be swept away, and with them the fear of the prison sentence that would have ruined her life. Yet with them would also go Ronald Silver. A man older by far than any she ever thought she would have any feelings for. He was not a handsome man, and certainly he had none of the height and bulging muscles of her teenage dreams, but, however it was defined, Ronald Silver was a man above all the men she had ever met, or even read about. She had been blackmailed into prostitution, and unexpectedly had found that it was pleasurable and suited her well. In comparison, her life before he had come into it had been empty. How would it be when he went out of it? She shook her head—she, didn't want to think about that.

'A man came while you were out, with a special delivery parcel. It's over there,' she said, pointing at it. Why should Ron's face suddenly harden and look so serious, when before it had been relaxed and happy?

Silver picked the box up with both hands, as though he were judging its weight, then looked round for somewhere to put it. The oak bureau had doors at the bottom that locked, but the parcel was too big, unless something already there was removed. He took out what looked like a black attaché case, one that was scuffed a little on its base. That made enough room. He stood the case on the floor by the now relocked bureau. Angela watched his movements, and noticed the white printed letters on the case.

'Is that a computer, Ron?' she asked impulsively, then wished she hadn't spoken. Until now she'd been reasonably successful at curbing any interest in Silver's activities. The warning of that horrid solicitor, Marston, still rang in her ears, but her words had caused no problem, in fact, it was almost as though Silver welcomed the distraction of his thoughts.

'That's right, love. A laptop computer. Do you know how to use one?' he asked, laying it on the table and opening it up.

She shook her head as she came over. 'I've only seen them in adverts, but I imagine they operate in just the same way as a normal PC.'

'I should think so.'

'Don't you know, Ron? It's yours, don't you use it?'

Silver scratched his head and smiled. 'Well, I had intended to, but, well, circumstances change. There's always more than one way of killing a cat. One has to alter one's plans as the situation develops. Like a general has to watch for events or natural features on the battlefield that he can use to his best advantage. That's the secret of success in life: turning fortuitous events to your own benefit. You're doing well with that computer, Angela, you'd better keep it. You'll make better use of it than I would have done.'

Angela looked at him with a puzzled frown and reached out an impulsive hand to put on his. 'You've given me so much, Ron, and I don't think I deserve it,' she said shyly.

'It's a pleasure to give you presents simply because you don't expect them. Now, if we're going to go and visit your grandmother, we'd better get a move on.' Silver went off to the bedroom to change into clothes more suitable for such a visit.

The nursing home, near the church at the centre of the small, still rural, village, had probably once been the vicarage.

Its Victorian builders had certainly provided ample living space for a large family, and for those servants necessary to maintain an incumbent in a style of life long since past; even so, that accommodation was obviously inadequate for its present use, for on both sides extensive single-storey wings had been built on.

There was a pile of plastic rubbish bags in the entrance hall, and the reception desk was not manned. So, unannounced, Angela led Silver down the corridor towards her grandmother's room, her hand tightly gripping his arm.

They passed an open door, against which rested a broom and a mop. It was apparently a communal sitting-room, for several elderly people sat around in high-backed chairs, with rugs wrapped round their legs. A few read books or newspapers, or knitted, others merely stared dejectedly before them, at nothing in particular. The large television in one corner of the room was blank and silent, and the nearby radiator was only lukewarm to Silver's touch. The whole atmosphere of the place was cool, rather dank, and tainted with the musty, pungent smell of urine.

'Are all old people's homes like this?' He frowned as he stared about him.

'It wasn't as bad as this when she first came, in fact it had a nice friendly feel, but the new man's changed things. He just laughed at me the other day when I tried to complain,' she replied dejectedly.

Her grandmother's room was small, yet it was shared with another. There was very little space not already occupied by beds, cupboards and chairs.

An expression of pleasure spread on the face of the little white-haired old lady who sat in the chair by the right-hand bed, blinking and peering up at her visitors.

With Silver she was very quickly set at ease. He had such a pleasant relaxed manner that she soon forgot he was a stranger only just introduced. He led the conversation round to times and events long since past, yet easily recalled in her still active mind; then with subtle deftness, he lured the other occupant, a tall angular woman, to join in the general chat. A chance remark brought out the fact that both of them had once been to Rome, a place which Silver apparently knew well, and so a lively, obviously enjoyable exchange of reminiscences developed. So much so that it suddenly seemed as if that cool bland room had become actually warm and cosy, full of good cheer and happiness.

271

Quite how Silver had managed to create such a result, Angela could not work out, but it had the strange effect of making her want to cry. That would not do, of course, so she blinked back her tears and joined energetically into the conversation, to take her mind off things.

After a while Silver announced that he was sure that they had much to talk about amongst themselves, and that, if they'd excuse him, he'd leave them for a while, and get some fresh air.

'What a charming young man, my dear. I really do like him,' Angela's grandmother said enthusiastically when he'd gone, squeezing the hand that lay so comfortingly on her own.

Silver strode nonchalantly along the corridor until he found a door with 'Office' on it.

He did not knock. He just opened it, and went in.

In a large padded chair, behind the desk, lounged a well-built, dark-haired man in a loose grey suit, probably aged in his late thirties.

He looked up in surprise at his unannounced visitor.

'Who the hell do you think you are? Have you no manners? Bloody well knock before you come into my office. Get out, and don't come back until I say you can,' he snapped angrily.

Silver stayed where he was, by the door. His eyes had narrowed at those rough words of welcome but his stern expression did not change.

'Are you Alexander Macklin?' he asked grimly.

'So what if I am? You heard what I said. Get out. We're full up, if that's what you want to know. Leave your name with the nurse outside. She'll put you on the waiting list. One of these old biddies is sure to pop off soon.'

With the identity of the man thus confirmed, Silver walked slowly over to the desk. That made Macklin's eyes widen, as his anger started to boil into rage.

'What the hell do you think you're playing at? Get out when I say get out. I own this place.'

'You think you own it, do you, Macklin? Did you ever read the small print on the loan agreement that you took out to buy this place?' Silver demanded, his eyes glinting coldly. 'You didn't? Well you should have done. Your debt was assignable. That means your lender can sell it if he wants, to anyone he likes. Didn't you read that? Well, I've come to give you some good news, your lender has decided to sell. Your debt has been bought by someone else. Now, aren't you a lucky fellow?'

A startled look of apprehension and concern appeared on Macklin's now bloated face.

'There was another clause you ought to have read,' Silver went on remorselessly. 'It says that if the principal of the first part is satisfied that the business is not being run in a proper manner, then he has the right to take whatever steps are necessary to protect the asset value which secures the loan. That means, if you want it spelled out in plain English, they can put the toe of their boot right up your fat backside. You don't believe me? Amazing! Get on the blower to Smithers at your finance company. He's the fellow you dealt with, isn't he? Go on, do it,' Silver snapped, a note of undisguised malice clearly ringing in his voice.

Macklin's face showed a series of expressions in quick succession, aggression, disbelief, doubt, and lastly, fear, but he picked up the phone and dialled a number.

What he learned in his short conversation confirmed what Silver had said, and his hand trembled as he put the receiver down, yet there was still truculence in his voice as he muttered the words, 'No bugger's going to tell me how to run my business.'

The reaction to that short speech was astonishingly quick. Silver moved with the speed of a striking snake. Suddenly Macklin found his left wrist being gripped and twisted in a hand that was exerting an unbelievably vice-like strength and power. He was a strong man himself, yet his strength seemed of no account as he was dragged from his chair, forward on his stomach, across his desk. That was humiliation enough, but there was more to come. He found the rounded point of his own brass letter-knife being pressed into the soft flesh under his jaw, preventing him from crying out, and forcing his head up. It gave him no choice but to gaze directly into Silver's eyes, and they glowed with such a ruthless ferocity that they struck a sickly terror into the pit of his stomach.

'No? No?' purred Silver's menacingly icy voice. 'Well, I'm going to tell you how to run your business, and what is more, you will obey me. The old men and women who are your guests, you are going to treat with love and respect. Yes, indeed,' Silver snarled the words out viciously. 'Not as you would treat your own parents, if there ever were any such unfortunate creatures prepared to acknowledge you. You will treat them, as though they were my parents. My parents, do you hear? Is it beginning to penetrate into that thick skull of yours that unpleasant things might happen if you don't?'

The question was rhetorical, for Macklin could make no reply. He dared not even gulp. Smooth and rounded the point of that letter-knife may have been, yet still it had torn the skin under his chin, and he could feel a drop of blood running slowly down his throat.

The next moment he was pushed contemptuously back into his chair, but any relief he might have felt at that was only short-lived. He stared in wide-eyed horror as his letter-knife was stabbed viciously down into the open palm of his left hand. Then that wrist too, was freed from Silver's steel-like grip, Macklin gave out a high-pitched cry of agony, but his deeply rasping intakes of breath soon smothered his groans of pain. He turned his watering eyes away from the hatefully implacable face of his visitor.

'We know where we stand now, do we?' Silver said smiling calmly. 'You will now have someone turn the central heating of this place up, and then you will ring an agency and arrange to hire the proper number of experienced staff needed to run an old people's home properly.'

Macklin looked at the bluish patch in the centre of his throbbing left palm, from which a globule of dark red blood had exuded, gulped, then picked up the phone and did as he was bid.

'Excellent,' Silver commented, now seated comfortably in the best visitors' chair. 'You have a doctor who calls here regularly, I presume.'

'Of course. He comes each day. He'll be along any time now.'

'While we're waiting for him then, outline to me how you will organise interesting activities for your guests, and not just during the Christmas period either. Things that will stimulate the use of their minds so that they will not be deadly bored, as they are now.'

Silver thought he detected a flicker of dissimulation pass across Macklin's face, and he smiled sardonically. 'Don't think for one moment that my visit is the only one you'll get. Far from it. Others will come after me, but they will not be like the local council inspector whom you butter up. They will chat with your guests and your staff, and if they find they're not happy, they might easily lose their tempers with you. Nasty, vicious people they are, when they're angry. Not mild, understanding and considerate, like I am. Do I make myself clear?'

Presumably he had, for Macklin nodded. He was obviously a competent person at his job, when he wished to be. He set out a programme to find the individual hobbies and interests of each of his guests and the steps needed to facilitate and encourage them. Then he outlined a scheme for general entertainment, plans that covered a range of interesting activities.

He had just finished doing that when there came a knock at the door. A young sandy-haired man with a pale freckled face came in.

'Ah, Dr Maclure,' Macklin said, the relief at having an outsider present clearly recognisable in his voice. 'I have someone here who wishes to talk to you about one of our guests.'

Maclure held out his hand to Silver, and smiled. 'Of course. Who is it?' he said in a lilting Scottish voice.

'The lady in number twelve, the one with advancing glaucoma.'

'Oh yes, I know who you mean,' he replied, nodding his head. 'Mrs..., well, her left eye is a lot worse than her right, but as you say, it is advancing. That's a pity, because otherwise she's quite fit and alert for her age. I've put her down for an operation, but it'll be between six to nine months, I'm afraid. The waiting lists, you know. I've done my very best for her, I assure you.'

Silver's smile was now a friendly one.

'So she's fit enough to have the operation, then?' he asked.

'Oh yes, she's fit enough. As I say, it's just a question of the waiting lists.'

Silver nodded thoughtfully and pinched his bottom lip between his forefinger and thumb. 'But, privately?' he asked.

Maclure smiled. 'Privately, she could have the operation tomorrow. No problem.'

'Would you arrange that then, please. I'm sure there's no need for the patient to be aware it's not being done under the National Health Service, is there? If you'll be kind enough to ascertain the costs involved then the matter of payment can be settled here and now. I have an extensive overseas trip in the offing, and delay would be inconvenient for me.'

The doctor stared momentarily at the face of this unexpected benefactor. There was something dominating about his personality, in which stature played no part. When Maclure had come into the room, he had been aware of a latent atmosphere of tension. He'd observed the blood on Macklin's throat, the clenched hand that seemed to be bothering him, and the smile that seemed so wooden and artificial. It was all very strange, very unusual. Still, it was no concern of his. He made a couple of very satisfactory phone calls, and blinkingly accepted a wad of fifty pound notes as though it were a commonplace activity for medical operations like that to be pre-paid, in cash.

'There's your receipt, thank you,' he said. 'She'll go into hospital this evening, and she'll have her operation tomorrow morning. I'll go and tell her, if I may. She'll be delighted.'

'Really?' Silver said complaisantly, as they drove out of the car-park.

'Yes. It's something to do with the NHS changes the government has made for fund-holding GPs. I didn't quite follow it, myself, but that doesn't matter. She's going to have the operation tomorrow. So she'll be able to see properly for Christmas. Isn't it marvellous?' Angela enthused.

'It certainly is.'

'And then a nurse came in with some cups of tea, and she said that something strange was going on. Extra staff were being hired, and there was a Christmas party, with real entertainers, to organise. They were getting so excited. What a change to come over that place in such a short time. I could hardly believe it. They seemed to think that you might have had something to do with it, Ron. They say you were in Mr Macklin's office for an awfully long time.'

Silver shrugged his shoulders. 'A well-built fellow, in his thirties, was he? Yes, I did see him about.'

Angela looked at him with suspicion, and bit back another question, because that would have been tantamount to the prying, which was forbidden. 'It must be awful to grow old,' she commented instead.

Silver chuckled out loud. 'But it's always other people who seem to grow old, Angela. It's the shock when the truth really comes home, that's the danger. It's even worse if you weave a fence around your life and isolate yourself in your own little world, because that becomes your Land of Eternal Youth, your "Tir na n'Og" of Celtic mythology. When you step out of it, you can't get back in. That means you're left alone and lonely. Like Rip Van Winkle, if you accept that he didn't sleep, but led a life of utter boredom instead, which is saying just about the same thing. The solution? Be like the Celts of old, Angela. Engrained in their culture is the belief that over each hill there's a valley that's greener than the one they're in. Was it Kipling who wrote that it is better to travel, than to arrive? Keep wide awake and keep moving, Angela. This world is greater than any lifetime,' he advised. Then he went on to say:

281

'Savour and relish each new terrain,
Each new smell or flavour.
Where the sun sets
Over that snowy mountain,
Across that sparkling sea,
Are delights beyond description,
Just awaiting thee.'

15

'If you must have bombs going off, Sidney, I'd very much appreciate it if you'd arrange for them to be in confined spaces,' Packstone said with a wry smile, as he spread the layout plan of Dr Wade's house and surrounding gardens on Walsh's desk. 'Debris goes such a hell of a long way outside. I haven't set this one up on the computer. It didn't seem worth it, since we know whereabouts the centre of the explosion was.'

'What did the bomb consist of, Mr Packstone?' Brenda asked.

'The same as the Medical Research Centre, TNT. This was a smaller quantity though,' Packstone replied, pulling out a handkerchief from his pocket and using it to vigorously polish the lenses of his spectacles.

'And the detonator?' said Reg Finch, asking the all-important question.

Packstone held his glasses up to the light from the window to see if they were free from smears before slipping them back on to his bony nose. 'We've found this piece of steel tube.' He laid it on the desk for them to inspect. 'It was impacted into the paper boy's bag. Internal and external diameters are the same as the piece we found at the lab site, and it compares metallurgically too, so as far as I'm concerned, they're from the same rod. Most probably the detonator was of a similar design. Simple, and apparently quite effective. What was it you said the paper boy saw, Brenda? An egg box?'

'Yes, with a thick elastic band round it,' Brenda replied promptly.

'That might have been necessary to keep the spring attached to the firing pin compressed. An egg-box bomb? How innocuous and innocent. There's nothing lethal or threatening about an egg box, is there? The depths of deception in the criminal mind never cease to astound me,' Packstone admitted. 'In spite of being alerted to danger, the Wades—and even Sergeant Masters himself, I wouldn't be at all surprised—would have picked that box up, if it hadn't been set off accidentally. The boy was lucky too, Sidney—if he hadn't had that bag stuffed with papers on his back, you might have had another death on your hands. That bit of tube penetrated to quite a depth, you know. It would have torn right through him.'

'One death's enough, Richard. Anything else?' Walsh asked.

'Not at the moment. Keep at it. You're up against someone fiendishly clever this time,' Packstone said in all seriousness as he gathered his papers together and went out of the office.

'Fiendishly clever just about sums it up,' agreed Finch.

'Well, we've just got to put on our fiendishly clever thinking caps, haven't we?' Brenda announced determinedly.

'We have indeed,' Walsh agreed. 'Now, obviously DaSilva didn't plant this last bomb himself, but we've only two suspects for his accomplice this time—the milkman and the paper boy. In either case, a small bribe for what they might have been told was a simple practical joke, would suffice—'

'That's all very well, boss,' Reg interrupted sceptically, 'but if the milkman did it, he'd have come up with a different story than the one he did. He'd have said the box was already there.'

'Oh, I don't know about that,' Brenda added doubtfully. 'If it had been on the doorstep with the empties, it would obviously have been left for him to take away for some reason. No, what I think is significant is that neither of them had any bribe-sized money on them.'

'So what?' Reg asked. 'Obviously Da-Silva had struck the bargain and paid up the day before, and he'd have handed the bomb over then.'

'I doubt that, Reg,' Walsh said, shaking his head. 'With the egg box only secured by a rubber band, neither the milkman nor the paper boy would have been able to resist the temptation to open it up, to see what the practical joke was about. No, the deal must have been struck that morning, while they were on their rounds.'

'In which case where's their money? Where's their bribe? They wouldn't have done it for nothing,' Reg said emphatically.

There was silence for a moment, then Brenda raised a finger meaningfully, like a cricket umpire does to a bowler's successful appeal. 'DaSilva could have had the money in an already stamped envelope, for them to write their address on and post to themselves. The bribe money might be being delivered first thing tomorrow morning.'

'That's a good thought. I hope you're right, Brenda,' Walsh acknowledged with a smile. 'Reg, you organise Arthur and Alison to call at the houses on both the milkman's and the paper boy's round. Someone might have seen DaSilva striking his bargain.'

'I can't do that yet, boss,' Reg interjected. 'Alison and Arthur are both out with DaSilva's picture, going round the bus drivers and car-park attendants. It'll be after lunch before they get back.'

'Oh well, set them on it as soon as you can. Brenda, you get on to the postal sorting office. We want to be tipped off about what letters or parcels will be delivered at those two addresses, then we can have someone there to witness what's in them when they're opened. Now, before you both go, I'd like you to put your names on this Christmas card I've bought for old Professor Hughes,' Walsh requested. 'I thought it'd be nice if it came from the three of us, and I've bought a bottle of Hine brandy for him as well. He'll like that. Heaven knows when I'm going to find the time to call in and see him, but I suppose I'll just have to make time, won't I?'

A white delivery van, with a well-known national name and insignia emblazoned on its side, drew up outside the main gates of the Medical Research Centre.

After a few moments the driver could be seen to reach round behind the passenger seat, and then get out with a parcel and a clipboard of papers in his hands. He walked slowly over to the lighted security office.

He seemed to be surprised when he realised that both of the wrought-iron gates were firmly closed, that the car-park inside was completely devoid of vehicles, and that most of the building behind was in darkness. His gloved hand pulled back a sleeve to expose a watch, then he shrugged and carried on walking to the little side access gate. He peered through the steamed-up office window, saw that there was indeed someone inside, then opened the door and went in.

'Cor, it's nice and warm in here,' he said, holding his hands towards the glowing electric fire. 'Where is everyone, mate?' he went on, in a distinctly cockney voice. 'Blimey, it ain't bleeding Christmas yet. 'Ave your lot skived off already, then? It's all right for some, ain't it? Our place don't finish till tomorrow night. Well, there you are.' He placed the parcel on the table. 'I ain't Santa Claus. That ain't a present for you, mate, but it's wanted urgent like. Immediate delivery. Look at all them there labels, more than we've got lights on our Christmas tree. An' there's only you blooming here. It's a funny old game, ain't it?'

'What is it?' the gateman said, as he picked up the parcel and stared at all the different labels on it. Prominent and familiar were the initials of a well-known computer manufacturer. 'I ain't expecting nothing. No one's told me there's anything urgent coming. Is there an order number on it?'

'The advice note's in the envelope, on the back, mate, and don't go tossing the bleeding thing about, not till you've signed for it. Special computer discs or something.'

'Where's the order number? Here it is. "Phone. M. O'Neil." Well, at least he's given a number.' He thumbed through the outstanding order copies in his tatty, black arch-lever file. 'The lazy bitches in the office ain't typed it yet, and it looks as if they've started a new book too. Typical. Well, let's have a look at them.'

The package was already torn at one corner. It took only a moment to insert a fingernail and rip off the narrow section of the brown paper that was free of the wide bands of clear plastic tape. The attempt to rip off a bigger area failed. The sticky tape bound thickly round the parcel seemingly had the breaking strain of a steel hawser, and all he achieved was to hurt his finger. So he studied what he could see. Clearly there were four black plastic boxes, each much the size of a normal videotape. 'Oh well, it looks all right to me,' he muttered. 'I'll sign your sheet for you, but it'll have to wait there until they comes back off holiday,' he went on, turning to put the package on a shelf.

'Suits me, mate, but you won't be popular if you keeps them things in here for a whole bleeding fortnight,' and he drew a line with his gloved finger on the steamed-up window. 'Damp, see, that's a killer for them sort of things. Look at them bloody labels. "Store in a temperature and humidity controlled environment." See, and there's another on the side, there, "Warning, anhydrous crystals in packing effective only twelve hours." Them's those bags of salty stuff what takes the moisture out of the air. You ought to get them things in your computer room where it's safe. If anything goes wrong then, it ain't your fault, is it, mate?'

'Good idea. It's better'n cluttering this place up, too—I've 'ardly enough room to swing a cat round as it is. I'll drop it in when I do me rounds. Cheers then, mate, 'ave a nice Christmas.'

The white van backed round, and drove away.

'No luck so far, Reg,' Alison Knott admitted as she sat down in Reg Finch's tiny office. 'I've seen all but two of the local bus drivers, and none of them recognise this man Long's picture, if that's really what his name is. The other two will be back on duty tomorrow, so I'll pop in and see them then. Right, so you want me to call on the houses on the milkman's route, do you? Arthur's doing the ones on the paper boy's round. Their rounds probably overlap, but never mind, I'll sort it out. I'll have a cup of coffee first, and then I'll get on with it.'

It was quite late in the evening when Walsh put his files in his briefcase and left his office. He'd spent the last three hours rereading all the files and reports on the recent bombings, and checking that all the logical and obvious follow-up steps had subsequently been taken. Yet satisfying himself that the case was being investigated in a sound and professional manner did nothing to ease the concern and tension he felt in his mind. He felt he was as far away from apprehending DaSilva, or any of his accomplices, as he had been when it had all started.

This case of the Medical Research Centre bomb was quite extraordinary. The way it had all unfolded had virtually been predicted with great accuracy. The surprise announcement of a possible cure for drug addiction, even to such a responsible conference audience, had brought about the immediate response, from both himself and the chief constable, that trouble at the Medical Research Centre could be anticipated. He could remember his own relief when he'd learned that the Home

Office had also had the same concern, and had appointed Superintendent Anderson to oversee the laboratory security. Then had come the information that the hitman, the elusive DaSilva, trouble-shooter for the international underworld of organised crime, had presumably been sent to arrange for the destruction and elimination of that research. The idea of decoy bombs had proved accurate too, but such predictions had still not prevented any of them from being planted. The important one at the Medical Centre ought to have wiped out, in one foul stroke, the two researchers involved and their stored data, but a fortuitous telephone call had saved the life of one of those, and a similar unforeseeable accident by the paper boy had foiled a follow-up attempt. However, being forewarned had not meant that he was forearmed. Neither stroke had been parried, and he was still none the wiser as to how they had been accomplished.

With such depressing thoughts predominant in his mind, it was hardly surprising that his wife, Gwen, did not find him a scintillatingly exciting companion for what little of the evening remained.

It was very late when a lone car drove through the near-empty city streets.

It slowed and stopped in the road behind

the looming bulk of the Medical Research Centre building. The driver's window was wound down, and an observer, had there been one, would have seen the driver operate a small device with a long extended aerial—one not unlike the apparatus used to control model aircraft in flight. It was moved slowly from side to side, as though it might be direction-finding. If it was, it found what it was after when the aerial pointed straight at the deserted rear of the building. A button was then pressed, and the car drove off, away out of the city.

Some five minutes elapsed, then, from inside the building, there came a low-pitched double thud of explosions. The first, a few milliseconds in advance of the other, blasted out small, jagged, hardened aluminium fragments which, like shrapnel, tore and rended their way through the light steel cabinets of the computer room. Then the second explosion erupted in a napalm-like burst of searing heat and flame, which quickly reduced all the equipment in that wide low room to a red-hot, distorted, twisted mass of unrecognisable debris, and all the data that computer installation had once contained was as if it had never been.

Walsh had hardly been in bed a restless hour before the telephone rang to tell him of the latest bombing incident. He'd got dressed and gone to view the wreckage of the Medical Research Centre's computer room for himself. It was a rather pointless thing to do, for there was nothing he could do there, except make himself even more depressed than he already was. After a while he'd left the experts to delve into the debris by themselves, and had sent Brenda Phipps and Reg Finch to wake up and interview two of the off-duty guards, while he himself went to rouse out the third.

As luck would have it, that third guard was the one who had been stupid enough to take an unchecked parcel into the computer room, in spite of all the warnings he and his colleagues had been given.

Walsh's fists had clenched white in the anger of his frustration, and he had been unable to prevent himself launching into a tirade of insulting epithets—which had left not only the guard white and shaken, but himself as well.

His momentary loss of self-control had been an utterly pointless and unproductive exercise, and afterwards he'd been glad that neither of his two assistants had been there to witness it. He'd pulled himself together eventually, and gone back to the lab where Packstone and his crew were still sifting through the foam-smothered wreckage of the latest, and by far the most efficient, bomb attack.

Eventually, though, he'd dragged himself away and gone back home to an anxious Gwen, to bath and shave, and eat a welcome breakfast.

It was not a good start to the day.

'Hang on a minute. I've seen him somewhere,' the overweight white-haired bus driver said cautiously, as he took the sketch from Alison Knott's outstretched hand. 'It ain't getting on me bus, that's for sure. I don't look at faces when I'm taking fares, I don't even know me neighbours when they get on, so it must have been somewhere else. Let me think.' To help him do that it was necessary to light a cigarette and then to drum his fingers on the none too clean table in the bus station messroom.

Alison waited expectantly. This was the first positive response to the picture of John Long, since the landlord in the Black Cat.

'It's coming,' the driver said at last. 'It were a couple of weeks or so back. That's right. That's it. He was in that shop in Huntingdon when I went to look at getting a new parka. I lives in St Neots, see, and the missus says I can have a new one for Christmas, 'cos me old one's getting all tatty like. Yes, and this bloke was in there—buying up the shop too, he was. That's why I remember him, see. You goes in normal to get a new pair of boots, or a new hat, or something you've worn out. It ain't often you see anyone buying everything at the same time. I remember saying to meself, "Either his place 'as burned down, or his missus has kicked 'im out, and he can't get at his stuff." It's got to be summat like that, ain't it?' he went on, tapping a finger on the side of his nose to indicate just how shrewd an observation that really was.

'He sounded as if he was sure, did he, Alison? Well done. That's good news. You'd better get straight over to Huntingdon and check it out,' Reg Finch replied to Alison Knott's telephone call. 'If the people in the outfitters' shop recognise the picture as well, give me a ring straight away, and I'll tell the boss we've got a confirmed sighting. Then it'll be all systems go, in Huntingdon, like as not.'

Sidney Walsh arrived in his office still tense and frustrated by the early morning bombing, and with a mind that just would not concentrate. After an hour he gave up trying to do anything constructive. He hardly needed an excuse to get out of headquarters, to let his mind relax and settle down, but he found one in the form of the Christmas card and bottle of brandy he'd bought for Professor Hughes.

Now was a good time to deliver them.

He strolled the short distance round the murky damp greenness of Parker's Piece and thence into the tranquil stone solidity of Downing College.

To Walsh's surprise it wasn't the cheerful, rotund professor who answered the door, but a bustling, comfortably plump woman, wearing a flowered apron.

'Yes he's in right enough, but he's feeling right low, he is, the poor old fellow. He's had the flu real bad, he has, and it's proper taken the stuffing out of him. Come on in. A bit of company'll do him good. I've still got his bed to change yet, but don't mind me, I'll be out of the way soon enough. I've other rooms to do before I come back and fix him a bite for lunch. We can't have him fading away, can we? I won't let him go outdoors yet awhile, not even over to the dining-room. I don't want that cold settling on his chest, not at his age, I don't.'

Walsh found the professor in his spacious sitting-room, well wrapped up in a thick, brightly coloured tartan dressing-gown, one that had a startlingly rich mass of interlaced gold braiding on the collar and lapels. He reclined comfortably in one of the deep armchairs that was pulled up as close as was safe to a roaring log fire. His round face was pale and drawn, but his eyes were bright with a welcome when he recognised his visitor.

Walsh drew another chair up to the fire. 'I'm sorry that you're not feeling up to much, Professor, and I'm sorry about the bomb in the computer room as well. That news can't have cheered you up very much,' he announced lamely.

Hughes smiled wanly. 'No, it certainly didn't. This bomber was too clever for us. I'd like to meet him one day.'

'I wish I could arrange it for you,' Walsh muttered despondently. 'You've lost a lot of expensive equipment, and years of research data.'

'Well, it's done now, so there's no point in losing any sleep over it,' Hughes said, with a suspicion of a chuckle. 'You look more depressed about it than I am. Cheer up. If our loss is causing you so much concern, let me put your mind at rest, but I must hold you to the strictest confidentiality. When you first came to see me I did project some possible scenarios in my mind, and the computers and the research data were obviously vulnerable. So I immediately took steps to have all Wade's and Chambers' handwritten notebooks photocopied, and last week I had all the data in those computer installations secretly duplicated in London, through a special direct line. They seemed sensible precautions to take. What I did is only known to a very few people, of course. So, in respect to the research data, there's no real harm done. As for the computers? They were insured and can be updated and replaced quickly enough. The work on the Wade—Chambers drug addiction project will be carried on, elsewhere. I'm not at liberty to divulge the precise location.'

The plump lady came in with a hot drink for the professor and coffee for his visitor.

'There you are, Mr Hughes,' she said cheerfully, 'that's hot honey and lemon, with a good dollop of rum in it. It'll do your throat the power of good, it will. It's a waste of time me telling you not to talk on too much, 'cos you men won't listen to good sense. Are you warm enough? Let me put another log on the fire, and I've got you a nice bit of fish for your lunch. You'll like that,' she chatted on.

Hughes smirked and pulled a long face when she'd left. 'I certainly do get well looked after, don't I? Bless her heart, but I mustn't grumble.'

Walsh smiled sympathetically, and a little more cheerfully. 'Well, maybe things aren't as bad as I thought. I should have realized that you would work things out for yourself. Now, Brenda, Reg and myself have this present for you, and a Christmas card.' He took them both out of the plastic bag he had brought with him, and handed them to the invalid.

Hughes's eyes brightened with obvious pleasure as he took them. 'Now that really is very thoughtful of you all, very kind indeed, and such a nice stained glass nativity picture too,' Hughes commented as he drew the card out from its envelope. 'I must admit, I do prefer cards with a religious theme. One gets so tired of robins on snowy gateposts, coaches and horses—and even worse are the so-called funny ones. Now, on the top of the bureau over there are some photographic reproductions of our now famous illuminated Vulgate Bible. I'd like you each to have one. Oh yes, and on the mantelpiece there are two reserved tickets for the service of Nine Lessons and Carols, in King's College Chapel—the one that's televised each year. Perhaps you and your wife might like to go? I don't feel well enough to be there this year. Now, there was something else I was going to say to you when we next met. I would have phoned you, but this cold quite took it out of my mind. What was it now? Yes, you brought me some copies of the poems you found in Dr Chambers' rooms, didn't you? I can remember puzzling over them for hours. It was that strange name or heading, "Cato ap Tiri", that kept bothering me.'

The professor was interrupted by the insistent bleeping of Walsh's mobile phone.

'Excuse me, Professor,' Walsh said, taking the instrument out of his pocket and answering the call.

It was Reg Finch, to tell him that Alison Knott was now in Huntingdon, and had confirmed the sighting of DaSilva, alias Long, in the outfitters' shop.

'That's excellent news, Reg. We're actually getting somewhere at last. I won't be long here. Wait for me in my office,' Walsh replied much more cheerfully, then he put the phone back in his pocket.

'I was saying that the name or title, "Cato ap Tiri", was bothering me, Inspector,' the professor went on. 'Then it dawned on me that it might be an anagram. It's possibly a coincidence, of course, but if it is an anagram, then I wouldn't be surprised if you'll find that interesting.'

Walsh had already started to get to his feet while the professor was still talking, but he stayed long enough to duly and politely express his thanks, and say his goodbyes and merry Christmases, before leaving the pale old professor to doze peacefully before the cosy flickering flames of the fire, while his nice piece of fish was being prepared.

Outside the cold raw wind stung the warm skin of his face, but that went unnoticed. Earlier his brain had seemed seized up into a solid block, but now it was starting to work again—in fact it was starting to race away, as though it needed to make up for lost time.

He walked slowly at first, his fingers holding the three presents in the plastic bag tightly, then his pace quickened. Possible answers to many problems were starting to present themselves, and they were fitting together into a very neat pattern indeed.

He found himself running the last few hundred yards or so back to headquarters, even crossing the lanky damp grass of Parker's Piece and getting his shoes soaking wet.

16

A thin watery sun had broken through the high scudding clouds, and its faint light dappled the leaves of the shrubs lining the shingled drive, into various shades of patchy dark and yellowed green.

Two cars, escorted by a police motor cyclist, drove up to the front of the house in Newnham.

The new door in the still damaged red-tiled porch was opened to Walsh by the police minder, still stationed there for the protection of Dr Wade and his wife.

'Dr Wade's in the sitting-room,' he replied to Walsh's question, his facial expression showing surprise at this sudden invasion by so many of his colleagues, 'but his wife's just popped out to do some shopping.'

'In her own car, is she?' Walsh asked quickly.

'No, she's not, as a matter of fact,' the minder replied casually. 'She's got her old man's. Hers had got a flat battery—she'd left her lights on last time she used—'

'Christ!' Walsh exclaimed in alarm. 'Where's she gone? Who's with her? How long ago?' he snapped.

'Only a few minutes. You must have passed her on your way here. Arthur Bryant's with her. She's only going to Sainsbury's.'

'Which way will she go? Reg, get Arthur on the radio...' Walsh said hurriedly.

'Down Long Road. I doubt if Bryant'll hear his phone, sir,' the minder explained helpfully. 'She always has the tape player in the car going flat out fit to bust your eardrums. Opera mad, she is. *Carmen* it was when I went out with her—'

'We'll have to go after them, Chief,' Brenda Phipps interrupted, pulling at his sleeve urgently.

Walsh was trying to think quickly, but he shook his head. 'With all that traffic? We'd never make it in time.'

'We might—on that. Come on,' Brenda yelled insistently, running towards the police motor bike which was parked on its stand while its rider stood watching the proceedings with interest.

That interest grew into alarm when Brenda leapt astride his machine, started the engine and pushed it off the stand, all in one slick movement. Walsh, now fully galvanised into action, pounded up and clambered on the back. 'Get going,' he grunted.

Police motor cycles are not expected

304

to do stunts like front-up wheelies, but Brenda achieved one with no apparent difficulty at all. As the bike roared away down the drive, stones and shingle sprayed in all directions.

Police motor cycles are not intended to carry pillion passengers either. There are no comfortable padded seats provided for them—the space behind the rider contains panniers, aerials, boxes of gear and radio equipment. However, Walsh was not concerned about his personal comfort at that moment, and it was on them that he precariously perched himself.

Brenda's wheelie was nearly his immediate undoing, and he only prevented himself being ejected to the rear by clinging tightly to Brenda's shoulders. The reverse situation, of course, applied as soon as she braked hard at the end of the drive. Walsh slid painfully forward, but that gave him the opportunity to get his arms gripped firmly round her waist. Hopefully that would prevent him from sliding about, but even so, his position felt extremely insecure. The panniers dug painfully into the base of his spine, and there was nowhere to put his feet, to steady himself. So he tucked them up behind him as best he could, and hung on for dear life as they roared away down the middle of the road. The traffic was jammed solid at the first roundabout, but that circumstance did not bother Brenda: she kicked down a couple of gears and went round it anyway—the wrong way. She missed an oncoming car by only inches, then accelerated flat out along Fen Causeway, towards the River Cam. The motor bike hit the hump of the bridge at speed, and promptly left the ground—only for a moment, but that was plenty of time for Walsh's backside to rise up a foot, and then come crashing back down again. Then it was hard braking and howling gear changes, to the junction with Trumpington Road, by the Leys School. Inevitably the traffic lights were red, but Brenda timed a sharp right turn superbly, and slipped through a narrow gap in the stream of cars crossing her path, then they were accelerating again. Somehow, while she was doing all that, Brenda had managed to find the siren switch. From somewhere beneath Walsh there suddenly came a screaming howl that was not of his own volition, and the light on the pole behind him started flashing.

The driver of a police patrol car, just turning out of Lensfield Road, saw the helmetless pair careering along on what was clearly a stolen police motor bike; he promptly switched on his sirens and headlights too, and set off in pursuit.

Walsh saw that patrol car out of the

corner of his eye, and would have shrugged his shoulders phlegmatically, had it been safe to do so. Instead, he raised his head to peer with squinted eyes over Brenda's left shoulder, looking for Wade's car. The registration number he could not remember, but it was a big white Rover, and nearly new. He closed his eyes as Brenda negotiated a queue at a set of traffic lights in her now usual way, by going passed on the wrong side of the road. Then she swung the bike in a sharp left turn, into another road. This was called Long Road, but it wouldn't seem long, not at the speed they were travelling, Walsh thought.

There, up in front, was a big white car, a big white Rover. He jerked at Brenda's waist and screamed, 'That's it,' in her ear.

Walsh turned his head and grimaced ferociously at the car's driver as Brenda pulled across in front, and started braking. He daringly released one arm and pumped it up and down vigorously—the traditional signal for slowing down. Then Brenda pulled out, to let the car come alongside. There was Mrs Wade's face, alarmed and anxious, but she clearly recognised him, and the driver's window was sliding down.

'Don't brake!' he screamed at her, having to compete in audio volume with the orchestral sounds from within, and the roar of the motor-bike engine without. 'Turn that bloody thing off!' he yelled, a compelling urgency in his voice. 'Don't brake. Let the car roll to a stop in neutral, and don't touch the handbrake—whatever you do—or the doors. Don't touch anything in fact,' he went on, his voice cracking with the emphasis he was putting into his words.

Mrs Wade was clearly scared out of her wits, but she was doing what he'd demanded.

The slope of the railway bridge brought the car to a momentary stop, but before it started to roll back, Mrs Wade sensibly turned the steering wheel, so that the rear tyres ran into the kerb, and the vehicle came to rest. Walsh sighed with relief as he got off the motor bike and ran over.

'Hello, Inspector. Fancy meeting you here,' Patricia Wade said in a voice that wasn't as jocular as it was meant to be.

'Hello, Mrs Wade,' Walsh replied automatically, then had to shake his head a little in order to resume reality. 'Don't touch anything. Leave the engine running. I want you out, and quick,' he croaked hurriedly. 'I think there's a bomb in the car. Anything might set it off.'

'What the hell's going on?' demanded the authoritative voice of the sergeant from the pursuing patrol car, but he changed his attitude quickly when Walsh turned angrily towards him. 'Oh, sorry, sir, I didn't recognise you. Er, can we be of any assistance?'

'Yes!' Walsh snapped angrily. 'Get rid of all these cars.' He waved an arm at all the waiting traffic. 'Turn them round quick, and I mean bloody quick. There's an unexploded bomb here—well, so far it's unexploded.'

The sergeant blinked, clearly thought about making a comment, but changed his mind.

'I want you out through the window, Mrs Wade,' Walsh went on quickly, turning back to the car. 'Swing your feet round towards Arthur. Quick! Come on.'

Mrs Wade sat across the car, with her back to Walsh. He reached in through the open window, and got his hands under her armpits, and lifted. 'Right. Now straighten your body. Go all stiff.'

With Arthur's help, Mrs Wade was lifted clear through the window of the car like a corpse on a plank. Then she and Walsh were running away. Arthur Bryant needed no help. He dived out through the open window head first, landed on his arms and back, rolled over, then was on his feet and running with the rest of them.

They'd gone perhaps thirty feet when

the explosion came. Walsh gave Patricia Wade a hefty thump in the middle of her back, which sent her reeling flat on her face on the grass verge, then he dropped down himself with his fingers clasped protectively round the back of his head.

For some reason, lying thus prone in the muddy gutter seemed a wonderfully comfortable place to be. He felt relaxed, and loath to make the effort to get up. He waited until the patter of falling debris had ceased, then reluctantly pushed himself to his feet, and just stood still, feeling dazed and stupid. He turned his head to look back. The driver's door of the white Rover had been blown off, the boot lid was up and there was a flicker of flame from the interior. The petrol tank hadn't yet ignited, but it might.

'The bomb must have been triggered when the weight came off the driver's seat, Chief, or else it was the heat from the exhaust pipe.' Brenda had appeared from somewhere, muttering in a voice that was unnaturally dulled and slurred. Walsh stared at her. Her face was pale and she was blinking her eyes as if to try and make them focus properly.

'That was a little too close for comfort,' he replied, trying to speak in as near normal a voice as he could.

More uniformed policemen had arrived,

and in the distance, past the confused mêlée of manoeuvring turning cars, there were the flashing blue lights of ambulances or fire engines. He grunted in relief; there were plenty of people here quite competent enough to sort all this confusion out. He need not worry about it. Anyway, it was time to start concentrating on other things. There was Patricia Wade, muddy and dishevelled, just sitting on the grass, sobbing quietly to herself, and here was Reg Finch, striding confidently towards him. There'd be a car up there somewhere that could take them back then perhaps he could get a cup of coffee. That would help settle his nerves. They felt a bit raw just at the moment.

The spacious sitting-room of the Wade house was tastefully hung with tinsel, brightly coloured paper-chains and other decorations. A string across the top of the wide french window held dozens of cards of robins, Santas and snowy candles, and in a corner, the lights on a small Christmas tree glowed and twinkled a merry cheer. It was a very pleasant festive scene.

Walsh lounged back comfortably in one of the armchairs and sipped at his hot cup of coffee. He made to brush at the muddy knees of his trousers with the back of his hand, but stopped himself. It would do no good while the material was still wet. When it dried out it might perhaps brush off, but more likely the trousers would end up at the cleaner's, if they weren't torn somewhere and not fit to wear. In his job he hardly ever wore a suit out properly.

'We'd just got near the railway bridge on Long Road when the inspector came up on the back of a motor bike...' Mrs Wade was standing in the middle of the floor, excitedly relating the details of her adventures to her husband, who lay slouched in a chair by the french window.

'What on earth's going on upstairs?' James Wade suddenly demanded, interrupting his wife's breathless narrative. 'And I'm sure I saw a dog go past the door a moment ago. I don't like dogs.'

'Oh, that'll be Brutus.' Walsh chuckled aloud. 'He's a fine little fellow, full of fun; and he'll lick you to death if he gets half a chance. He's a real expert. He can sniff out explosives a mile away. We're just giving the place a quick check over, we want to make sure there's no more nasty bombs lying about.'

Wade frowned deeply. 'Don't you let him go running around outside in the garden. I don't want dog muck all over my lawn. I really must insist,' he demanded emphatically.

Walsh raised a hand casually. 'Have no fear. The dog's well trained. There'll be no problem.'

Wade was clearly not happy with that simple answer, because he opened his mouth to say something else, but by then Patricia Wade had recommenced recounting her experiences.

'Then the inspector came up on the back of this police motor bike,' she repeated. 'Well, I thought it was some sort of joke at first, you can imagine, can't you?'

She was interrupted again, this time by one of Packstone's forensic team—a human explosives expert. He acted very strangely. He merely opened the door, looked over at Walsh, smiled broadly, nodded his head vigorously, then punched the air emphatically with a closed fist that had its thumb stuck up in the air. He went off without actually saying a word.

' "Don't brake, don't touch anything," he shouted at me,' Mrs Wade went doggedly on. "Just let the car roll to a stop." Well, I was starting to get more than a bit worried by then.'

Reg Finch was the next one to come in. Surprisingly, he wore a pair of white gloves, and he held in one hand a clear plastic bag containing some papers. Like the previous visitor, he too seemed reluctant to use his voice, being merely content to look at Walsh, and nod.

'Originals?' Walsh asked briefly.

Another nod.

'Fingerprints?'

A nod.

'Both of them?'

The next nod was accompanied by the broadest of grins, and then Reg went to sit down on the settee next to Brenda.

Walsh took another sip of coffee.

'Anyway, they dragged me out through the car window, would you believe?' Mrs Wade went on. 'Then we ran away as fast as we could. We hadn't gone far when the car just blew up. The inspector pushed me flat on the ground, because there were bits flying everywhere. It was horrible. I, er, we could have been killed.'

James Wade was looking unusually alert and very thoughtful, apparently studying the tips of his fingers intently. For a moment it looked as though he had not been listening to any of his wife's story, but then he made the correct response due from a loving husband.

'You obviously saved my wife's life, Inspector. I am very grateful, very grateful indeed.'

'I'll bet you are,' Walsh observed shortly, putting his now empty cup down on the table beside him. He then blinked his eyes

314

a couple of times, flexed the fingers of one hand for a moment, and seemed to make up his mind about something, for he sat himself more upright and leaned slightly forward.

'Tell me, Mrs Wade,' he asked quietly. 'When you first learned that Justin Chambers had been blown into a million different pieces, did it never occur to you that you, yourself, might be the killer's next victim?'

Patricia Wade looked at him in utter astonishment, speechless—for a moment.

'Me?' she said incredulously. 'Why me? The bomb that killed Justin was meant to kill James as well, to wipe out their research project, wasn't it? Me? What's it got to do with me? I don't know anything about neurology or biochemistry.'

Walsh pursed his lips and nodded slightly. 'What about the bomb outside your front door? It doesn't seem to me that your husband is even the slightest bit interested in what goes on in a kitchen. Is it likely that anyone would expect him to open up an egg box and put its contents in the fridge? No, I really can't see that that bomb was intended for him. It doesn't make sense—but if it wasn't intended for him, who was it intended for? You perhaps?'

Mrs Wade's dark eyes now looked

315

enormous and very puzzled, and her lower jaw hung loosely down, leaving her mouth wide open, a space that was soon filled by a knuckle of her right hand.

'With your husband so distraught that he could hardly do anything for himself, who would expect him to be the next one to want to use a car? Someone's got to do the shopping, and that someone is you. Did you really leave your car's lights on the last time you used it? Is it likely? How long is it since you last did a thing like that?' Walsh asked calmly.

Mrs Wade was clearly so bewildered by what he was saying that she was nearly in tears. 'You're being ridiculous, Inspector,' James Wade said scornfully, rising from his chair and taking his empty glass over to the little table where the brandy bottle stood. 'Why on earth would anyone want to kill Patricia? It's nonsense. Utter nonsense.'

'Of course it is.' Walsh agreed soothingly, nodding his head slowly. 'Mind you,' he went on, 'I can understand why someone might want to kill a person referred to as "Cato ap Tiri", though.'

Those words had a dramatic effect.

Patricia Wade's head jerked up as enlightenment dawned on her. She turned suddenly towards her husband with her arms raised threateningly, her fingers crooked into eagle-like talons—from a near-weeping woman to one of raging fury in less than one second.

'You bastard. You bloody bastard!' she screamed. Her eyes glowed with such anger that he reeled back from her and gave a whimpering cry of fear.

His facial expression changed quickly from desperate alarm to shock, back to fear again, then into the panic of apparent madness. Suddenly, with an athleticism that belied his previous laboured actions, he pushed his wife violently away from him, snatched the brandy bottle from the table and hurled it straight at Walsh's head, then he turned and burst out through the french window, breaking the string that was stretched across it, and sending all the Christmas cards fluttering and wafting like falling autumn leaves to the floor.

Walsh dodged the bottle easily enough and was on his feet like a shot, running after him—but so too, unfortunately, were Reg Finch and Brenda Phipps. They each negotiated the sprawling Mrs Wade satisfactorily enough, but all that achieved was a muddled congestion of eager chasing bodies at the door. Walsh heard the bolts on the side gate being drawn back, then running footsteps crunching the gravel of the front drive—then he was outside, and in hot pursuit.

It was hardly the fault of the driver of the green Mercedes. Even if the laws of this country were framed in such a way that those grown infirm by the passage of time could be prevented from getting behind the wheels of powerful vehicles, it is by no means certain that the result of this particular incident would have been any different.

The octogenarian driver braked almost as soon as the wild-eyed Dr James Wade ran out on to the road and into the path of his car, but by the time the brakes were really biting, there had been a crunching impact. James Wade slewed across the broad bonnet, hit the windscreen hard, and went flying away through the air, like a limp rag doll.

Angela ran up the stairs of the luxury block of flats in Huntingdon, her auburn hair flying wildly in disorder, then she stood panting at the door, fumbling to find her key in the contents of her handbag. The angles and hollows of her face seemed to have filled out during the past week or so, allowing her mere prettiness to develop into something more akin to radiant beauty. Now those features held an expression of excited and happy anticipation.

She flung the door wide and burst in, shouting, 'Ron, Ron! Grandma's had her operation. She can see again. She's...'

She stopped suddenly. There was a feeling about the place, a feeling of emptiness, that now she was aware of it, grew stronger and more real.

Her happy expression disappeared almost immediately, to be replaced by a lip-biting look of anxiety. She ran into the bedroom, and what she had feared was confirmed. Ronald Silver's clothes were gone from the wardrobe.

So, the moment of parting had come. Inevitable though she had known it would be, she had pushed it firmly to the back of her mind, as though by refusing to contemplate it she could delay or even prevent its execution. Her feeling of loss and desertion was almost overwhelming, but after a few moments she raised her head. There had been something especially deep in their relationship, in their feelings for each other. She had felt that too often for it to be in doubt. Ron might have gone, but he would not have left her without a word of some sort. Somewhere there would be a message.

There was.

She found it in the sitting-room. A single sheet of paper, lying on his favourite chair by the fire. She sank to her knees and picked it up, blinking back the watery mistiness from her eyes.

'My dear,' it read, 'circumstances have brought my stay here in England to an end sooner than I had anticipated after all. My work is done. I am not now in a position to give you instructions, but I do beg that you will comply with the arrangements that I have set in being. I am well aware that your venture into crime was solely because of your father's inability to maintain your grandmother's nursing home charges, and I respected you for that, but on that score let your mind be at rest. No further demands will be made on you, or your father, for her accommodation, and she will now be cared for properly. As for yourself, you may not like Marston, but he has been charged with arranging for you to be trained as a nurse, and his influence is considerable. Phone him in the New Year and he will tell you what arrangements he has made. They will include a regular allowance and access to funds when necessary. You will not find him ungenerous, and neither will he again make demands of you. Now I have come to the most difficult part of this letter. I had expected to meet in England a girl who was hardened and selfish, one whom I could callously use for my pleasure, but instead, I met you. To my eternal shame, I did not send you away. I am one of life's rolling stones. One who is devious and disreputable, who turns fortuitous circumstances to his own selfish gain. Until now I have been unrepentant. In you I found what I had never expected to find—anywhere. A mind akin to my own and companionship of which I would probably never tire, besides unconscious beauty, but I fear I could not have held you long, had I even tried. I am afraid that this rolling stone may gather no moss, or sweet flowers. I must be content with treasured memories. I hope you will think of me with some sort of affection.'

It was unsigned.

Angela let the paper fall. As she had read those words it seemed as if her mind could actually hear his voice speaking them. He was the man who had held her in his arms, and had loved her. His words said it was so, and her heart told her that it was true. He had called her a sweet flower, and he wanted to be remembered—with affection. Now she could admit honestly that her feelings for him were as he felt for her, and that was cause for a momentary glow of happiness, and a fierce determination to become the kind of nurse of whom he would be proud, but then there came the realisation that his gentle hands would never again caress her—never again would she hear his chuckle, or see his eyes lighten when they looked at her.

Her bottom lip trembled in an expression

of utter dejection. A feeling of desperately miserable loneliness engulfed her. She put her head down on her arms, gave a heart-rending sob, and burst into tears.

The setting sun had nearly disappeared below the far horizon, but its rays still bathed the vast expanse of Texas desert a rich golden red. In fifteen minutes, by contrast, all would be pitch black, then the stars would start to twinkle, and the temperature would drop dramatically.

The two men in the chairs by the swimming pool had seen that memorable sight more times than they could remember, yet they still watched the event in awe and silence.

'Fancy DaSilva framing that second doctor for the death of the first. I tell you, that guy's a genius,' one said, reaching for a tall glass from the table that stood between them.

'He sure is, and some crazy animal rights activists get blamed when he blows up their damned computers. I'm hanged if I remember when I last laughed so much.'

'With those two researchers out of action and all their data destroyed, it's all neat and tidy; buttoned up just fine. Still, as Ramon says, now they know a cure for addiction is possible, they'll keep on looking for it, but that won't be for many a long year. DaSilva's worth every last darned nickel.'

'Yeah, just what did he cost us this time? Orphans or missionary nuns?'

'His usual fee, that's hefty enough, but quality costs, as I'm always saying, and we're into old people's homes this time, but don't you worry, it's a new kind of investment for us. Marston reckons it could pay well if it's run right, and he'll see that it is. There's a dear old lady to look after, but she's in her eighties, and there's the bird Marston found for DaSilva. He obviously fancied her because we've got to look after her while she's training to be a medic or something. "That's no so bad," as my old granny from Fife used to say.'

'Old people's homes? Now that could be a good new line for us, couldn't it? We could set up a whole chain of them and centralise things. Good asset stability in the real estate side too. We've got to do something with all our cash surpluses. Maybe we can turn these events to our own advantage. What do you think?'

'By George, Sidney, your little grey cells must have kicked into top gear all of a sudden. What on earth put you on to Wade? How is he? Will he live?' the chief constable demanded, pushing the plain white porcelain coffee pot over to

Walsh's side of his broad desk.

Walsh shrugged his shoulders. He ignored the coffee, and instead helped himself from an open box of chocolate liqueurs, a more hospitable sign of the festive season than the few scattered Christmas cards.

The CC frowned. 'Lay off the cherry brandy ones, they're my favourites. You have some of the others,' he grunted.

'The latest reports on Wade don't sound good,' Walsh said slowly, allowing the chocolate in his mouth to dissolve, rather than biting it and releasing the liqueur too quickly. 'He's got serious internal injuries and a fractured skull, with bits of bone driven into his brain. If he does survive he may not be sane, but whatever happens, it'll be a long time before he's fit enough to be brought to trial.'

The CC pulled at his chin and nodded wisely.

'So, what suddenly made you think Wade might be doing most of the bombing round here, and not that fellow DaSilva?' he asked.

'Well, it was those Celtic love poems we found in Justin Chambers' secret drawer. We thought they might refer to someone who DaSilva could have been using as a hostage, to force Chambers to take that bomb into the lab, if you remember, but we dropped the idea when Packstone's computer program showed that the bomb had been put behind the drawer. By then, though, I'd asked old Professor Hughes at Downing College to read them, in case there was anything obvious that we'd missed,' Walsh replied casually.

'And?'

'Well, the poems appeared to have two titles. The second meant the Land of Eternal Youth, in Celtic, but the first, "Cato ap Tiri", didn't make any sense—in any language,' Walsh explained, 'until Hughes had the bright idea that it might simply be an anagram. The letters that make up "Cato ap Tiri", rearranged, make "To Patricia", and Mrs Wade's name is Patricia. There's no doubt what kind of relationship those poems were referring to, and if you assume Mrs Wade was Chambers' lover, and assume James Wade found out, then this whole business takes on an entirely different hue.'

The CC was frowning. 'Are you telling me that Wade deliberately told that conference all about the secret "cure for drug addiction" project, as part of a plan to murder his wife's lover, and then her?'

Walsh smiled. 'It looks like it. Wade's got a brilliant mind, and it wouldn't take much savvy to work out that we'd get panicky about the possibility that the news might find its way into the wrong ears.

Even if we hadn't been tipped off about DaSilva, when that bomb went off in the Medical Centre we'd have immediately blamed it on one of the drug cartels, wouldn't we?'

'Ah!' exclaimed the CC, waving an extended finger in the air to emphasise what he was going to say. 'Surely Wade would also have realised that if the drug barons did indeed find out about his precious project, then he really was putting his own life in danger. You can't see him doing that, can you?'

'Well, yes. We're trained to worry about any breach in security, but from Wade's point of view everyone at that meeting was a top-ranking official. He probably reckoned that the chances of his news leaking out were pretty negligible.'

'All right. So how come, if the bomb in the lab was a booby-trap, Wade didn't blow himself up as well as Chambers?'

'Because the booby-trap wasn't set until Wade had the phone call summoning him to the lab director's office. When Wade fixed the bomb behind the computer desk drawer earlier in the week, he probably left the little hook that was attached to the trigger device taped up somewhere safe. Then, when he'd got a good excuse not to be around for a while, he opened that drawer a little way, reached in to get a pen or something, and—'

'Untaped the hook and clipped it over something solid,' the CC interrupted brightly. 'Then he got the hell out of the way. When Chambers opened the drawer properly, off went the bomb. So all Wade's nerves and tears were acting, then?'

'I think so, but by then, of course, we'd had one of DaSilva's red-herring bombs go off. That must have given Wade a hell of a shock, so maybe he didn't feel quite as safe as he thought he was.'

'So his next step was to murder his wife in a way that would make us think someone was trying to kill him. How did he manage to plant the egg box on his own doorstep without our man seeing him? Have you worked that out?' the CC demanded.

Walsh smiled again. 'The Wades' bedroom has an *en suite* bathroom over the porch. I think Wade waited until he'd heard the milkman come, then he went in there and doubled a long piece of string through the elastic band on the egg box, and lowered it out of the window, down to the porch. He might have had to swing it a bit to get it in just the right place, but then all he had to do was let go of one end of the string and pull the whole length up out of sight. Luckily for Mrs Wade, the paper boy came along and messed that plan up.'

'So Wade had to resort to another bomb, and a more risky one too, because our chaps had already checked both of those cars at least once, and for all he knew, we might do so again. By running her car's battery flat, he forced his wife to use his, and if he'd succeeded in killing her, we'd have thought the bomb was intended for him. He's a clever bugger, isn't he?'

'He's not as clever as he thought he was. He left the rest of his explosive under a paving slab outside the garden shed, which was a bit silly. Our forensic man and the sniffer dog had no trouble finding that. When Reg Finch found the originals of Chambers' love poems in a little box in Patricia Wade's knicker drawer, and they'd got both hers and her husband's fingerprints on them, it all seemed pretty conclusive. Mind you, when Patricia Wade cottoned on to what her hubby had been up to, I thought I was going to have his murder on my hands too. She was ready to kill him there and then, and from the look on his face before he flipped his lid completely, Wade thought so too.'

'Has she admitted she was having it off with Chambers?' the CC asked.

'Not likely. Once she'd seen the state of her husband in the ambulance before it drove off, she clammed up tight. If he dies, she gets all his money, and with no scandal to her name,' Walsh said with a half-smile.

'So you can't pin anything on her, more's the pity, because she was the cause of it all. Unfortunately there's no law saying that she can't drop her knickers whenever she feels like a bit of nooky, even if it does result in a man getting killed,' the CC said reluctantly. Then he laughed. 'I bet I know someone who's over the moon about all this, and that's DaSilva. I know you think you've got a good lead on him in Huntingdon, but it's a waste of time you trying to follow that up. He's probably high-tailing it out of the country right now. His job's done, but I bet he's claiming he set up all this business between Chambers and Wade. I can't say I'd blame him, either, it's what I'd do if I were in his shoes. Right, what are your plans now?'

'My plans?' Walsh repeated slowly, as though the question had taken him by surprise. 'My plans are to go home, have a shower, and change into some nice clean clothes. Then Gwen and I are going out for dinner tonight, at Reg Finch's place. His wife is a superb cook, so I expect to have a damned good evening. I won't be coming in here tomorrow, that's for certain. I shall have a nice lazy morning; I might even go into town to browse round the shops and buy some presents. Then in the afternoon Gwen and I are going to the service of Nine Lessons and Carols in King's College Chapel. We've got reserved seats right up near the choir. I'm really looking forward to that. I've had enough of police business for a while. Peace on earth and good will to all men—and women, that's going to be my motto for the next few days.'

He got up, reached over the desk to the box of liqueurs, and deliberately picked out the last two cherry brandy ones.

'These are my favourites too,' he said with his mouth full, yet at the same time managing to grin at the expression of consternation on the CC's face. Then he turned, and made his way to the door.

'Have a nice Christmas yourself. I'll see you in the New Year,' he said quietly as he went out.

The publishers hope that this book has given you enjoyable reading. Large Print Books are especially designed to be as easy to see and hold as possible. If you wish a complete list of our books, please ask at your local library or write directly to: Dales Large Print Books, Long Preston, North Yorkshire, BD23 4ND, England.

This Large Print Book for the Partially sighted, who cannot read normal print, is published under the auspices of

THE ULVERSCROFT FOUNDATION

THE ULVERSCROFT FOUNDATION

. . . we hope that you have enjoyed this Large Print Book. Please think for a moment about those people who have worse eyesight problems than you . . . and are unable to even read or enjoy Large Print, without great difficulty.

You can help them by sending a donation, large or small to:

**The Ulverscroft Foundation,
1, The Green, Bradgate Road,
Anstey, Leicestershire, LE7 7FU,
England.**
or request a copy of our brochure for more details.

The Foundation will use all your help to assist those people who are handicapped by various sight problems and need special attention.

Thank you very much for your help.

Other DALES Mystery Titles In Large Print